THE LADY AND HER DUKE

The Ladies of Sommer-by-the-Sea
Book 3

Ruth A. Casie

ARE YOU SIGNED UP FOR DRAGONBLADE'S BLOG?

You'll get the latest news and information on exclusive giveaways, exclusive excerpts, coming releases, sales, free books, cover reveals and more.

Check out our complete list of authors, too!

No spam, no junk. That's a promise!

Sign Up Here

www.dragonbladepublishing.com

Dearest Reader;

Thank you for your support of a small press. At Dragonblade Publishing, we strive to bring you the highest quality Historical Romance from some of the best authors in the business. Without your support, there is no 'us', so we sincerely hope you adore these stories and find some new favorite authors along the way.

Happy Reading!

CEO, Dragonblade Publishing

**Additional Dragonblade books by
Author Ruth A. Casie**

The Ladies of Sommer-by-the-Sea Series
The Lady and Her Quill (Book 1)
The Lady and the Spy (Book 2)
The Lady and Her Duke (Book 3)

Pirates of Britannia Series
Donald
Hugh
Graham
The Pirate's Jewel
The Pirate's Redemption

CHAPTER ONE

June 20, 1815
Royston Mills, Baycliff Woods

THE BLAST OF a pistol shattered the quiet afternoon. Shouts and screams rose, their sound carrying into the surrounding area. In a clearing by the lake where the wood bordered the village, the shock and chaos subsided into a deafening silence.

Lord Ian Wallace knelt next to his business partner, Bennett Sutton. His bruised and bloody face was a mess of soot and gunpowder. Wallace glanced over his shoulder, signaling his valet.

"Water. Quick. His eyes need to be flushed." Wallace wavered between restraint and rage as he ministered to Sutton. "Stay calm and whatever you do, keep your eyes closed." His hands ran over Sutton's torso checking for injuries. He found none, other than the small tremors he assumed were from shock.

"I'm dying." Sutton spoke not in disbelief, but in resignation, as if dying was an undisputed conclusion.

Wallace's chest tightened at the sound of those words. He had heard them before from the injured men he commanded in Spain. For a moment he was back on the battlefield going from man to man: comforting them, waiting for medical attention and, in too many cases, saying good-bye.

"Swear to me." Sutton, agitated and breathing hard, reached up and grabbed his lapel. "Swear to me you'll marry my niece, Ivy-Rose."

What niece? Sutton had a niece?

"Swear it!"

"Yes, yes. I swear." In a fit of rage, he'd say anything to escape from the madman. It was luck that Sutton's gun misfired. He gazed at his friend and partner in disbelief. From the moment his valet pulled him to the ground, he'd found it difficult to comprehend why Sutton tried to kill him, tried to shoot him in the back.

Sutton tugged on his lapels. "No, on your honor as a gentleman. Swear it." Another tug. Bennett's strength was waning.

Wallace's anger softened. The man had to be kept calm. Roddy, his foreman, and Lord Ryder Whitaker had gone to fetch Dr. Price. The doctor had left the clearing when Sutton called off the duel.

"Swear it." The man sounded as if it was his last breath.

"As a gentleman, I, Lord Ian Wallace, 4th Duke of Blackhall, promise to marry your Ivy-Rose." He bent closer to him. "Is that better?"

Sutton released his lapels and slumped onto the ground, his breath coming in spurts.

Lenard returned carrying a basin of warm water.

Wallace stood aside and gave his valet room. They had been together a long time. Lenard was his personal attendant at Cambridge as well as in Spain during the war. Together they had seen worse. Now he flushed the gunpowder and soot out from Sutton's eyes. It would serve Sutton right if the pain was unbearable.

"Much better." Sutton's voice faded to a calm stillness.

Wallace wasn't sure if his partner referred to the oath he gave or the warm water.

"Your Grace, I cannot find any wound." Lenard kept streaming water over the man's face.

The battlefield images flashed in his head. Some had outcomes that were more severe than others. But that was war, not a card game gone wrong.

"God's blood, where is that doctor?" He glanced about.

Sutton raised his face to Lenard as the man ran more water over him and, with a gentle touch, wiped him dry.

"You have my thanks." Quiet at last, Sutton winced when he tried to lay down on the ground.

"Over here, Dr. Price." Whitaker and Roddy led the doctor to the injured man.

"I thought Sutton had the good sense to call off the duel." Dr. Price pushed his way in front of Wallace. "Where did your bullet hit him?"

"I never fired my weapon." Wallace stood back to let the doctor do his job.

"His pistol misfired when he aimed at Wallace's back." Whitaker stepped forward. "I stood in shock when he raised his pistol and took aim."

The doctor, on his knees, paused and glanced up at him.

"That's not at all like Sutton. Wallace, what did you say to him?" The doctor resumed examining Sutton's head.

"Not a thing. I convinced him to call off this ridiculous duel. I thought to give him time and hoped he'd have more sense in the morning. I was leaving the clearing, not far behind you when the shot went off."

"There are some abrasions from the powder blast and irritation from the gunpowder, but no wound." Price examined Sutton's hands. Scrapes, a bit of a burn in places, but nothing fatal. "Sutton's a lucky man."

The doctor stood up cleaning his hands with a cloth from his bag.

"Help me bring him to my carriage. We'll take him to the inn. I want to watch him until tomorrow rather than have him brought back to Sommer-by-the-Sea now."

Roddy and Lenard lifted Sutton, made their way through the gathered onlookers, and laid him in the back of the doctor's carriage.

"There's room enough for you and me up here." Roddy tapped Lenard and pointed next to the driver.

"I can go with them if you prefer." Whitaker stood next to him. "I know you're the man's partner, but no one would blame you for washing your hands of him."

"That won't be necessary. I'll go with him. I'm staying at the inn." Wallace got in the carriage still thinking through the events. He agreed with Dr. Price: this wasn't at all like Sutton.

The door closed, Whitaker signaled the driver, and the carriage pulled away.

"I don't know what's gotten into him." Wallace stared at Sutton propped up on the seat across from him.

"I've known that man since he was a boy and agree this is out of character for him. But don't you worry, Your Grace. We'll have him all to rights soon enough."

The carriage pulled up to Weaver's Inn. News of the incident traveled faster than he imagined. More onlookers buzzed about them like a swarm of angry bees. Wallace led the way for Lenard and Roddy to bring Sutton up the stairs to his room.

"I'll stay with him for a while. Head injuries can be nasty." Dr. Price stood over his patient and checked Sutton's breathing again.

"Ale for you both and watered ale for Mr. Sutton." Lenard put the tankards on the table. "Your Grace, I have the papers you gave me earlier. I'll put them in your room."

"I'll take them. I can review the documents while I sit with him." Wallace nodded toward Sutton.

"If that will be all, I'll be in the tavern if you need me." Lenard put the folio on the table.

"I'll go with you." Roddy looked at the patient lying in the bed and shook his head. The two men left and closed the door behind them.

Dr. Price sat at the table and took a tankard of ale. "How did this start?"

Wallace sat next to the doctor and reached for the second tankard.

"I found him troubled over several issues when I came up from London. He was in a fit over worker demands. He also expected a sizeable amount of fleece, but instead received a smaller delivery than promised.

"I had an issue to discuss with him, but in his state, I knew it would be impossible. I thought to divert his attention, a game of cards to take his mind off everything. Once he was himself, we could address the business problems and go over my visit to Cambridge. But Sutton drank too much, took risks no man in his right mind would take, and lost miserably."

"And his mood went from bad to worse." Dr. Price glanced at his patient, shook his head, and took a draw on the tankard.

"Yes, it did. I was at a loss what to do. Sutton wouldn't stop playing despite losing one game after another. I couldn't imagine the situation getting any worse, but it did.

"I dealt the cards. How Sutton preened like a peacock, so sure the winning hand was his. He drank and taunted me. He drained his flask dry and had Mr. Jackson fill it to the top. I was astounded when the deed to his home landed on the table."

"His cards..." The doctor closed his eyes and moaned.

"A beginner would know better than to bet on the cards Sutton held. He had no chance of winning." Wallace let out a strained laugh. "I conceded defeat and laid my cards face down, but Sutton demanded to see them. I refused. He reached across the table and turned them over. Then he went mad. Sutton grabbed a pen from the bar, sat down, and started writing. I stayed his hand. I didn't want his home. I thought to entice him with the best two out of three games, but he refused. *I pay my debts.*"

"Sutton is a proud man and a man of his word. But I've never known him to be this reckless." Price sat back, his legs out in front of him, staring at the tankard in his hand.

"Man of his word? We wouldn't be here if our workers believed him. I told them over and over the new mechanicals would not replace them. But fear does strange things to people. If things go as Sutton and I plan, there will be more work for more people and more money, not less.

"I offered to speak with the workers and explain the plan. That's when Sutton exploded. I tried my best to calm him, but now I understand. Sutton didn't calm down during the game. If anything, his card playing was more intense, more erratic, more irrational." He stared at his partner. "My strategy to calm him with the card game did the opposite. It pushed him over the edge."

"Don't blame yourself. From what you've told me, Sutton was already agitated. It wasn't one thing. It was everything."

"My partner accused me of siding with the workers and called me out in front of everyone demanding satisfaction. A duel." Wallace glanced at the doctor. The incident still beyond belief. "I refused. I told him I had enough of weapons in Spain. Businessmen didn't settle disputes with weapons. To everyone's horror, he slapped my face. I remember his odd smirk, daring me to ignore the affront.

"*Choose your weapon. I refused. Pistols. You didn't think I'd want to be near you with a blade. At least with a pistol I have a fighting chance.*

"I still didn't give up.

"All the way to the field and even when we arrived, I tried to dissuade him. I would have gladly shot myself to put an end to his stupidity. At last, the fight went out of him. You witnessed how we called off the duel, shook hands, and sent everyone home. Sutton was still holding his loaded pistol. I told him to take his anger out on the maple tree, the one by the lake." He paused and glanced at Sutton. "I thought he came to his senses."

"That is how I remember the morning." Dr. Price nodded.

"I turned to leave with the others, only to hear Sutton's pistol discharge. Lenard pulled me to the ground. When we got to our feet, it was Sutton who was down.

"I was back on the battlefield. His... his gun misfired." Wallace's voice was a whisper. The blast of the explosion filled his mind followed by Lenard tugging him, pulling him down and covering him with his body.

After several heartbeats, Wallace cleared his throat and glanced at the doctor with a silent plea for an explanation. There was none.

"Sutton and I met at Cambridge. We became as thick as thieves. I thought we had developed a fast friendship and would have wagered nothing like this was possible. I forgave him many things over the years, but this? How can I be a partner with a man who would kill me if he didn't get his way? And over what, speaking to our workers?"

Dr. Price's sympathetic expression didn't make him feel any better. The doctor went to his patient, touched Sutton's forehead then put his ear to his chest.

Wallace stood by, unable to pull his gaze away. His partner appeared at ease, calm for the first time in days. Like his old self. Wallace downed half the tankard not out of thirst, but rather out of the need for something to do.

God's blood. What happened? His explanation of their early relationship was not an exaggeration. In Cambridge they were like brothers. But did he really know Sutton? Neither of them talked about their family. All he knew of Sutton's family was they were prosperous sheep farmers. He wasn't even aware Sutton had a niece.

Wallace downed the rest of his ale. They had lost touch after graduation. Five years ago, he went back to Cambridge to honor a retiring professor. Sutton was among the guests. Like any reunion, they spoke for hours. The years faded and they easily renewed their friendship. They found they both were adamant. Industrializing was the way of the future. He was impressed to learn Sutton had struck out on his own and started a textile company using mechanicals.

He glanced at his friend. He should be furious and nowhere

near the attempted murderer. Instead, he sat here drinking ale worried about him.

Dr. Price's expression faded from concerned into pleased. Wallace let out a breath and sagged against the chair.

"All seems in good order. His breathing is normal, I do not detect a fever, and our patient is comfortable and calm." The doctor gathered his things into his medical bag. "I'm going home for dinner and a good night's sleep. I suggest you do the same."

"Thank you. I'll stay a bit longer in case he rouses. I'm sure everything will turn to right in the morning."

He saw the doctor to the door and went back to Sutton's bedside.

Lenard had done a good job of cleaning his face. Scrapes and cuts. Nothing very deep. Bluish patches on his face warned of bruises starting to form. Sutton slept on his stomach, snoring gently with his head pressed into the pillow. He could well have been back at university after an evening of debating and drinking.

"What were you thinking?"

There'd be no answers now. Time for that in the morning.

Wallace took a seat at the small table near the hearth and removed the papers from the folio. One look at the documents and his mind shifted from Sutton to the work at hand.

The folio held mechanical drawings, cut-away views of the carder, spinning mule, water frame, and loom mechanicals, showing how they worked.

His partner's ability to identify potential problems and present credible solutions excited him. As they worked together, he realized Sutton responded better to the diagrams than to standing and looking at the apparatus. That was of no concern to him. It was the results that mattered.

Wallace stopped and stared blankly at the empty hearth. He appreciated the details in the diagrams. For years, his responsibility focused on drawing very different mechanicals and situations. He sketched battle placements and troop positions then brought them back to Whitehall. At least men's lives weren't at stake with the drawings in his hand. Or were they? This unrest was disturbing and growing more urgent. Shaking his head, he returned to the drawings.

Impressed with his partner's grasp of the mechanical inner workings, he went through the comments on each diagram and added his own.

"Water."

Wallace turned toward the bed. Sutton rolled to his back, licked his lips, and gripped the linen covering him.

Wallace dropped the papers on the table, picked up the watered ale, and hurried to Sutton's side. Snaking his arm under his shoulders, he raised him a bit and put the tankard to his lips. Ale dribbled down his chin from taking such large gulps.

"Easy now, not all at once. This isn't a race." He put the tankard down.

His partner gazed at him. "You've always been a friend. After all the years in service. We picked up where we left off."

As he lowered him onto the bed, Sutton groaned and arched his back.

"What is it?" Wallace went to lift him, but Sutton stayed his hand.

"No. It stopped. We have much to talk about. I want you to tell me about Cambridge." Sutton fidgeted trying to find a comfortable position.

"I have a more important issue to discuss with you. I cannot be a partner with someone who believes in settling a disagreement with a duel and attempts to put a bullet in my back."

Sutton went still. His eyes trained on Wallace. "What's this about a bullet in your back? Who would dare do that?"

Wallace bent down and glared at him, eye-to-eye. "You."

Neither of them turned away.

"I may not be a good shot, but as broad as your back is, I couldn't miss it if I aimed at it."

Wallace straightened but didn't take his eyes off the man.

"Then what were you aiming at?"

"I fired at the maple tree as you strongly suggested." Sutton blinked, trying to focus his damaged eyes. "Why would I want to kill you? We've been friends since Cambridge."

Wallace grunted. Sutton's words brought him up short. A surge of guilt left him flushed and confused. Sutton was telling the truth.

"You thought I would… We may have our disagreements, but we've always been open and trusting with each other. I'm dying, and I go knowing I have been a fair and honest man." Sutton didn't even try to hide his yawn, his eyes closing.

"You're not dying. Get some rest. I'll return later and we can talk more. About…"

Wallace didn't bother finishing his sentence. Sutton was sound asleep.

He shoved the papers into the folio, left the room, and went to the tavern. Lenard sat at a table with tankards of ale ready.

"How is Mr. Sutton?"

"He woke for a bit. I left when he couldn't keep his eyes open. I find it curious. He denies shooting at me. But rather, he says that he followed my advice and aimed at the maple." Wallace paused. "I believe him."

"I didn't wait to find out where the bullet came from. I pulled you down when I heard the pistol go off. I would agree that Mr. Sutton wouldn't hurt you, but Your Grace, after these last few days can you trust his word?"

Wallace valued Lenard's opinion and took his time to think it through. "We have the means to prove where he aimed. There is still enough light for a walk in the woods. There's only one maple tree by the lake."

Did he want to know? Really want the truth or take Sutton's word? Lenard stood and waited. He downed his ale and stood.

"Best we get to it." He led the way to the door.

A hard, dry cough caught his attention. "Lord Wallace."

Alfred Bromley, the manager of Royston Textiles, waited for his attention. "Bromley. I'm on my way out."

"How is Sutton? Nasty accident. Is it serious?"

"Your concern is gratifying. He's resting at the moment."

"That's good news. I'll let the others know. Please, don't let me stop you." Bromley stood to the side and let them pass.

The sky was ablaze with reds and oranges as the sun began to sink below the horizon. The summer breeze shook the leaves as they made their way through Baycliff Woods. They emerged from the forest onto the field.

"The spot is up ahead." Lenard headed for the area where they prepared for the duel.

Wallace, close behind, scanned the peaceful field and found where Sutton had stationed himself. He bent and picked up Sutton's sooty cravat as well as a piece of flint, the correct size to fit the flint jaw of a pistol.

He stood and glanced toward the maple where Lenard headed. The tree was not anywhere near where Lenard pulled him to the ground. He trudged over to the tree, but Wallace knew what he would find.

He ran his hand up the trunk and found the splintered bark, the wound weeping with sap. He closed his eyes, relieved he had been wrong.

"We're finished here. I want to speak to Sutton. I need to make things right. Not tomorrow, but at once."

They hurried back to the inn through the fading light, content that the bullet was in the tree.

"Curious. The pistol didn't misfire. If it had, the shot would still be in the chamber. It's not like Sutton to mishandle the weapon."

"It wasn't like Mr. Sutton to call you out. He wasn't himself."

Wallace nodded as they entered the inn. Lenard went upstairs.

"Has the doctor returned to administer to Mr. Sutton?" Wallace asked Mrs. Jackson, the innkeeper's wife.

"No, Your Grace. No one's been to see him. Mr. Sutton's been as quiet as a mouse."

Wallace nodded and headed to his partner's room. He opened the door and was shocked at what he faced. A rusty sweet odor hit him. Lenard stood in front of him, his face white as a clean sheet.

"I'll fetch the doctor." Lenard hurried past him before he had time to ask any questions. He didn't have to. The familiar odor of blood and death filled the room.

"Wallace? Is that you?"

He rushed to Sutton's side. Sutton's skin had a bluish tinge. Blood was everywhere. In a controlled panic, he tried to find the source of the bleeding. Sutton stayed his hand.

"Is Lenard gone?"

Breathing hard, Wallace began to swab and search. Blood oozed from his partner's nose, ears, eyes, and mouth.

"Yes. Rest easy. He's gone for the doctor." Wallace rinsed out the cloth and stared at the basin as the water turned red.

A dry laugh escaped Sutton's lips. "Price. Can't do. Anything. For me. I'm dying." His halting words punctuated with shallow breaths led Wallace to believe his partner could be right.

Sutton beckoned him closer.

Wallace placed the warm damp cloth over Sutton's blood-encrusted eyes and bent closer to him, as he asked.

"Secure and protect. Sacred. Coffer." Sutton, his voice a whisper, was almost out of breath.

Wallace looked at him, unable to understand why blood oozed from every opening.

"What? Where?" He let the damp cloth rest on his eyes hoping he cleared them enough for Sutton to open them. It was a small act, but something he could do to ease his friend.

"Sommer-by-the-Sea. Guard. With a silver lock—" Sutton went into a fit of coughing.

Wallace raised him up a bit to help subdue his discomfort. He glanced at the door silently commanding Price and Lenard to rush in. No one was there.

"Should I add the coffer to my promise to marry your niece?"

He thought to lighten the mood. He pulled the cloth away with care.

Sutton's eyes fluttered open.

The fear in his friend's eyes made Wallace stop. "What is it? What must I do?" Anything to have your rest easy."

"By your oath." The man was out of breath.

"As a gentleman, I, Lord Ian Wallace, 4th Duke of Blackhall, promise to secure and protect the sacred coffer in Sommer-by-the-Sea *and* marry your Ivy-Rose." He bent closer to Sutton. "Is that better?"

All the fight seemed to drain out of his friend as he laid on the bed staring at him.

"Did you. Find the bullet. In the maple?" His voice was a whisper.

"You knew I would go?" Wallace sat on the chair next to the bed.

"You are. The most thorough. Person, I know. Next to Katherine." He tried to laugh, but all he let out of his mouth was foul air.

Wallace wiped the blood that trickled down his chin.

"I suppose. This wasn't. The greeting. You expected. Your first time here. And to the factory." His breaths came in spurts. "Tell me. About Cambridge."

"It can wait."

"But I can't. Tell me now."

"I spoke to several doctors about creating a clinic for our factory workers. I received as many opinions as people I interviewed." Why was this so important to him?

"You'll make the right decision…" Sutton gasped for breath, unable to fill his lungs but forced out another word. "It must be done."

"Rest. Lenard will be here with the doctor any time now."

Sutton gripped his hand. He arched his spine and reached for his back. Wallace got on his knees next to the bed and spoke into his ear. "Hold on a little longer."

Wallace stood by helpless as his partner fought for every breath, one tortured breath after another. Each breath was shallower than the last, until there were none.

The door flew open. Dr. Price rushed into the room.

Dazed, Wallace got to his feet. Lenard pulled him away.

"What happened after Lenard left?" Price examined Sutton.

"I tried to help him. No matter what I did I couldn't stop the bleeding. From his mouth, his ears, even his eyes." Wallace, who had been staring at Sutton, looked at the doctor. "He said he was dying. He said the words before, but I thought he was distraught. You said he would be better by the morning. But when Lenard and I returned from the tavern we found him…"

"Go on. I must know the rest." Price continued his examination.

"I told him you would be here soon. We settled into a light conversation. He asked about my trip to Cambridge and appeared to be comfortable until he started gasping for breath. He reached for his back before he… died." Wallace bowed his head still trying to make sense of what happened.

Dr. Price rolled Sutton onto his side and gave his back a thorough examination.

Curses fell from his lips as he returned Sutton to his back, placed his arms at his side, and raised the linen to cover his face.

"What happened? I couldn't find any wounds, yet he bled from every opening in his body. A few hours ago, he was improving." He searched the doctor's face, but the man was as shaken as he was.

"He died from a venomous poison. I witnessed this one other time, in Africa. A man brought a young boy to me bitten by a boomslang snake. The poison is slow-acting and causes this type of bleeding."

"Snake? Africa? This is England. The only snakes here are in Parliament."

Dr. Price let out a nervous chuckle.

"I stood by and did nothing as he died. On the battlefield I gave aid, comfort. This happened so fast." He stopped the images of the past. No sense going down that path. It wouldn't help Sutton. He closed his eyes. It wouldn't help him.

"There is nothing you or anyone else could have done for him. Death was inevitable with this venom."

He understood the doctor's words, but they still didn't make sense.

"An African snake here in Baycliff Woods? Surely someone would have seen a snake. Where is the bite mark? You gave him a thorough examination hours ago and found nothing." Wallace wasn't blaming the doctor simply trying to understand.

"I don't think he was bitten." Price lifted the linen from Sutton's body and rolled him on his side for Wallace to see his back.

Wallace and Lenard both glanced at it.

"Do you see the reddened spot in the middle of his back? It hadn't festered when I examined him earlier. If you examine his back now, you will find a small puncture."

Wallace bent down for a better view. Sutton's back had a modest-sized, round irritation. On closer examination he saw the small puncture.

"This was intentional." Wallace stood to his full height and stared at Price. "He's been murdered."

CHAPTER TWO

"SOMEONE JABBED SUTTON with something small and sharp." Dr. Price gently settled Sutton on the bed and straightened the sheet covering him.

"A needle or a dart?" Lenard's question startled Wallace and Price.

"Yes. I would suspect, one dipped in the venom then thrust into Sutton's back. This venom takes time to act. Under normal circumstances, the poison could have been administered at any time yesterday. But if the afternoon was any indication of his state of mind, I suspect he arrived at the clearing already agitated."

"His disposition worsened as the day progressed. I kept trying to calm him. Once he called off the duel, he settled down." Wallace didn't need to delve deep into his memory. Sutton's agitation had left a decided mark.

"The venom spreads faster when the victim is agitated." Price spoke from experience. "If the attack happened earlier in the day, symptoms may have presented sooner. But they didn't. Someone administered the venom at the dueling field. Do you remember who was in attendance?"

"It would be easier to ask who wasn't there. The clearing was a circus. Everyone gathered around Sutton begging him to settle the dispute without a duel." Wallace ran his hand through his hair.

"Murder." None of this made sense. "Who would want to kill him? And why?"

"Your Grace," said Price. Wallace gave the doctor his attention. "You mustn't say anything about snake venom to anyone." Wallace nodded in agreement. "It will only start a panic. Without a militia in the area, things could get out of hand. People will be beating the ground looking for something that doesn't exist."

"You have the right of it. The sooner I bring him back to Sommer-by-the-Sea the better for everyone. We'll leave in the morning."

"There is nothing left for me to do here." The doctor took his medical bag and went to the door. "And, Your Grace."

He glanced at the doctor.

"There was nothing you or anyone could have done for him. There is no cure. This snake's venom is a death sentence. I'll tell the innkeeper to lock this door. You don't need anyone disturbing him. Let him rest in peace."

Wallace nodded as the doctor left the room. Absolving him from saving Sutton's life did not make him feel any better. Reeling from the speed of the events over the last few hours, he sat next to Sutton half expecting him to sit up and tell him they had it all wrong.

The thin linen covering the body sculpted Sutton's face like a mask. Every bone evident, but no rising chest.

Breathe. Damn it. Breathe. Please. One breath.

At last, Wallace closed his eyes, his head bowed. "I give you my word I will marry your Ivy-Rose, secure the sacred coffer, and find out who did this to you, so help me God." His pain-soaked voice was a whisper.

"Excuse me, Your Grace."

Wallace glanced at the door surprised to see Myles Jackson, the innkeeper standing in the doorway. His usually tough veneer had been traded for a compassionate expression.

He glanced at the shroud-draped body, got to his feet, and left the room. Behind him, he listened to the lock engage as Jackson turned the key.

The innkeeper caught up with him at the head of the stairs. "Everyone thought his wounds were trifling. Soot and gunpowder. No one thought Mr. Sutton would die."

"Me neither." They started down the stairs.

"Without knowing anything, people make up their own answers. Some of it may be upsetting to you. I sat your friend at a table where the two of you can talk and not be disturbed."

"You have my thanks for the warning." The last thing he wanted to do was talk about the duel, Sutton's death, or anything else at the moment.

He went down to the tavern. Lenard sat at a table off in a corner away from most of the others. A barmaid brought them bread and cheese.

Wallace and Lenard glanced at Jackson who saluted them and went about his business.

"The poor devil. Sutton's pistol misfired. I hear tell the man barely made it to his bed before he died." Wallace glanced at the table where the man sat. He didn't recognize any of the men.

"Poor devil? My arse." Another man at the same table shouted out silencing the room. "His pistol misfired all right, trying to shoot his partner in the back. I say good riddance. The way his workers are treated, I say good riddance, indeed." The man raised his tankard in salute.

Wallace scanned the room relieved that no one joined in the salute.

The man's eyes skittered around the room. Finally, he put his untouched tankard down.

"You're all wrong. I was with him." Everyone turned toward Roddy. "Let me sum it up for you. Mr. Sutton settled the issue and called off the duel. The two shook hands and Lord Wallace started to leave the clearing. Mr. Sutton discharged the pistol to clear it of gunpowder before putting it away."

"Wallace is no better than Sutton. The two of them were scratching at each other to take advantage of us. If Sutton hadn't fired first, Wallace would have." An agitated rumble went through the crowd.

Wallace's forearm muscles tightened, and his hands flexed as a rage worked its way through his body. Lenard put his hand on Wallace's arm. His valet knew him well.

"That would have been impossible unless His Lordship hit Mr. Sutton over the head with his pistol. He had no intention of dueling." Roddy stood so everyone would hear him. "The two knew each other since they were lads. Before Lord Wallace joined the regiment and went to Spain and Mr. Sutton to North America. Neither man is ruthless. Not like some we know. Disagreeing for sure, but there was no animosity between the two."

A swell of agreement from Sutton workers filled the room.

"Take advantage of us?" Roddy went on. "If giving us wages that are enough to support our families, seeing to their wellbeing, and working side-by-side with us is taking advantage of us then it's fine with me. To Lord Wallace and Mr. Sutton." The men lifted their tankards. The Sutton workers drank them dry followed by the thunderous clap of empty tankards slammed onto the tables.

"You don't know what you're talking about. They may take care of you. You're their foreman. What about us?" Another man in the crowd tried to provoke others to join in.

Who was this instigator? Wallace didn't want to stand but he couldn't make out the man clearly.

Roddy went over to the man. Wallace noticed other Sutton men stood with him.

"Us? Certainly, that doesn't include you. You're not a Sutton Textile man. Who do you work for, Royston Textiles?"

"He's not one of ours." The shout came from somewhere in the crowded room.

The agitator's eyes darted around the room. He didn't find any allies. Even the people at his table sat back, putting some distance between them and him.

"What do you know about…us?" Roddy pressed the man, his hands fisted at his side.

"That will be enough. Cool your tempers or I'll clear the place and you'll die of thirst with no other tavern for four hours," Jackson bellowed with a club in his hand.

Roddy stepped back and went to a table across the room, his men behind him. The temperature and tension in the room lowered.

"Sutton knew how to handle a pistol; even with drink in him, he could load and prime without any issues. He did it often enough in battle." Wallace glanced at the table as if the answer lay in plain sight.

"I watched him the entire time waiting for him to stop the duel. I don't remember him loading his pistol. Someone handed the weapon to him. I can see the man's arm, well dressed." Wallace shook his head. "But I didn't see his face."

"Do you think someone tampered with his pistol?"

"I think the accident with the pistol was a distraction from what was really planned." Wallace could feel it in his bones. It could be linked to the workers and their grievance, but murder was a drastic measure.

Wallace cut a slab of bread and ate it and every so often nibbled on a piece of cheese. The events kept running through his mind. It was not the situation at the mill that concerned him. At the moment, he was not looking forward to telling Sutton's family.

"I had so much to discuss with him. The factory. Cambridge. Now I'll never have my answer," he mumbled under his breath, and drank some ale to wash down the disappointment.

"Your answer?" Lenard stared at him waiting for an explanation.

"I researched what we needed to do to create a factory medical clinic. There are several possibilities. Sutton had a direction, a plan. We were going to discuss it."

"There are others who can assist with the decision, even the workers. They must have some ideas. Did Mr. Sutton say anything?"

"Sutton was lucid for a short time." Wallace finished his ale and stood. "When you went to fetch Dr. Price, I wanted to talk about it, but...."

"From Mrs. Jackson." The barmaid interrupted and put down a plate of stew in front of each of them. Before he could say anything, she was gone. He got a quick nod from Jackson when he glanced at the bar.

The rest of their evening was spent reminiscing about Sutton and Cambridge.

THE FOLLOWING MORNING was deceptively bright and comfortable. Wallace stood at the bedroom window staring at the clear-blue sky with a tinge of pink. It was a good day for the four-hour carriage ride if they started early. The roads would be dry and somewhat easy to travel.

The crunch of gravel grabbed his attention. His gaze drifted to the yard below. A wagon draped in black crepe with Lenard driving and Roddy sitting next to him came into view. He rubbed the back of his neck. He wanted this over but didn't look forward to it starting.

For Sutton it was the ride that would take him home to his final resting place. Other than family, none were as close to him as Sutton. Bringing him home was a duty he didn't take lightly. It brought back the nightmare when he rode in front of the carriage that brought his father and brother home.

The second son of Geoffrey Mitchell Ian Wallace, the 3rd Duke of Blackhall, Ian was proud and supported his older brother's responsibility. Father had trained his heir well and never forgot he had two sons.

'Each of you have a responsibility, your own duty to the king. Geoffrey, your duty is to serve in Parliament. And you Ian, it is your duty to

serve in the army. You both will do what you must to the best of your ability. You are a Wallace.'

As a lad of six, Ian proudly stood by as his father bought and signed the papers for his commission. Rather than go off to service as a young lad, his father made a provision for him to study at Cambridge. There would be time enough for him to serve his king after graduation. So, like his brother, he too went off to Cambridge.

Geoffrey trained to be a duke. A hint of a smile spread across Ian's face. That left him to follow his passion.

Mechanicals fascinated him, how they were constructed, how they worked, how they could be improved. In Cambridge he studied drafting and brought that skill to the battlefield and quickly became an asset to Wellington's army in Spain. He drafted schematics of military fortifications with precision and beauty.

As a retired soldier, Wallace's passion never wavered. He found more outlets for his skills drafting mechanicals, each part intricately documented, and at times, found ways to improve them. When Sutton told him he needed a partner to modernize his textile mill, Wallace didn't think twice.

That seemed so long ago, another lifetime. He needed to put those memories away. At the moment, his energies needed to be focused on bringing Bennett Sutton home.

The last of his clothes packed into his portmanteau, he was ready to meet Lenard in the tavern for something to eat. He opened the door and stared across the hall at Sutton's door. He should look in on him. He hesitated. It wouldn't be a short visit and there was a lot to do once they reached Sommer-by-the-Sea. Best to get started.

In the tavern he picked up the local newspaper, found Lenard, and took a seat.

The loud discussions continued from the night before with new participants. People complained about the coming future and rallied they would put a stop to mechanicals replacing people, taking away their jobs, leaving many without a means to survive. Others defended the growth and opportunity industrialization provided. Wallace understood change was never easy, but it was also inevitable.

He drank his morning coffee and read the paper. The local news covered petty thievery and a small article about the workers. Turning to the news from London he froze.

Wallace leaned forward and reread the article.

"The very eligible and handsome Lord Wallace, 4th Duke of Black-hall is finally off the market. He's made his vow. Does Lady Ivy-Rose T. even know she snagged the wealthiest and handsomest man in London? And does Lady RH realize she's missed her opportunity? This should be something to watch unfold. All the best to the happy (?) couple. No matter who becomes the next Duchess of Blackhall."

He groaned as the essence of his oath, made openly in front of witnesses, stared at him in the newspaper. He couldn't deny the article. Enough people heard him. He folded the sheet and put it in his pocket.

At least he had some time. Sutton had mentioned Ivy-Rose was in a seminary. There was no need to take immediate action. There would be plenty of time when she reached a marriageable age. For now, he would see to her wellbeing, be her guardian while she attended school.

With that issue resolved, at least for the moment, he faced the next one – bringing Sutton home.

"If you're ready, Your Grace." Jackson stood at the table. "It would be best to take care of this while the inn is quiet.

CHAPTER THREE

T HE JINGLING KEYS on Jackson's belt echoed as Wallace followed him down the hall. The noise from the tavern faded to a hushed buzz in this part of the inn, something Wallace hadn't noticed before.

"We'll take Sutton down the back stairs. They lead directly to the yard."

"You have my thanks." He walked next to the innkeeper. "With what I heard downstairs I would rather not listen to what is being said. I wouldn't be able to remain silent."

"Those men, the ones that are so vocal, are not from Royston Mills. From what Roddy told me they are not your men either. Your men don't make any trouble. These men? All they do is complain. I'm ready to toss them out on their ears." Wallace appreciated Jackson's frankness.

"Then why are those men here?" Wallace shook his head as they came to Sutton's door. "What do they hope to accomplish?"

Jackson, the key in his hand, glanced at him and let out a deep breath.

"Speak to Roddy. These men talk as if they have direct information when all they do is take hearsay and make it sound like the truth. Go to your foreman if you want accurate information." Jackson sprung the lock and pushed the door wide open.

The two men stood at the doorway, stunned. Clothes, papers,

everything, tossed as if a windstorm had swept through the room.

Wallace headed for Sutton but stopped in his tracks at the scene before them. Sutton's legs dangled off the bed. His clothes in disarray, the bed linen pulled away. Wallace hurried over to Sutton and settled him on the bed.

"He doesn't deserve this." Jackson scooped up the odds and ends on the table and in the bed.

Wallace retrieved the linen from the floor and covered his body.

"I'll brain the person who did this when I find him." Jackson's anger spiraled into a full rage.

While Jackson made quick work of gathering everything in the room, Wallace scanned the papers strewn on the floor and put them back into the folio. Nothing appeared to be missing. They would have to wait until later.

"That's everything. I'll fetch Roddy and Lenard." Jackson handed him Sutton's belongings and left for the yard.

Wallace stepped to the window. He needed more light for a better look at what Jackson had handed him: a brass button, pocket watch and fob, wallet with several small denomination banknotes, a card case with Sutton's calling card as well as those of others. He put the items his handkerchief and stuffed it into his pocket.

A movement outside caught his attention, but it was the window that he stared at. He pulled at the sash, but it wouldn't budge. A glance at the lock gave him the answer.

"They're coming," Jackson said, entering the room.

"I examined the window. It's locked from the inside. Whoever entered came in through the door."

"Impossible." Jackson stood with him finding the very idea absurd. "I got the only key, and it never leaves my side."

There was no sense arguing with the innkeeper. Unless the intruder came in through the window and locked up after himself before going out the door, someone else had a key.

"The carriage is ready." Roddy and Lenard stood at the door.

"What's that?" Wallace stared at a well-made coffin, lined with Sutton Textile's finest material.

"We couldn't send Mr. Sutton home laying in the back of a wagon. The carpenter here offered to fashion a coffin. One of our men went home and told everyone. He returned before daybreak. The women made the lining, fitting it as best they could, given the amount of time they had."

"Lord Wallace, you and Roddy go down to the yard. Lenard and I will get Mr. Sutton and bring him down."

He didn't argue. He and Roddy made their way to the carriage and waited.

"The men would like to know what you plan to do with the factory." Roddy was clearly upset. "Some are saying that without Mr. Sutton you'll be selling or worse, closing the factory down."

A shadow of annoyance crossed Wallace's face but quickly faded. He shouldn't be surprised that the gossip and rumors were running rampant. Sutton was not even buried, and people are jumping to their own conclusions about the factory and about his death. No sense in being angry with Roddy. He was only the messenger.

"My task is to bring Sutton home to his family for them to bury and mourn him as is proper." He considered closing the factory for two days out of respect for his partner, but that move would cause more anxiety. "As much as it pains me to say, it will be business as usual at the factory. Your question tells me the workers are anxious. Closing, even to mourn for one day will only add to the rumors. Workers can be given time to pay their respects. You can tell everyone Sutton Textile is not closing nor are there any plans to sell."

"I would not mention it—"

"You did the right thing. With all that I heard in the tavern I can understand why the men are concerned." Wallace turned to mount his horse but hesitated.

"Who did you hear the rumors from? Most of our people returned home yesterday."

"Several men from Royston Textile are at the inn. They made it sound as if the sale was a certainty."

Four men rode into the yard as Lenard and Jackson reached the yard with the coffin. Roddy nodded to them.

"Lord Wallace, we're here to accompany Mr. Sutton home."

Sutton may have been a bit crazed yesterday, but he had put together a fine unit of men. Loyal. Honorable.

"I thank you for his family."

Roddy and Lenard mounted the wagon. He mounted up and led the procession out of the yard and onto the road that would take them into Sommer-by-the-Sea.

They'd divided the business responsibilities between them from the beginning of their partnership. Sutton took care of the day-to-day in the village. He took care of the financing and trade, which kept him in London most of the time. As often as Sutton had invited him, Wallace had been to the coastal town once, when he signed the partnership papers.

COMING OUT OF Baycliff Woods two and half hours later, he smelled the briny ocean air. The open road ahead stretched for miles. The day was balmy with a clear summer sky. They were on the final part of the journey, ninety minutes from Sommer-by-the-Sea.

The rhythmic clinking of the horse's metal tack and the beat of their hooves mesmerized him. He welcomed the escape from the last day's events and guilt, his inability to prevent them.

He needed to meet with several people. Sutton's solicitor, Judge Scofield, was easy to talk to. With any luck, Scofield would tell him the document Sutton signed was not binding. Nothing would please him more than to tear it up.

Someone had to speak to the village vicar. Making burial arrangements was the family's responsibility, but how could the task be left to a young girl? Surely the vicar would help.

The most difficult visit was the last one, visiting the seminary. Telling an adult someone near to them had died was bad enough, but a little girl? He would tell her she had to be brave and not worry. Things would stay much the same as now. She would continue to live at the seminary. He would see to her wellbeing, she could call on him when needed, and yes, count on him.

But if she shed tears? Sheer fright rushed up his spine. Before the panic took over, he gave his head a shake. He would console her. Perhaps a small gift to distract her. Yes, that sounded right.

"Your Grace."

Wallace came to a halt and rode over to Roddy.

"This road continues to Newcastle Upon Tyne. Here is where we turn off for Sommer-by-the-Sea." Roddy nodded to his right. "That road divides. The way to the village is on the lower road. Mr. Sutton's house is on the upper."

"You and the others take Mr. Sutton home. I will be there as soon as I finish in the village."

Roddy nodded and started the wagon toward High Cliff Road. Wallace headed down Kings Lane into the village.

He passed several farms as he rode down the lower road and came to the outskirts of the village. The road wound around a bend and in the distance came upon the larger townhouses. He crossed the bridge and came to Westmore Commons.

A gentle breeze from the ocean cooled the warm summer day. In the distance, several boat masts peaked above the rooftops. Sea birds flew overhead, squawking on their way to the beach.

He passed the town square busy with people hurrying about the market. The merchants' stalls filled with villagers buying vegetables, hand pies, baked goods, fish, leather items, material, clothes – the variety of goods went on and on.

After leaving the market, he headed to the village hall and the judge's house across the lane.

"Lord Wallace, come in, come in. It's good to see you." Scofield welcomed him and led him into his office. "Welcome to Sommer-by-the-Sea."

"Thank you. I regret I come with sad news."

"Please, be seated." The judge motioned to the chairs by the cold hearth.

He settled into the chair and waited a heartbeat before he began. "Bennett Sutton has passed on. I was with him and several of our workers in Royston Mills. We've brought him home."

Gone was Scofield's open, welcoming expression. At first it was replaced with surprise then astonished grief. "Was it a factory accident?"

"No." There was no way for him to make this pleasant. "Sutton was murdered."

Judge Scofield sucked in a breath. The judge's sad expression changed to disbelief then anger filled the man's dark penetrating eyes. "Tell me what happened and why you think he didn't die of natural causes."

Wallace explained the events and Dr. Price's findings.

"I've known Elliott Price a long time. He is an excellent doctor." Scofield's shock had ebbed away.

"There is another issue. Sutton signed a paper to cover his losses at the card table." Wallace removed the paper from his pocket and handed it to the judge.

Scofield read the document, glanced at him, then read it again. He put the paper down, folded his hands, and stared at him. "Where there any witnesses?"

Wallace's stomach dropped. "Everyone in the inn."

The judge's stare didn't falter.

"Sutton did this often. However, this is not like the others."

"What do you mean, not like the others?"

"The other documents were real, but he never signed his own name."

"They weren't binding." Wallace smirked.

"He signed them Oliver Cromwell, Arthur Pendragon, and most recently Napoleon Bonaparte. But this, this is Sutton's name, his own signature. I still must speak to the witnesses, but from what you've said, the paper is binding."

"I thought as much. Although I admit, I did hope you would find some irregularity."

This wasn't the outcome he hoped for. All that he needed to do now was inform Ivy-Rose, give her Sutton's belongings, and take care of matters at the factory.

He could still hand the house over to Ivy-Rose, although how would she maintain it? Should he sell it? No, of course not. Where would the poor girl go after the seminary?

"Are you feeling well?" the judge asked.

"Quite fine." *Perhaps keeping the house is a better idea.* He could give her the house as part of her dowry.

"I will speak to the vicar, Mr. Hendrickson, and make the necessary arrangements." The judge put Sutton's note into a folio on his desk. "I'll also confirm the note."

"That is good of you." Wallace got to his feet, "I need to speak to his niece."

"Then you'll be off to Mrs. Bainbridge at the Sommer-by-the-Sea Female Seminary on Wisteria Way. Please call upon me should you have any questions. I'll see you at Thornton Abbey after the burial."

"Thornton Abbey?" Wallace hesitated on his way to the door.

"Sutton's home on High Cliff Road. As Sutton's partner you'll need to be present when I read the will. I will move all the papers through probate as fast as I can."

Wallace left the judge and strolled through the market browsing, still not sure what he wanted. He passed a book seller and a florist. Neither appealed to him for his mission. *What do you bring a young girl?* He was about to give up when he came to a knickknackery. The perfect place to find something for Ivy-Rose.

He entered the stall and quickly became overwhelmed by the shelves filled with dolls. Dolls filled several shelves. How was he to pick the right one?

"Excuse me, sir." A woman and a young girl squeezed past

him.

"Of course." He touched the brim of his hat and stood to the side to let them pass. The young girl was very definite about which doll she wanted.

"Which color hair do you want, black or brown?" the mother, or at least he thought the woman was her mother, asked.

The child examined the dolls intently. It almost made him laugh. She scrutinized the dolls as if the purchase was important.

"I'll take the one with the brown hair."

"You made a good choice," her mother said. "Let's go home. Your new friend can join us at dinner."

The woman paid for her purchase and left the stall.

Wallace went to the shelf and picked up the doll with black hair. Moments later he too left the stall and found himself across from a florist. As an afterthought, he bought a bouquet of summer flowers for the headmistress.

The mixture of grief and distress that plagued him since yesterday lifted as he glanced at his purchases. His mouth curved into an unconscious smile as he headed toward the seminary on Wisteria Way.

CHAPTER FOUR

L ORD WALLACE ARRIVED at The Sommer-by-the-Sea Female Seminary and rapped on the door.

"Good day, sir. Can I help you?" A woman wearing a chatelaine answered the door.

"I'd like to speak to Mrs. Bainbridge." Wallace took his card from his vest pocket and handed it to the woman.

"This way, Your Grace. I'll tell Mrs. Bainbridge you're here."

The housekeeper left him in the parlor and closed the door behind her. The pale green wallpaper, white trim, and touches of Chinese art surprised him. The room was elegant for a village school. Before he could examine his surroundings further, the door opened.

"Lord Wallace." Mrs. Bainbridge, a woman about his age, glided into the room and commanded control of the interview by only uttering his name.

"Please pardon the intrusion. I hope I'm not taking you away from anything urgent. I brought these for you." He handed her the bouquet.

"You are not intruding at all." The headmistress took the offered flowers. "You do have me curious. What could the Duke of Blackhall possibly want at my seminary?"

"Ivy-Rose." His low confident voice along with the single name shifted the control of the situation to him.

The flowers almost dropped to the floor, along with her pleasant expression. She gave him a questioning stare.

"Let me explain. My partner is Bennett Sutton."

Mrs. Bainbridge's face brightened, but only a bit.

"I'm bringing sad news. Mr. Sutton passed away. I'm afraid I have the duty to inform the child of her loss."

Mrs. Bainbridge nodded her understanding, glanced at him, and rang for her housekeeper.

The door opened moments later. "Yes, Mrs. Bainbridge."

"Ellen, please tell Lady Katherine to join me."

The housekeeper left.

"What's that?" Mrs. Bainbridge gestured to his other purchase.

Wallace raised the doll to show her. "I admit to knowing little about children. I thought to give Ivy-Rose something to take her mind off Sutton." He stared at her uncomfortably. "Now, that doesn't sound like a good idea."

There was a soft knock on the door.

Mrs. Bainbridge took the doll from him and handed him the flowers.

"I suggest you don't call her Ivy-Rose." Mrs. Bainbridge glanced toward the door. "Come in."

"You wanted to see me?" Lady Katherine Thornton glided into the room.

It was Wallace's turn to be confused. He was not certain why he held the bouquet. Expecting a child, instead, he stared at an elegant, graceful, and attractive woman in a peacock blue dress that complimented her raven black hair and sparkling violet eyes. Her only jewelry, a silver locket around her neck. *Perfect* was the word that came to mind.

He glanced at Mrs. Bainbridge, who tried not to smile. Wallace gave her a nod and gathered his thoughts. *So, this is Sutton's niece.*

"Lady Katherine Thornton. May I present the Duke of Blackhall, Lord Wallace, your Uncle Bennett's business partner." The headmistress turned to him.

"Thank you, Mrs. Bainbridge." His eyes never left Ivy-Rose, or more correctly, Lady Katherine.

"I brought these for Mrs. Bainbridge and…" He picked up the doll and showed her. "And this was for you. I thought you were… Sutton spoke of you, but he didn't make it clear that you were a grown woman."

Katherine gaped at him, then Mrs. Bainbridge. Unable to contain herself, she started laughing. "It seems we are both the brunt of my uncle's humor. He led me to believe you were a fat, dreary old man."

So like Sutton to mislead. He pressed on his stomach and looked at her. "I seemed to have lost a great deal of weight and dreariness working with your uncle. I would say it is all for the better."

"Lord Wallace, I can see why you and my uncle get along. Thank you for your thoughtfulness. We meet at last. He speaks of you often." She let out a deep sigh. "Sometimes the man expects everyone to know what's in his head."

To Wallace, the situation would have been funny if his mission wasn't so grave.

"Why don't the two of you sit down?" Mrs. Bainbridge sat near the door.

Katherine gestured to a chair and sat in the one across from him.

"If you're here to meet with him, I'm afraid Uncle Bennett's gone to Royston Mills on business. I'm sure—"

"No, that's not why I'm here. I was with him yesterday."

She sat there, happy and unsuspecting. What he had to tell her would be devastating and for that, he was sorry.

"Lady Katherine, I'm sorry to tell you that your Uncle Bennett passed away last night."

The gentle smile dropped from her face, replaced with a blank stare.

"What happened?" Her voice was too soft and low for him to

make out what she asked. Her lips told him her question.

He planned a simple explanation for a young girl. Not to withhold the truth from her, but to give her time to adjust. Over time he would tell her everything that happened. But now? Giving a simple explanation would never do. *No. This woman will demand every detail. Where to start?*

He glanced at her lovely, anxious face and made his decision. The truth. Nothing less would do.

"Your uncle was uncomfortable with the recent situation with the workers. It's why we went to Royston Mills, to speak with the owner of Royston Textiles."

"Yes, I am aware."

"Sutton became anxious about the workers who spoke out against him. I thought a game of cards would distract him. Unfortunately, that did not work."

"Uncle Bennett did not play cards very well." Her eyes softened. "He never won when we played."

"Yesterday he was reckless with his playing and his betting." Wallace chose his words with care. "We played a private game, just the two of us."

"Let me guess. My uncle was losing badly."

"Yes." She was taking Sutton's passing remarkably well. "I wouldn't take my winnings."

"Ah, but my dear uncle demanded you must." She nodded and her mouth curved into an unconscious smile.

His fingers ached and for a fleeting moment, he imagined running them along her moist lips.

Unnerved by his wandering thoughts, Wallace couldn't remain in his seat any longer. He rose and walked to the window. "One thing led to another. Sutton challenged me to a duel." He turned and faced her.

She sat ramrod straight with a penetrating stare. He didn't like being on the receiving side of her glare. No, not one bit.

KATHERINE SAID NOTHING. She had given this man the benefit of the doubt. Her chest heaved as her anger grew, but she waited for him to finish his tale. She had never met Lord Wallace, but her uncle spoke of him often. He described Wallace as a fair and generous man. Was *that* a tale as much as the appearance Bennett described?

Lords are never fair or generous. They are always after something. She had warned him, but would he listen?

"Now, now, Ivy-Rose. Don't worry about things of which you know nothing. And Wallace? To know the man is to love him."

Ivy-Rose, indeed. She removed her handkerchief from her waist. Her uncle used her middle name to irritate her, and it worked. How he liked her to call him Uncle Bennett. And how she refused him the honor, except in public of course. Ten years older than her, they looked more like brother and sister than uncle and niece.

Her eyes never left Wallace's. She could understand why Bennett was taken in. Wallace appeared friendly, fit, and fine looking. Taller than most and based on the fit of his coat, he had no need for shoulder padding. His dark, thick hair and well-trimmed beard added a bit of mystery and wildness to his overall image. But it was his eyes that held her captive, hazel eyes whose color seemed to change with his temperament. At the moment they were clear, honest. That remained to be seen.

"We got as far as the field of honor. I convinced him a duel didn't settle anything. We decided to continue our discussion in the morning and were leaving the clearing."

"If he canceled the duel, why did you shoot him?"

She steeled herself not to gasp as his clear hazel eyes turned a shade of blue she had never witnessed before. The muscles along his jaw tensed as he struggled to control his anger.

Katherine didn't intimidate easily, and she didn't now. No,

Lord Wallace walked up and glared at her, silently incensed by her accusation.

"I did not shoot your uncle. I had no intention of dueling. Your uncle was in his cups. His own second tried to reason with him."

"Whose word do I have but yours? I can't imagine you would confess." Lords, dukes, earls, none of them took responsibility for their actions. *They just give orders and treat people…*

It didn't matter how *they* treated people. She quieted her mind. She stayed in Sommer-by-the-Sea to get away from the *ton*, their narrow-mindedness, horrid rules, and men who cared nothing for the consequences they left behind.

"I couldn't have shot him if I wanted to. I never loaded my pistol." He remained quiet while she took in that information. Then, he told her the truth. "Your uncle didn't die of a pistol shot. Your uncle died of poison."

"Poison?" Katherine gasped, touching her throat.

Wallace took her hand. She didn't pull it away. She glanced at his face filled with concern, not arrogance.

"Dr. Price found a small puncture in his back. He suspects a thin weapon, its point dipped in deadly snake venom."

"Snake venom? A puncture. Not a bite?"

"No, not a bite." She fixed on his gaze that demanded she pay attention.

"Bennett Sutton was murdered." His voice turned deep, warm, and smooth like good French brandy.

Katherine closed her eyes and took a deep breath. Had her reaction been too harsh? Her mind filled with so many thoughts. All of them bombarded her at once.

Mrs. Bainbridge came to her side.

"Katherine?"

She nodded, not wanting to say anything. Lord Wallace went to give her a glass half-filled with sherry from the sideboard, but her hand shook too much to hold it.

He put the glass to her lips.

"A sip." She glimpsed at the concern in his eyes as he coaxed her to drink.

Katherine did as he said. One sip, then she gently pushed the glass away. The amber liquid warmed her insides and set something free. A single tear ran down her cheek.

He took her handkerchief and with a gentle touch, captured the tear.

"I swore to your uncle, and I will swear to you." He spoke to her softly but with determination. "I will find who did this and bring them to justice."

"I'm sure this was not easy for you." His words were beginning to settle in. The shock of Bennett's death was one thing, but murder? She glanced at him, struck by his sincerity. His words were not empty. Lord Wallace had every intention of finding Bennett's murderer.

"There is more I must tell you." Wallace downed the rest of her sherry. "We locked Sutton's door last night. This morning we found the room tossed. Someone was searching for something."

"Robbery?" Mrs. Bainbridge asked. She hadn't left Lady Katherine's side.

"No. I have your uncle's personal effects." He took the wrapped handkerchief from his pocket and handed it to her. "There's a gold watch and fob along with his wallet and a sizeable number of banknotes, along with some odds and ends. These would have been taken if robbery were the objective."

She unwrapped the small package, her heart pounding. Tears welled up as she gazed at Bennett's pocket watch. He was never without it. She let out a breath and rewrapped his belongings.

"You're quite correct. It wasn't robbery. What would someone want from Bennett?" Katherine mumbled.

"I have no idea. But I fear you may be in jeopardy. I intend to make arrangements with the magistrate for your safety."

"The magistrate cannot help. There is no militia in our village." Mrs. Bainbridge joined in. "And Lord Barrington is in London. I believe he's returning home within the next few days.

We can speak to him then."

"Lord Barrington? Reese Barrington?"

"Yes. Do you know His Lordship?"

"I do. I meet with him and his brother Edward from time to time. I didn't realize he lived in Sommer-by-the-Sea."

"Lord Barrington retired here. He and his former officers created a men's club of sorts, The Sommer League. More recently, they've been called upon to assist in caring for the area since we do not have a militia stationed in the village. The closest is at Bamburgh Castle." A determined glare filled the headmistress' eyes. "Lady Katherine. Under these circumstances, you cannot stay at Thornton Abbey by yourself."

"Nonsense. I'm not alone. Mr. and Mrs. Russell as well as my staff are with me."

"Be reasonable. They are not young, nor are they able to protect you. Stay with me here."

"Absolutely not. I will not be routed from my home."

"Lord Wallace, speak some sense into her."

"Lady Katherine, I am in need of lodging. I didn't plan on staying in Sommer-by-the-Sea. Perhaps I can stay as a guest at Thornton Abbey and provide you with the protection Mrs. Bainbridge insists you need."

"That would be impossible." Mrs. Bainbridge registered her adamant disagreement.

Indeed, your request is... Katherine turned and glared at Mrs. Bainbridge. "Why not? Thornton Abbey has a history of hosting visitors. You know yourself I've opened the abbey to others many times."

"Your uncle lived with you."

"I'm not alone. My staff is with me." Katherine glared at Mrs. Bainbridge one corner of her mouth twisted upward. "If you are so concerned for my reputation, you are welcome to stay at the abbey as well. I believe the Seminary is closed for the summer."

CHAPTER FIVE

L ADY KATHERINE'S SUPPORT of his bold suggestion surprised him. Then again, the woman was full of surprises. He suspected the headmistress' objection drove Lady Katherine's response.

Wallace found the mischief in her eyes captivating. When riled, her violet eyes brightened with fire. For a fleeting moment, he wondered how they appeared when the lady was overcome by passion.

"Thank you." Mrs. Bainbridge glanced at him. "I accept your gracious offer."

"Roddy and the other Sutton workers brought your uncle home." Wallace paused. "I took the liberty and spoke to Judge Scofield before I came here. He will speak to the vicar."

Wallace, watchful and concerned, recognized as the reality of the situation made its way to her face. The light in her eyes, her smile, both turned somber.

It took all his strength to remain still when she struggled to control her quivering lip. The muscles in his arms twitched, wanting to embrace her, protect her.

She turned from him to the headmistress.

"You're welcome at the abbey any time you choose to arrive." Lady Katherine turned to him. "I'll be a few minutes."

He didn't have time to respond. The woman glided out of the

room in the same fashion she had glided in.

"Katherine is a strong woman." Wallace stared after her.

"I agree. Thank you, Your Grace. I wouldn't want anyone to face this alone."

Wallace scrutinized Mrs. Bainbridge. "You didn't object to my staying at the abbey." The hint of a smile touched his lips.

"Why, Your Grace, whatever gave you that idea?" Her innocent expression made him chuckle.

"Ordinarily, I would say Lady Katherine is well-protected by her staff. But this is not an ordinary situation. Either way, we both got what we wanted."

"Yes, we did." Although he didn't know why he made the suggestion. He had every intention of staying at the factory.

"If you will excuse me, I, too, must gather my things." Mrs. Bainbridge picked up the doll, put it on the mantel, and stood back. "I think it looks lovely there. Don't you?"

"It does." Wallace could feel the heat running up his neck and was thankful his beard would hide the flush of his cheeks.

"Your gift is a kind and thoughtful act. An action that wouldn't enter the mind of many men, especially those of the *ton*. I can see why Bennett chose you for his partner. Please, help yourself to some refreshments while you wait for Lady Katherine." Mrs. Bainbridge left the room.

Everyone in England, including him, were aware of Mrs. Bainbridge and her female seminary. A unique place for unique young women. One didn't apply, but instead had to be personally invited and interviewed by the headmistress. Each of her charges had a unique gift. And at the moment, he wondered what gift Lady Katherine had cultivated.

Wallace took a cup of tea and a biscuit, sat on the very comfortable sofa, and waited for Lady Katherine. The next hurdle faced him: how to tell her about the ownership of the house and that they were to be married. He glanced at the door, then his cup of tea. He should have taken a full glass of brandy.

HALF AN HOUR later, Katherine sat atop her horse, Lord Wallace riding next to her. They were on their way to Thornton Abbey.

"Before your uncle passed away, he said something strange." They walked their horses along High Cliff Road. "I waited to say anything because he made it sound as if he gave me a great secret. He made me pledge to keep it safe." Wallace glanced at her. "Secure and protect the sacred coffer with the silver lock."

Katherine's eyes widened.

"What is this coffer, what does it contain, and where is it? I must know so I can fulfill my pledge to Sutton. All I know is that it is here in Sommer-by-the-Sea."

"There is an old legend associated with the village, one we celebrate every year on the twenty-second of June. My family is descended from Lord Stephen Thornton, a fourteenth-century Templar knight.

"Lord Stephen was a knight who, with his sword, never lost a battle. His sword became a symbol of his prowess. Its name, *Invincible,* was etched on its blade. When the Templar brotherhood needed him, he answered their call. His great sword didn't fail him. Minstrels sang about him and *Invincible,* sowing the seeds of the legend. Only the true of heart could wield the power of the sword, be invincible.

"Those against the Templars, King Phillip in particular, were determined to possess the weapon. Lord Stephen was just as determined that *Invincible* never fall into their hands."

"In a show of faith, when they arrested the Grand Master, Lord Stephen surrendered. Pope Clement V exonerated the Templars. That is, all but the Grand Master and the faithful with him.

"Before his execution, Lord Stephen secreted his sword out of France and sent it here to his father Aldus. He sent word he would rather die than allow the sword to become the possession of the unholy, for surely the charges against his Templar brothers was the work of the devil.

"Lord Thornton hid the sacred sword here in Sommer-by-the-Sea. Today, the village is said to be protected by the sword. We've been invincible against the French, Viking and Scottish invaders, foreign spies, pirates, and smugglers."

"It's a good legend." Wallace nodded, deep in thought.

"Yes. Some believe that the secret to its hiding place is passed down to the most senior Thornton."

They reined in their horses in front of Thornton Abbey. Wallace glanced at her. "That would be you, wouldn't it?"

Katherine whipped her head around to face him. "I… I hadn't thought about that. My father broke tradition. It was his misfortune to sire a single daughter. No son. The title and the secret passed to his trusted brother-in-law. My father and Bennett were always at odds, but in truth they were devoted to each other. My father thought of him more as his brother than someone who married into the family.

"My uncle accepted the honor with a stipulation that the succession would be through my children. Bennett saw himself as a temporary protector of the title."

Wallace helped her dismount and glanced at her before she turned to lead the way to the door. Her expression was one he experienced before, on the battlefield when junior officers took over for his fallen commanding officer. He knew the feeling all too well. Based on the few hours they spent together, he did not doubt Lady Katherine's ability to take on the burden of the title as well as Sutton Textiles, even now in its hour of disruption.

Wallace followed her, shaking his head. To think, he had brought her a doll to give her strength when she had a legendary sword.

KATHERINE APPROACHED THE front door. It wasn't real until now.

Her uncle was gone.

Before they reached the last step, Mr. Russell, her butler, opened the door. Her housekeeper and staff solemnly stood in a line with their heads bent. The men wore black armbands. The women pinned black ribbons on their caps.

The house seemed different. Weighted down. She held back the tears that threatened until she glimpsed the black crepe draped wreath waiting by the door to be hung.

Thoughts and the heart-aching loss of her father bubbled up from that deep place she kept hidden. Everything changed then, too.

One day they played on the beach and the next her father couldn't get out of bed. A fever, Mother said. But he never recovered.

Neither did her mother. She became a shadow of herself, demanding to be moved out of her room. But the other side of the house wasn't far enough. Mother couldn't bear being in the abbey, the place her father loved.

The invitation to Mrs. Bainbridge's Female Seminary arrived soon after. Weeks later she moved into her new home and her mother left to stay with her ill sister, Aunt Nora, Bennett's mother.

Katherine glanced up the stairs. When she graduated from the seminary, she closed the rooms and hall where her parents' rooms were located. Every time she walked down that hall ghosts bombarded her.

Mrs. Russell, her housekeeper, moved her to her mother's room in the guest quarters on the other hall.

Bennett joined her at the abbey when he returned from the war in the Americas. He challenged and vanquished her ghosts, then happily moved into their domain.

A heavy sigh escaped her lips. Bennett. His body laid behind the closed parlor doors as her father's had all those years ago.

"Your Grace, please excuse me for a few minutes. My butler

will show you to the library."

"Of course, Lady Katherine." She turned to the butler.

"Mr. Russell, we'll be having guests. His Grace, and Mrs. Bainbridge will be staying on as our guests. Please make the necessary arrangements." She glanced at her guest, then back to her butler. "I should think the blue room would be most appropriate."

Her butler nodded and led Lord Wallace to the library as she climbed the stairs and made her way to her room.

Ivy-Rose. The blue room? You haven't lost your sense of humor. You're right, you know. The room is the color of his eyes. Now come, see what I have for you.

Katherine closed her eyes as the echo of Bennett's voice floated up from the foyer.

Don't look down. Bennett isn't striding toward the stairs calling after you today, tomorrow, or ever again. She wiped a tear from her cheek and continued up the stairs unable to stop her chin from trembling.

"Ivy-Rose, tears? I've never seen you cry. Don't start now. You're made of stronger stuff."

Bennett's voice faded from a hushed whisper into nothing.

Her toe caught on the stair tread, tripping her. She squeezed her eyes shut and gripped the banister.

In her heart… in her heart she wanted Bennett, to argue with him about his new designs, the cost, and too much salt in the stew. An hour, she bargained, a minute, a moment to say goodbye.

She entered her room and closed the door behind her.

WALLACE WATCHED HER go up the stairs and noticed her guarded glance at the parlor. He started for the steps when she tripped but the determination on her face held him back. Lady Katherine wore her sorrow with dignity. That didn't stop him from feeling her pain. He thought her a beauty when she glided into the seminary parlor, but her fragile yet regal ascent up the stairs left him breathless.

Wallace waited until the latch on her door clicked shut before he turned and followed the butler into the library.

At first glance, this was a man's room, but he found subtle female touches that didn't intrude upon, but rather enhanced, the room. Artwork, and small ivory and porcelain figurines placed with care on select shelves.

Bookcases filled two walls. Comfortable chairs flanked the hearth on the far wall. He faced a set of double doors that led to the terrace. A large pedestal desk stood to his right and a library table and chairs were across the room.

He did not find it surprising that Lady Katherine took over the library. He found her intriguing and wanted to learn more about the lady.

"Your Grace."

Wallace glanced at Mr. Russell.

"Your man brought your things. I showed him to your room and had a fresh basin of hot water sent up."

"Brilliant." He joined the butler at the door. "Lead on, Mr. Russell."

They made their way into the foyer. Now, Wallace observed the abbey with a critical eye. After all, the place belonged to him. Now all he had to do was tell her.

CHAPTER SIX

WALLACE FOLLOWED THE butler up the wide, carpeted staircase, appreciating its fine workmanship. He could practically see his image in the polished walnut banisters. The cream-colored walls with white decorative trim continued throughout the hall. Wallace didn't know what to expect from Bennett's home, but it was nothing like this. Thornton Abbey had all the trappings of a well-established, well-maintained, and well-heeled estate.

Before agreeing to a partnership, Wallace had his solicitor investigate the family and Sutton's business. He already knew the family's long history of sheep farming. His sister, Fiona, married well to the Earl of Thornton, who was in trade.

Eight years ago, Lord Thornton succumbed to a fever while working with his younger brother-in-law. Lady Thornton retired to her sister's home in Bath. But never any mention of children.

At the top of the stairs, Mr. Russell led him to the left toward the south end of the house, the opposite direction Lady Katherine had gone. They turned down a hall that led toward the back. Sections here needed repair and painting. Stains on the ceiling showed more damage. While the carpet was passable, it needed to be repaired, thoroughly cleaned, and in some areas possibly to be replaced.

It was understandable in a house as large as this one with few in residence that some unused areas would suffer. The staff would have to be spoken to and an inventory of repairs created.

"Here we are, Your Grace." Mr. Russell opened the door.

He entered a sizeable bedroom and sitting area with a hearth. The tall windows looked out at the garden. Lenard was in the dressing room unpacking his portmanteau.

"Thank you. That will be all, Mr. Russell."

The butler nodded and left.

He stood and spun around, taking in the room. It was indeed blue, Prussian blue with white accents, including white crown molding in a clean keystone pattern that ran high on the wall. A crystal chandelier hung from the center of the coffered ceiling.

The room didn't matter at the moment. Wallace needed to rid himself of the road. He removed his coat and shirt and went directly to the wash basin.

"There appears to be two areas on this level." Lenard worked the clothes brush on Wallace's coat.

"What makes you say that?"

Lenard laid out the coat and grabbed a linen for Wallace.

"We've been relegated to the part of the house in need of repair."

"How odd. I wouldn't expect her to be subtle after what I witnessed." Wallace's mouth rippled with amusement as he combed his beard. "Lady Katherine should tell us how she really feels about us staying at Thornton Abbey."

"I think Lady Katherine is the master of subtlety. Mrs. Russell mentioned this was Mr. Sutton's side of the house. Lady Katherine is on the other."

Wallace looked in the mirror at his valet's reflection, surprised at Lenard's information. He glanced at the basin, nodded, and then took another look at his grooming accomplishments.

"Anything else I should know?"

"The other rooms on this hall do not appear to be currently occupied. From their appearance, no one has used them for some time."

Wallace, satisfied with his results, stepped away and shrugged into a clean shirt. Lenard helped him into his coat, brushing the last bit of dust from his lapel.

"Come with me. I want to tour this area before we go downstairs." Wallace was at the door, Lenard a step behind.

Starting at the far end of the hall, there was a suite of rooms with two bedrooms and a parlor. The dustcovers draped the beds and upholstered furniture. Drawn drapes were over the closed and locked windows. From the dust that had accumulated on the dressers and tables, it was obvious the rooms had not been used in several years. This must be the lord and lady's suite. There was nothing personal left, but their presence was unmistakable. No wonder the rooms remained closed.

The other rooms were in the same condition with dustcovers and locked windows. Wallace came to the last room before reaching the grand staircase and poked his head inside.

His mouth hung open. He expected to see a closed bedroom, not a room that was spotlessly clean and filled with industrial designs. In place of furniture were parts of looms, spinning Jennings, and weaving mechanicals all in various stages of disrepair.

"This must be Mr. Sutton's—"

"Playground, Lenard." Wallace walked between several tables strewn with his drawings and designs, along with the actual parts in support of the images. "That's what he called it. Actually, he called this room his *drawing room*. Now I understand why he found that so funny. After our encounter in Royston Mills, I can understand why Sutton worked here. He could work without worrying about distractions."

Wallace stared at one of the building designs he crafted. They had converted Sutton Mill to Sutton Textile with spinning and weaving done in the same factory. After speaking with Francis Lowell from America, they considered creating housing for the displaced farmers.

The Sutton workers' jobs had never been in jeopardy. Not

even the cottage workers. Yes, the mechanicals would be able to make most of the fabric cheaper and faster, but their plan included producing handmade printed and embroidered materials. The company had a set of customers who still wanted premium textiles, and the workers would reap the benefits. Their plans, the ones shared with Roddy and the others, proved that no one would suffer.

Someone was trying to undermine them. Would that include threatening Sutton? He was the one involved with the day-to-day business. A cold shiver ran up his spine. Did Sutton have any idea that he was in jeopardy? His unhinged behavior? The erratic card games? The oath?

"God's blood. He did." He raked his hand through his hair. "How did I not see this?"

"Your Grace, this is odd." Lenard stood at a table, a cloth in his hands. "It was under this cloth."

Wallace went over to Lenard to examine what he found. "A lock. He never mentioned anything like this to me. This must be something for the factory."

Lenard replaced the material the way he found it. They left the room and made their way to the staircase.

Wallace had a better appreciation for Sutton's home. Thornton Abbey was grand even with many of its rooms closed. The repairs needed appeared to be manageable. It's curious that the staff maintains one half of the house and not the other. Was the Thornton estate facing financial difficulties? He started down the staircase. That must be why Sutton made him promise to marry Ivy-Rose.

He chuckled at the surprise of finding Ivy-Rose to be a beautiful woman rather than a child. But the problem of how Lady Katherine could take care of herself with Sutton gone persisted. The more he thought about it, the more he realized the financial predicament Lady Katherine would face.

By your oath.

Sutton's demand and his vow screamed in his head. He

couldn't deny it. He bloody well made it twice. If the gossip was in a Royston Mills paper, it wouldn't be long before people read it in the Sommer-by-the-Sea and London papers. He stepped into the foyer.

Lady Katherine needed to be informed before anyone else brought the article to her attention. Accustomed to Sutton's pranks, surely when he explained the situation she'd find it amusing. Wallace made his way to the library.

She is a beautiful, intelligent woman. He slowed his steps. *Why wasn't she married?* She was past the age of her first season.

Was she already spoken for? No one in their right mind would let her get away. She didn't mention contacting someone dear. *No one has come to her aid.* A wave of relief swept over him, leaving him almost giddy. Yes, the best thing for him to do is tell her about her uncle's desire, the oath, and settle the entire incident.

Wallace quickened his step to the library door. Tell her Sutton made him take an oath. *"I thought you were a child."* No, no. *That will never do.* He hesitated. How to start? *Tell her, without any fancy dressing.*

Lady Katherine, before Sutton died, I took an oath in front of witnesses that I would marry you. I understand that this is sudden. But, you see, the announcement's been in the papers. I'm sure we can decide how to proceed.

Satisfied with his plan, he let out a deep breath, opened the door, and stepped inside.

Empty. He glanced in every direction to make certain. No one was there. He wasn't sure if he was disappointed, annoyed, or relieved.

There was no need to mention the article in the newspaper. Not until he explained the situation. He went to the sideboard and poured himself some liquid courage.

"Lord Wallace." Lady Katherine came into the room.

"Ah, Lady Katherine. Just the person I wanted to speak to." Gone was her peacock blue dress. In its place she wore black crepe. She carried herself with strength, but her lovely violet eyes were swollen and red. The lady had been crying.

"Yes, Your Grace. What is it you'd like to discuss?" She placed the small bundle with Sutton's belongings on the desk and turned to him.

He saw her pain and refused to add to it. The situation was something that didn't need to be addressed this moment.

"It can wait." He stepped to her side. "Can I pour you some sherry?"

"Brandy, please." Her brow wrinkled for a moment then smoothed as a small smile touched her lips. "Bennett taught me how to appreciate liquor."

"Brandy's not the usual drink for a lady of the *ton*." Momentarily shocked by her request, Wallace poured her a glass of the amber liquid.

"That explains it. I'm not a usual lady of the *ton*." For a moment, there was a touch of mischief in her face, but it quickly vanished.

Lady Katherine looked at him and took the offered glass.

His fingers gently brushed hers, a fleeting touch, but it was enough to send shivers of excitement through him. Her glance told him he knew she felt it, too.

"Would you like me to escort you to the parlor?"

Her skin paled. The brandy splashed in her glass.

Without a word, Wallace removed the glass from her trembling hand, placed it on the desk, and waited.

She stared at him for several long heartbeats. Finally, she found her voice. "You are very perceptive. And kind."

"Lady Katherine."

They both turned to the door at the intrusion.

"The vicar is here." Russell stood at the door with a solemn expression. "I showed him to the parlor."

"Thank you."

She placed her hand on Wallace's forearm with a gentle squeeze. He placed his hand over hers and led her to the parlor.

They paused at the parlor threshold. Black crepe draped the almost bare room. The table that remained in the center of the parlor was the only furniture. Bennet Sutton, dressed in a linen shroud, laid there in peace.

Wallace let out a breath. Thankfully, Sutton looked like himself, not as he did in Royston Mills.

She stood rigid, clutching his arm, her lips quivering. He had expected some outward display. Instead, he observed an exceptional woman struggling to maintain control and hold on to her dignity.

When she raised her chin and glanced at him, she silently thanked him. He was caught in her beautiful violet eyes, the only touch of color about her.

He hoped it was for his strength, his presence. Would she feel the same once she knew the situation about her house and bloody hell, if she read the gossip sheets? He put that to the side and gave her a slight nod to show his support.

After what seemed to be an eternity, she let out a deep breath, gently squeezed his hand, and turned to the vicar.

"Thank you for coming." Her voice was soft and steady.

"I'm so heartbroken and I know you are aching. My prayers are with you." The vicar glanced at Sutton. "He was a good man, a good uncle, and a good friend. I, too, will miss him. May Bennett Sutton's life be for a blessing."

Mr. Hendrickson's honest words filled the air and beat down the building tension in the room. "There are a few necessary details we need to manage then I can leave you to your…reflection of Bennett."

"You are kind. But you can say the word mourning. I promise not to fall to pieces or have the vapors. Your Grace, let me introduce you to the vicar, Mr. Hendrickson." She turned to the vicar. "This is Lord Wallace, Bennett's partner."

"I'm sorry to meet you under these circumstances," Wallace said.

"I as well, Your Grace. Judge Scofield mentioned you brought

Mr. Sutton home. He spoke of you often. Especially when we played piquet. He must have admired the way you play the game. He invoked your name in conjunction with words I can't say in front of Lady Katherine or anyone else for that matter."

The vicar leaned close to him. "He usually lost and threaten to sign the deed to Thornton Abbey to me."

Wallace's smile broadened into laughter. "Did he do that with you, too?"

"Ah, Your Grace. He did it with everyone. Trying to right a wrong I suppose."

"Bennett played cards with Father. Bennett was surprised he won. Even ill, my father could beat him soundly. But he won. Father signed the deed to him. They left the cards on the table and celebrated." She looked up at Wallace. "In the morning, my father was dead. When Bennett turned over Father's cards, he had the winning hand."

The memory still cut deep. He saw it in her eyes. There was no comfort; even the vicar was at a loss.

"With the unrest in the village and factory," Lady Katherine interrupted the silence, "I want the burial done, tomorrow if possible. Can you arrange it?"

"It is most irregular." The flustered man mopped his brow. "Tomorrow is the annual Invincible Celebration. It will be a big event. As you know, it's the five hundredth anniversary of Lord Thornton's execution. It would be best if the service was the day after."

"Of course. It slipped my mind. You are right. There will be no privacy tomorrow with all the celebrating around the Thornton Mausoleum. The day after tomorrow then."

"I'll make arrangements to open the crypt and have it ready," the vicar said.

"I know. Bennett would not be happy if he was aware he was spending eternity next to my father."

She turned to Wallace. "My father treated Bennett as a brother rather than someone who married his sister. The two argued like brothers, all the time. When not arguing they laughed and enjoyed each other, until the cards came out. Father lost the house to Bennett, more than once."

Wallace glanced at her, then the vicar, but remained quiet. Now was not the time to inform her of the results of her uncle's last card game.

They left the parlor and entered the library and were welcomed by the sound of a hard dry cough.

"Mr. Bromley." Lady Katherine gave the man a small smile.

Wallace wanted to know why the man was here. Sutton told him while the Royston Textile manager was pleasant, he kept him at a distance.

"Lady Katherine. I'm here to offer my sincere condolences for your uncle's passing."

"Your concern is comforting."

"I wanted to come and offer any assistance that you need." He glanced at Wallace and the vicar. "I can see you are well-cared for. Please feel free to call on me should you need anything."

"You're most kind."

Three other gentlemen joined them in the library. Wallace recognized them at once. These were the men in Royston Mills who accosted Sutton about the evil of mechanicals. On high alert, he stepped close to Lady Katherine.

"We are here to speak to Sutton."

SHE GAVE THE man a scathing glare, puncturing his exaggerated sense of importance and causing it to quickly collapse. Her stare didn't waver. The man, on the other hand, was unable to look her in her eyes. He stepped back and smoldered.

"Who are you?" Her indignant tone set the mood of the discussion. She turned to Mr. Bromley. "Do you know these men?"

Bromley glanced at them. "I have seen them in Royston Mills by our factory. But I do not know them."

"I'm Ollie. This here is Tim and Frank. We thought to talk to Mr. Sutton. We saw him get hurt. We're here to see how he is."

Before she took a step, Wallace touched her arm and leaned close for only her to hear. "These are the men who confronted Sutton and me in Royston Mills. They made demands about the factory and for the workers."

She said nothing, but gave him a side glance, acknowledging his words.

"This way. I'll take you to my uncle." She walked regally down the hall and stood by the parlor entrance. The others followed. With the four men in front of the door, she swung it wide.

Wallace heard Tim gasp. Ollie and Frank weren't much better.

The men glanced at Sutton, then nervously looked at one another before approaching his body. Ollie stood closest to Sutton, the others a few steps behind.

"So, he is dead." Ollie's words were venomous. He leaned down to Sutton, poised to act.

Katherine bent close and whispered in his ear, determined to put an end to his intimidation.

Ollie's eyes widened. He straightened and struggled to swallow.

Pleased with herself, her face showed no emotion. She wouldn't give the brute the satisfaction.

Wallace stepped in front of Katherine and gently coaxed her behind him.

"I think you have seen what you came for." He hated people who intimidated those whom they perceived as vulnerable.

"With Sutton gone do you really expect to keep the factory?" Ollie stood in front of Wallace, his hands on his hips. "I tell you this as a friend. The days of Sutton Textile are coming to an end."

Katherine stepped forward and faced Ollie. "I hope that isn't a threat. You have no idea what I do to people who threaten me and those I care for. Do I make myself clear?"

"Ollie, we should leave." Tim turned to her. "Lady Katherine, I am sorry for your loss."

Russell stood at the parlor door with three others from the household ready to escort the men out.

"Come, gentlemen. We will leave Lady Katherine and Lord Wallace to do their reflecting." Mr. Hendrickson herded them out as if they were sheep.

"I'll help you." Bromley brought up the rear.

Wallace took her hand and moved her along.

"Where are we going?"

He stared into her lovely violet eyes. Over the course of the last half-hour, he watched as they progressed from a soothing, rich lavender to the angry, deepest purple.

"The library. We can both use some brandy after that encounter."

They made their way down the hall.

"What did you say to Ollie that nearly choked him?"

"The three have made their demands over the last several weeks. There was no love lost between any of them and Bennett." She took a seat in the library while he refreshed her glass.

Wallace watched as she stared at nothing in particular for several minutes. He had no intention of interrupting her.

"How strange. I expected Bennett to look… different." She raised her head and gazed at him.

"How?" Wallace handed her the half-filled glass and took a sip of his own.

"For a man whose gun blew up in his face, he looks quite handsome. Wouldn't you agree?" She took a sip of brandy.

He began to choke and cough.

"Oh dear." She put down her glass, hurried to his side, and pounded on his back.

He waved her away while he tried to catch his breath and rid his throat of the brandy that went down the wrong way.

"And I told Ollie I suspected he knew more than he's telling anyone." She freshened her glass and returned to her seat.

"You have a good point, but—"

"I also asked why he was here. He and the others do not work at Sutton Textiles nor did they like my uncle. Then I told him I knew his plan."

"What! Do you have any idea what you've done? You may have gotten the men to leave, but they'll be back. Don't be foolish and think you have solved anything. If he is rash enough to disrupt the factory and brash enough to come here and try to disgrace Bennett, threatening to expose him will only make him do something more reckless."

She shot out of her chair, straightened her back, and turned on him.

"What right do you have to scold me like a misbehaving child?" She glared at him almost forcing him to take a step back. "Foolish? You cannot fight such aggressive people with words. No, Your Grace. I will protect my own. This is my house, and I will say what I want, to whom I want to say it. When this house is yours, I'll seek your counsel."

She downed the brandy, put the glass on the table, and left the room.

Bloody hell. *That didn't go well.* He looked at the door and stifled a groan.

What would happen when she found out he *did* own the house? He poured himself another glass of brandy and downed it.

As he stared at the empty glass, the beginning of a smile tipped the corners of his mouth. *Her eyes are even more magnificent when she is furious.*

CHAPTER SEVEN

T HE FOLLOWING MORNING promised to be a bright and comfortable day. From his perch on top of the rise, Wallace enjoyed the constancy of the waves crashing on the shore. Children ran on the beach teasing the waves, daring the water to catch them. Listening carefully, he made out their squeals over the roar of the surf and the seagulls' shouts overhead.

Rather than ride, Wallace walked to the cemetery and stood with Roddy at the Thornton Mausoleum, waiting for the villagers to gather.

"The village takes the celebration to heart. Many dress and speak in the fourteenth-century style. The costumes are one of the last remnants of the original event. The celebration has changed over its five-hundred-year history."

Roddy nodded to a villager who passed by. "In the beginning, villagers gathered at Thornton Abbey. The knight's father gave a rousing speech honoring his son and his dedication of the Knights Templar. Afterwards, he led a solemn processional to the cemetery, to the spot where his family erected a memorial stone. The local clergy gave a sermon about bravery and the holiness of God, but never mentioned the boy."

"How sad that a man couldn't mourn his son in public." Wallace had heard the stories of the atrocities committed to make the knights confess. War, holy or otherwise, was not a pretty sight.

"I understand the sword is the centerpiece of the celebration. Will it make an appearance today?"

"Oh, no. The sword has never been seen. Many came to Sommer-by-the-Sea searching but leave disappointed. Lord Aldus hid the weapon away. The whereabouts of the blade and what it looks like are unknown. Some say *Invincible* is made of gold while others say the sword's encrusted with jewels. In my mind, if the sword is real and exists at all, it is a simple, dull steel blade."

"Roddy." One of the workers came up to them. "You're needed at the factory. An order of fleece has arrived."

"Excuse me, Your Grace." Roddy didn't wait for him to reply but took his leave.

Wallace scanned the area as it quickly filled. Many of the men wore surcoats, the women in kirtles. He could well imagine being back in the fourteenth century.

Unable to find Lady Katherine among the people travelling down the winding path, he craned his neck for a better view. Wallace relaxed when he glimpsed Mr. Hendrickson making his way around the bend. Lady Katherine walked beside him with three other women.

She wore her black mourning dress and a solemn manner as people expressed their sympathy and wished her well.

"Good morning to you, Wallace." He turned and nodded to Lord Barrington.

"Your Grace." Mrs. Bainbridge came on the arm of Lord Barrington and settled between the two men.

"The pleasure is mine." He straightened his coat, not used to the loose fit of the older style. "I didn't know what to expect. It certainly wasn't this."

"The event grows every year. The celebration is a nice homage to the young knight and an excuse to dress and act as if it were the fourteenth century. Everyone enjoys the day." Mrs. Bainbridge glowed with excitement.

"You look like a fourteenth-century queen." Wallace gave her a courtly bow that made her laugh.

"Sutton mentioned that you are proficient with a sword." Barrington dressed simply in the style of the fourteenth-century courtier. "The celebration includes a pageant, a retelling of the legend of *Invincible*. The men who fight put their heart and soul into it. You would think those in the pageant were fighting for their lives. You must join us. We sit with Lady Katherine up front."

"I've heard about the pageant." Wallace glimpsed at his clothes. "Consider me one of the courtiers. Do the men train for the event?"

"Most definitely. Peter and Simon give the men instructions, mainly on how not to harm themselves."

"Sutton mentioned to me that you have a practice arena in your home for all types of sports."

"He exaggerates. I had one of the rooms in Sommer Chase refitted with equipment to help with my recuperation from my injuries in the war. I enjoyed the exercises and kept at it. My friends, all retired military men, train with me. Four of them will be joining us at the pageant. We're a friendly group. Come join us. You're always welcome."

"Do you know anything about our celebration?" Mrs. Bainbridge drew his attention away from Lord Barrington.

"Roddy told me a little about the celebration's early history. It sounds like a serious event that's lasted and bloomed over the centuries."

"I agree with you. Things change over time. What was important five hundred years ago has a different meaning today. That said, I do think the old lord would be pleased and proud to know his descendants and the village continue to honor his son, a tradition he started."

"There is a lot to be said about tradition. Roddy captured my imagination telling me about Lord Stephen." The event interested Wallace more than he expected.

"There is much more to the story. Young Stephen Thornton,

a handsome lad, had dark wavy hair and hazel eyes. Much like you, Your Grace."

Wallace's eyes widened at Mrs. Bainbridge's unexpected compliment.

"The story of Stephen and his invincible sword began long before he became a Knight Templar. As a young boy, his father taught him skills to help and protect his people. The villagers loved Stephen, their protector, who came to their aid when needed. He was quick to learn and when he grew into manhood, his father rewarded him with a sword that he carried proudly.

"When a raiding party attacked Sommer-by-the-Sea, Stephen took up arms and joined his father to protect his people. But this time the raiders outnumbered the villagers.

"Too many were dying. Stephen thought there must be a better way to settle the encounter. He stole out of the barricaded village and challenged the leader.

"The raiding chief said he would leave the village in peace if Stephen surrendered his sword.

"Without hesitating, the boy made a counteroffer. The sword would be his if he, and he alone, took it out of his hand. The raiding chief thought the challenge would be easy. But at the first parry, Stephen cut the man. The match went on for some time. First, one had the advantage, then the other. But, in the end, Stephen removed the challenger's sword from the raider's severed hand. The enemy left never to return. The villagers celebrated their good fortune and Lord Aldus had his son's sword engraved. *Invincible.*

"When the call came for Crusaders, Stephen and *Invincible* went willingly. For five years he served the holy order. No one could beat him.

"In the end, Stephen surrendered in support of the Grand Master. But he refused to surrender *Invincible,* for everyone in Christendom knew the legend. Before he left to join the Grand Master, he entrusted the things that held great meaning for his family with a Templar brother.

"The Templar brother carried the news of Stephen's execution to Thornton Abbey. Together with Stephen's parents, the three came here, to the spot where the memorial stone now stands. They knelt and prayed. When they were done the knight handed his father Stephen's most precious belongings, a silver locket, *Invincible,* and a note that the sword be hidden away for the next chosen warrior to wield.

"Many have searched, but no one knows where Lord Aldus hid *Invincible.* Some say it lies at the bottom of Sommer Bay, others say buried in France, still others say it never existed. It remains a mystery."

He experienced a mixture of emotions as Mrs. Bainbridge related the story. To him, the legend spoke about pride, humility, and duty. He understood why the village celebrated Lord Stephen every year. The story embodied the values and goals that guided the people and the community.

"As with any historic event, as those who lived through the incident passed on, the story took on a different focus. People couldn't identify with the young knight but *could* believe in an invincible sword. Over time, the celebration became... less of a memorial and more a celebration." Mrs. Bainbridge moved closer to him. "The story of the young knight turned into the story of his sword. The true deeds of Lord Stephen Thornton are told at the bonfire."

"Not every hero is a knight or a soldier." Wallace knew that better than most. "But you both know that. You've piqued my interest. Tell me more about the celebration."

"In honor of the four-hundredth anniversary of the event, Katherine's great-grandfather had the stone fashioned into a sarcophagus. An effigy of the knight and his name are engraved on the stone as a memorial since neither his body nor ashes were returned. Now, every year, the villagers gather here at the mausoleum. Afterwards we celebrate at the castle, listen to the legend of the great sword, and view the pageant. In the evening we eat, have a bonfire, and sing."

"What are you three talking about?"

Wallace glanced over his shoulder. Lady Katherine's expression held a mixture of emotions that stirred his heart. She came up behind him holding a small bunch of flowers.

"I was telling His Grace about the evolution of the celebration and impressing him with your pedigree. Your great-grandfather was astute at making sure the young knight got a blessing."

"It was my father's request when he was a young boy. For four-hundred years the priests wouldn't give the knight a blessing. They said the knight denied God and worshiped idols. Father reasoned how would God allow him to have an invincible sword if he was so bad? He went on to argue with the priest that it was terrible that someone who gave his life for God and his country to be denied a blessing. The old priest would not listen. He demanded that my great-grandfather stop celebrating a heretic."

"Your great-grandfather was a patient man," Mrs. Bainbridge said.

"The old priest left the parish and a new one arrived. He and my great-grandfather put their heads together. Great-grandfather had the mausoleum built to include the Lord Stephen's effigy and his parents. If you listen with care, the blessing is for those named inside. My father thought that was quite clever. To make my father even happier, great-grandfather went so far as to include a feast with the celebration. A gift from the Thornton family.

"Now, the day starts here with the rededication. After the blessing, everyone goes to the castle to enjoy food, games, and tournaments. The simple recognition has turned into an all-day celebration that goes far into the night."

Mr. Hendrickson stood on the mausoleum steps. A hush came over the crowd as everyone gave their attention to the vicar.

"Welcome all who are here. Today we celebrate a young and noble knight who saw to the wellbeing of his family and home to the very end..."

⟫⟫⟫✦⟪⟪⟪

AFTER WALKING OUT on Wallace yesterday afternoon, she thought about their conversation. Yes, he would be difficult at dinner, making it easier for her to ignore him. Except…

Wallace didn't attend dinner, which made her even angrier.

"Your Grace."

Wallace turned toward her.

"I gave some thought to my final words to you yesterday. I had hoped you would be at dinner."

"I took the opportunity to become familiar with the village."

And give her time to compose herself, she added silently. She was sure he thought himself the winner. In the morning, Mrs. Russell had breakfast ready for Lenard. It didn't take her long to find out His Grace had gone to the market in the evening and came upon Roddy who invited him to dinner.

Wallace was more than she could have expected. Bennett never told her how involved he was in the factory. He made it sound as if all Wallace did was provide funds.

"…young Lord Stephen Thornton. A boy of eighteen who…" The vicar continued his tribute to the young lord.

Bennett hated this annual celebration. Out-dated. No consequences. Impatient for it to be over, he made those in attendance aware just what he thought of the event until everyone sighed with relief when he left. A pang, a small pain, tore at her chest. When would she have to stop thinking of him?

"Lady Katherine, regarding last night. I did speak out of turn. But it was done out of concern for you and a debt I owe to your uncle. Before Sutton died, he asked that I take care of you. I ask your forgiveness if I offended you."

Her eyes widened. Her expression softened. "No apology is necessary. We were both at fault." She glanced at Mr. Hendrickson. "He's at the end. I'm not looking forward to going into the crypt."

"Lady Katherine."

She stared at the vicar. His hand extended toward her.

Wallace could feel her discomfort. He didn't ask. He took her arm, threaded it through his, placed his hand on top of hers, and walked with her to the mausoleum's door.

He stood watchful over her as the vicar said his words.

Without hesitating, after the vicar completed the service, he escorted Lady Katherine into the crypt.

They stood at the doorway of a modest open space. Above them, in the mausoleum's dome was an oculus. The limestone walls held all the family crypts except one.

The limestone sarcophagus stood in front of them with a life-sized sculpture of the young knight on its top. They stepped forward next to the tomb. Wallace examined the stonework closely. The carving was extraordinary, down to the locket around the knight's neck.

He could see a Thornton family likeness and for a moment was certain if the young knight opened his eyes, they would be a deep blue-purple. The knight's hair fell away from his face in curls onto the pillow. He wore his Templar vestments, his belt clasped over his surcoat pleated the material that appeared soft and supple. His hands rested on the end of his sword's pommel. The drawn sword, *Invincible,* pointed down, its tip resting between the knight's feet.

A ray of sunlight came through the oculus and struck the knight's sword. He hadn't noticed it earlier, but the small gems or glass pieces embedded around the sword glittered in the sunlight, giving the sword an unworldly look.

She broke the melancholy silence. "The affect is dramatic. My father enjoyed the magic."

"I can understand why." Her family had filled the legend and small space with magic. How much was true didn't matter to him. Sometimes it was best not to see how the magician works his trade. *Awe and delight are fine.*

"My great-grandfather had the dome built in such a way that

the beam of sunlight focused on the sword hilt. Father told me the hilt had been covered with glass gems at one time and when the sun struck the one in the middle of the hilt, the entire sword would shine. Now, only a few remain. He impressed upon me the importance of my responsibility as a Thornton to guard the knight and his sword."

She placed a flower next to Lord Stephen. Then she stepped to the wall to his right and the crypts of Lord Aldus and Lady Inga Thornton, the knight's parents, and placed flowers in the small vase on the wall.

She turned to the left and faced the crypt of Lord Lewis Thornton. Wallace watched as her lips moved without a sound and her hand trembled. For a moment he felt as if he were sharing something very private. He stepped closer and willed her his strength.

"May you rest in peace and may the Lord shelter you with the cover of His wings forever." She rested her hand on his name and placed her cheek on the stone. "I miss you, Father. Please don't be cross. Bennett is joining you tomorrow. Be kind to him. He's taken good care of me." Her voice faded into a hushed stillness.

She placed the rest of the flowers in the vase next to his crypt.

"Your father is proud of you." Wallace assured her and he stood close.

She glared at him challenging him to prove his point.

"Take a deep breath and let your mind go. You will feel it. There is no turmoil here, only peace."

She closed her eyes and took a deep breath, then another. He didn't rush her. Slowly a small smile tilted the corners of her lips. At last, she opened her eyes, looked at him, and nodded.

Offering her his arm, they walked out of the crypt to a hushed silence. The crowd made way as they walked out of the church-yard. He had no idea where she was leading him, but was willing to go wherever she wanted.

They passed the castle and watched as people made a large

pile of wood for the bonfire in the center of the bailey for the evening's celebration. There was activity around the outside. The archery butts and fencing pell were being cleared.

Lady Katherine guided him along the path that led to the cliff. They walked up the rise and were rewarded with a view of the North Sea and the coastline for as far as the eye could see. Great stones, some slabs, others flattened boulders, dotted the cliff and were convenient resting places.

They stood looking out at the horizon for several minutes.

"You have my thanks. Father died ten years ago and sometimes I still expect him to come through the door, happy to be home after a long trip." She waved her hand dismissively. "It is a childish fantasy. I know too well he is gone."

"Lady Katherine, saying good-bye to the ones we love is never easy. I was sincere when I said your father would be proud of you."

She let out a shuttering breath. "Those were the last words he said to me before he died. I had no idea he would leave us a few months later. Every year, I dread entering the crypt, facing the truth that he is gone."

He understood the emotional toll a day like today could be and was surprised when she put her hand on his. She didn't say anything, just stared at the sea and held his hand.

"I told Lord Barrington we'd find you here."

They turned as Lord Barrington and Mrs. Bainbridge joined them.

"I've always thought there was something special and calming about sitting here." Mrs. Bainbridge took a deep breath.

"I agree." Wallace breathed in the briny air and focused on the horizon. "I was here earlier this morning. The rhythmic sound of the waves is good medicine. The vastness can aid in putting things into perspective. Here I am getting poetic."

"Nonsense." Barrington also stared at the ocean. "Now you understand why I live here. The doctor's healed my body as best he could. The only physical remnant is this cane." He shook the walking stick to show them. "But I needed to do more to recover. I had to face the fact that my service as a soldier was over.

"As a second son, my father groomed me for the military from childhood. My military career was how I defined myself. Without it, I was a ship without a rudder. I had to find who I was and embrace that Reese Barrington. Until I did, I was of no value to myself, others, and especially the people who mean the most to me." He gazed at Mrs. Bainbridge and squeezed her hand.

"You're not alone." Lady Katherine swiveled around and faced Wallace at Barrington's declaration. "We'll have to share this boulder. No questions will be asked. No explanations will be necessary."

She smiled at him. "Next time we'll choose a larger boulder." With his arm around her, they gazed out at the North Sea. "Or maybe not. This one is just right."

CHAPTER EIGHT

WALLACE AND LADY Katherine walked up to the castle along with Lord Barrington and Mrs. Bainbridge. Stalls hosting a variety of games and sports were outside the castle walls.

The old archery butts had been cleaned and decorated, targets set, and distances marked off. Not far away, the sacks for the sack race sat stacked and ready. In another area, men poured water to create a wide mud puddle preparing for the tug-of-war. The pell with its wooden soldiers stood ready for the sword attacks.

"Do you play Pall Mall, Your Grace?" Lady Katherine stopped and nodded toward the metal hoops that had been set up. "We play in teams. Each year the course is different. You never know where the path will take you. One year the course went all through the village. We played through the tearoom. I don't remember ever laughing so much."

Thus far, the day was going well. The strain of the ceremony at the mausoleum had come and gone. Tomorrow would be difficult, but Wallace pushed that aside. Lady Katherine was entitled to a respite if only for today.

"I played when I was a boy." Wallace took her hand and brought it to his lips. "Lady Katherine, would you do me the honor of being my Pall Mall partner?"

"How can I refuse such a gallant request? Yes, I will be your partner." She spun around to Mrs. Bainbridge and Barrington. "Will you complete our foursome?"

Barrington glanced at Mrs. Bainbridge, who graced him with an adoring smile. Wallace suspected the woman would never deny the man anything.

He glanced at Lady Katherine, startled that he craved to see that same expression in her eyes when she looked at him.

"Your wish is our command. How could we refuse?" Barrington was downright jolly. "Wallace and I will sign us up in the bailey."

They walked through the castle gates. The bailey had been transformed into a medieval castle. Thornton and King Edward II's pennants hung from the ramparts. Garlands made of flowers and material draped from the north wall to the east one creating a floral roof with hanging lanterns.

"This is not a small event." He started toward the stalls. Lady Katherine held back, her attention drawn somewhere across from them. Ready to act, he followed her stare. Unable to ferret out the problem, he put a protective arm around her.

"Is something amiss?" He bent and spoke for her ears only but kept watch on the people across from them.

"Not at all." The cool tone in her voice told him differently. "Just getting up my courage."

Wallace couldn't be fooled. Someone here upset Lady Katherine.

They continued past an area where children played leapfrog and spun tops. Others, in a foot race, ran to the cheers of the crowd around them. They came around the next row of stalls, the place to register for the Pall Mall ahead.

"Kate, I thought it was you." Lord Whitaker strutted up to her, brandishing his cane and ignoring Wallace.

The momentary flare of fire in her eyes put Wallace on high alert. Whitaker? Was this the man who startled her?

"That's rude even for you, Lord Whitaker. You see His Grace standing next to me." Lady Katherine turned her shoulder to

Whitaker and spoke to Wallace. "Your Grace, please forgive Lord Whitaker's slight. He is a rude man by nature." She turned back to Whitaker. "Who gave you permission to call me by my given name? And don't tell me my uncle. I know better. So don't add any new lies to your list of offenses."

Shocked, Wallace remained quiet. But the horror on Whitaker's face was justified.

"Lady Katherine." Whitaker gave her a deep courtly bow. "I apologize. Blame my bad manners on too much of your Thornton ale. Please forgive my indiscretion."

"Why are you here?" Her tone didn't change.

"I was at Royston Mills when Bennett... Mr. Sutton..." Whitaker paused as he worked through his embarrassment and started again. "As an old friend, I thought you might welcome some support."

Barrington and Mrs. Bainbridge joined them carrying hand pies. The headmistress' expression left nothing to explain. She was not pleased with Whitaker.

"That is thoughtful of you. As you can see," Lady Katherine gestured to those around her, "I have all the support I require."

"Then I will leave you to your grief." Whitaker turned to leave.

"Lord Whitaker. You didn't apologize to the Duke of Blackhall. I believe a baron is several rungs lower."

Everyone held their breath, including him.

"Your Grace. I apologize for..." Whitaker gave Lady Katherine a sideways glance. "For my arrogance. It is unbecoming even for a baron."

"Accepted." He felt sorry for the man. What had he done to provoke Lady Katherine to take such measures? Her reaction seemed out of character.

"Lady Katherine." Whitaker gave her a swift nod then swiveled toward him. "Lord Wallace. I hope you will let me make amends. I assure you my behavior was a lapse of character that will not happen again."

Lady Katherine did not melt. She simply stared at him and said nothing. Finally, the man turned and slinked away and within moments vanished into the crowd of people, clowns, and minstrels.

How strange. Wallace stared after him. Whitaker had better manners than that. If anything, he overdid them. The man had never slighted him before. And yes, ignoring him was a slight. In most circles a very unforgivable one.

He glanced at Lady Katherine. He'd have to get to the bottom of this. But not now. Perhaps after tomorrow.

"What in heaven's name Katherine? I have never seen you this rude. Ever."

"My issues with Lord Whitaker are a personal matter of which he is well aware."

Lady Katherine took a hand pie from Mrs. Bainbridge and bit into it.

"Mrs. Russell was concerned these wouldn't be good. They are perfect." She glanced at Barrington. "Is that for you or is that for His Grace?"

A bit dumbfounded, Barrington stared at the pie in his hand.

"Whitaker doesn't have a good reputation in London." Barrington gave the pie to Wallace. "Or anywhere else for that matter. There isn't a house or gambling hell in London that will tolerate him."

Wallace knew Whitaker's reputation. They didn't travel in the same circles but did meet from time to time.

"I do not know his game, but I will find out." Lady Katherine's clipped tones signaled to him that Whitaker's actions were worse than he expected.

"No. Lord Wallace and I will take care of him. Antics are one thing, but his persistence is another. Seeking you out does not go well with me." Barrington looked at Wallace for confirmation and received a nod. "I'm glad Lord Wallace is situated at the abbey."

Barrington turned to Lady Katherine. "There are people who

you can count on."

"I suggest you tell Mr. Russell that if Lord Whitaker calls, he should say you're out. Say nothing more to him." Wallace finished his hand pie.

"Gentlemen. Lord Whitaker was an enemy long before he came here today. There was no reason for him to assume he would be welcome. But I will do as you suggest. I may have been harsh, but I will not be intimidated."

"I think you were brilliant. But let's not allow this incident to influence our day. Perhaps Lord Barrington and Lord Wallace should put us on the list for Pall Mall. We can play before the pageant." She could have kissed Mrs. Bainbridge for changing the subject.

"Come Wallace. We have our marching orders." Barrington tipped his hat. "Ladies."

The two men left to register for the game.

KATHERINE FINISHED THE hand pie and glimpsed at Wallace as he walked with Barrington. His displeasure went past the expression on his face. His body, all magnificent six feet, three inches pulsed with questions and anger.

"You never told me about Lord Whitaker—"

"I've told you what is fit for people to hear."

"Katherine. What are you hiding?"

There were times when she welcomed Mrs. Bainbridge's motherly concern. This wasn't one of those. She would deal with Whitaker.

Barrington and Lord Wallace returned carrying mallets and balls.

"We are fortunate. If we hurry along, we're next to start." Wallace offered Katherine his arm. "Yours is the red ball, mine the green."

Another fortunate interruption. She didn't want to put Mrs. Bainbridge off, but she didn't want to respond either.

What did an eighteen-year-old girl know about the *ton*. Each of her foolish mistakes glared at her, burned into her memory and she worked hard to forget them. However, her foolish antics seemed to work harder at reminding her.

Today, she acknowledged her youthful innocence and inexperience. All Whitaker saw when he looked at her all those years ago was an innocent who knew no better. An innocent with an awful lot of money. He stole a kiss here and fleeting touch there, maybe not so fleeting, but either way it was wrong. For him, she was a conquest. For her, he was a mistake.

Bennett put Whitaker in his place then, and again nine months ago. What would it take to rid herself of the man?

"THE NEXT STROKE is yours." Wallace handed her the mallet.

The course this year was more daring than in the past. They started outside the castle gates and across the field toward the cliffs. From her position, the next hoop she needed to go through was back toward the church which wasn't far away.

Katherine studied her ball and adjusted her stance, turned slightly, then gave the ball a solid hit. The players and onlookers watched her ball glide over the ground and bounce over ruts. Would her ball go off the course? To everyone's amazement, her ball hit Wallace's and stopped abruptly, teetering on the edge of the cliff. Wallace's ball, squarely hit, went off the course and down the side.

"Your Grace, I'm so sorry. I struck and sent your ball…" She glanced over the cliff's edge. "Into the weeds." She laid her hand gently on his chest and smiled. "I'll wait for you at the final hoop."

Wallace raised his eyebrow, gave her a most charming smile,

and took her hand. "Oh, milady, I won't be long. My ball will fly to be near yours so I may be back at your side." His teasing words stopped her in her place.

Katherine noted the crowd's collective sigh. She turned in time to watch her ball begin to slip from its spot. Little by little, the red sphere rolled until it, too, toppled over the cliff and plopped next to Wallace's and kept on rolling.

She turned to him, a shocked expression on her face. He tried to keep a serious expression but was lost when she burst out laughing.

He placed his mallet over his shoulder, turned, and extended his arm to her. "Shall we, milady?"

She shouldered her mallet and took his arm. "Most certainly, milord."

They found Wallace's ball first. Finding hers was another story.

"You would think a red ball would be easy to see in all these weeds, but I can't find it anywhere." Katherine swung her mallet at the clumps of weeds that lined the path clinging to the side of the cliff walk leading down to the beach.

Wallace searched on the other side of the path examining the gentle slope on the weed covered shoulder. He looked past the tall weeds to the steep decline and the rocks and beach below. There, nestled in the niche of stones Katherine's red wooden ball sat laughing at him. He glanced over at her. She still searched the weeds. The woman was determined.

"Come, let's go up to the castle. I'll find you another ball."

"No. We'll find it. The ball must be here." She didn't stop searching.

He took her hand and tugged her to the other side of the path and pointed to the red dot not too far below.

"Your hand, if you please."

"You don't intend to…" He let out a breath. "Yes, you do intend to go fetch that ball."

"Oh, no. Not fetch it. Play the ball through. But don't let me stop you if you haven't got the stomach for such a shot."

The smirk on her face warmed him in places that had only recently come to life.

He climbed over the edge, took her hand, and helped her. Walking along the rocks wasn't necessarily difficult, just daring.

They reached her ball as a stiff ocean breeze swept along the rocks. The wind blew her summer skirt and tugged her hair loose, blowing it in every direction. She didn't take any notice. Instead, Katherine focused on the task at hand. She stepped closer to the ball sending small stones over the edge.

"Be careful." He pulled her back.

"I need to be closer for the ball to go over the cliff and not down onto the beach." She stood on a teetering rock concentrating on the shot, lining up the ball, determined to succeed. "The problem is mathematical. Where and how hard you strike the ball are as important as your aim."

"Here, let me help you." Wallace put one arm around her waist to hold her steady and held her long black hair in his other hand. "If you go over the side, I will be there with you."

She glanced at him, ready to say something, but the wind caught his hair. Her heart skipped a beat. She wasn't sure if it was his romantically wild hair that curled softly around his face or the touch of his hand at the nape of her neck that sent her heart racing.

The sensation was more than pleasant. She hesitated to strike the ball, not wanting him to step away.

He bent close to her ear, to be heard over the pounding surf and her pounding heart.

"Take your time." Katherine closed her eyes at his soft whisper. *Please, don't stop.* She stretched her neck for more and was rewarded with a thrilling cascade of desire as wild as the ocean that crashed around them. It raced through her, from her thundering heart to her fluttering stomach, and back again.

"I could stay like this as long as you like." His husky tone lingered. "I'm quite comfortable, but we are creating a bit of a spectacle."

Katherine took in a deep breath and answered him with a swing of her mallet. The red dot flew in a high arc. From the crowd's cheers the ball must have landed in a good position on the path.

She turned to him still in his arms. "I think you can let me go now."

His hand stroked her cheek. He gazed into her eyes with a wistful expression. "I… I don't want to let you go."

The mystery in his eyes held her captive.

Katherine stepped back. It was too easy to get lost in the way he stared at her, the way he unlocked sensations that had been shut away a long time.

Looking resigned, he said, "We best move on before Barrington sends a search party for us."

The hike up the path and back onto the cliff was comical as they both tried to keep the other from succeeding. They laughed until they reached the top. Wallace, his coat off and his shirtsleeves turned up, reached the end of the course with her. Barrington waited at the final hoop, leaning on his mallet with Mrs. Bainbridge by his side.

"You played a good game." Wallace bowed to her. "You are a worthy opponent."

"As are you, milord." She gave him her best impish smile.

Wallace took a teal ribbon out of his pocket. He reached behind her, his fingers barely brushing the skin on the nape of her neck as he tied back her hair. "I may not be with you the next time you dare to walk along the rocks. I send you into battle with my protection." His hands lingered a bit before he moved away.

"Before you ask, I bought the ribbon earlier this morning when I wandered into the bailey before I went to the cemetery. When I saw the color, I thought of you."

"It's my favorite color. You could have tied my hair back all along." Her eyes lowered.

"Would you have rather I did?"

She raised her chin and stared at him. There was a trace of vulnerability about him that moved something inside her. No jest or humorous reply to that question would do. There was something intimate and exclusive as he tied the ribbon. Something special.

"No, not at all."

CHAPTER NINE

THE FOURSOME MADE their way to the castle gates. Several of the games were still in progress.

They glanced at Whitaker as they passed the pell. He hacked away at the wooden soldier. It was most unfortunate for Whitaker, but the wooden soldier appeared to be winning.

"I'd like to watch the archery. Marjory should be starting soon." Katherine scanned the group of archers at the butts. "Is she here?"

"Yes, over there." Mrs. Bainbridge nodded toward the target. "She's setting the target. She may be next."

Katherine and Mrs. Bainbridge went on ahead. Wallace and Barrington followed.

"Marjory Alastair is one of Honoria's seminary girls. Very few can beat her on the butts," Barrington said. "I enjoy her flare for the dramatic. When she is shooting, the crowd holds its collective breath. When she lets go of the string, everyone exhales and creates a mighty wind."

They both laughed at the image.

"Several other ladies from the seminary are standing with Lady Katherine and Honoria, Lady Euphemia Brandt, Lady Harriet Manning, and Lady Marianna Ravencroft."

"The ladies appear to be a close group."

"They are. Honoria is very selective in inviting young ladies to join the seminary. She is adamant that all the girls fit in. No exceptions. Each of them with a propensity towards something. Honoria makes sure their talent is cultivated. Each girl is encouraged to explore her talent and be her best."

"My father had a similar idea. My cultivated talent served me well."

"There you are, Barrington." Ernest Hawkins approached them.

"Hawkins, come and join us." Barrington gestured to the reporter. "Lord Wallace. This is Ernest Hawkins, the editor and proprietor of the village newspaper, *The Sommer Sentinel.*"

"Pleasure to meet you." Wallace tilted his head in a friendly acknowledgement. The reporter, paper and pencil in hand, stood rather awkwardly next to Barrington.

"Your Grace. It is a pleasure to meet you. I hoped to speak to you. Would you be so kind as to answer a few questions? I am putting together the next edition of the paper and your appearance in the village is of interest to everyone."

Wallace was momentarily speechless. "Interested. In me? Are you sure?"

"Oh, yes, Your Grace. The village is buzzing. You can't go anywhere without someone speculating. Everyone is aware you brought Mr. Sutton home."

"I understand." He should have realized rumors and gossip would run rampant in a small village like Sommer-by-the-Sea. "What would you like to know?"

Hawkins' dower face brightened, as he readied his pencil.

"My information, from a reliable source, informed me with certainty Mr. Sutton died as a result of a duel." Hawkins referred to some pages until he found what he wanted. "There was some impropriety at a card game, and he challenged you."

The pleasantness on Wallace's face faded at about the same time it did from Barrington's.

"Mr. Hawkins, Mr. Sutton did not die of a pistol wound. As a matter of fact, the dispute that brought Mr. Sutton to the dueling field was amicably settled and he called off the duel. I'm afraid your reliable source isn't so reliable."

"But that can't be." Hawkins' face blanched when he glanced up at Barrington and Wallace. "I mean… that's not what my source told me. If he didn't die from a pistol shot, how did he die?"

"When Mr. Sutton emptied the gun power from the pistol's chamber, his weapon misfired, the flash striking him in the face." Wallace's icy glare made the reporter dance from one foot to the other. "Get your facts straight. Don't you think Lady Katherine has gone through enough with the sudden death of her uncle? She doesn't need to hear blatant lies tainting his good name."

"Yes, yes. Of course."

"Next time confirm your source. Roddy and the men from the factory were at Royston Mills. I'm sure they can give an unbiased account of what happened."

"Thank you, Your Grace." Hawkins put his paper and pencil away. The man couldn't leave him and Barrington fast enough.

"That went well." Barrington watched Hawkins heading for a group of Sutton Textile workers. "It looks like he's going to speak to Roddy. I'm surprised at his questions. He usually only repeats what he reads in the gossip columns."

"Gossip columns. Bloody hell." He still had to face telling Lady Katherine.

"Is something in the gossip column bothering you?"

"It will bother Lady Katherine much more." He took out the sheet from the newspaper and handed it to Barrington.

"Ivy-Rose." Barrington gave him a sideways glance. "Only Sutton dared to call her by her middle name. I don't think anyone else knows she has one. And who is Lady RH?"

Wallace took the paper back and studied it. His dark brows furrowed as dates came together. "Rosamond Henley."

Barrington laughed. "How are you involved with Lady Rose?"

"I'm not. It was a favor for my brother. He introduced us at a house party in honor of her birthday. She asked that I dance the first dance with her. I couldn't refuse. I didn't stay long. I shipped out in the morning.

"When Father and Geoffrey died, she sent a note every so often. Not intrusive. Something a friend would do. I never thought she deserved the reputation everyone attributed to her."

"You wouldn't, and why am I not surprised?"

"I'm more certain than ever that Sutton planned this entire ruse. His intention was to coerce me into marrying Lady Katherine. Why?"

"What did she say when you told her?"

Wallace didn't move. He glared at Barrington.

Barrington shook his head. "You haven't told her?"

"When should I have told her, when I met her at the seminary? And what should I have said? 'Ivy-Rose, let me introduce myself, I'm Lord Wallace, the 4th Duke of Blackhall. I'm here to deliver the body of your deceased Uncle Bennett with my sincere condolences. He's been murdered, you see. And, my dear, he lost your house to me in a card game, and he made me give him my oath – in front of several dozen people – that I would marry you.' How does that sound?"

Barrington tried not to laugh. "I understand what you mean. You are in an unenviable position. But, look at the article." He pointed to the gossip item. "You must tell her before she finds out some other way. Like in *The Sommer Sentinel*."

Wallace let out a deep breath. "I know you're right. I thought she was a child. Sutton didn't tell me she was a grown woman. A beautiful one. I can't delay telling her. Then again, this entire issue may not be as bad as it sounds."

"Oh? Why not?"

"This oath cannot be binding." Was he trying to convince Barrington or himself?

"That would depend on how Lady Katherine and the *ton* interpret the situation. You may not care about her honor—"

"Of course, I care about her honor. I would never do anything to bring her shame." Wallace understood Barrington's point. His stomach sank.

"Tell her. Tonight. The London news will be here soon. I assure you if Mr. Hawkins gets wind of that tidbit, he will be chewing it all around Sommer-by-the-Sea."

"Barrington."

Four men, retired soldiers, he suspected, came up to Barrington. He didn't doubt they were military. They walked like soldiers. They were big like soldiers. They held themselves with pride like soldiers.

"Lord Wallace, this is James Wilmore, Peter Simms, Simon Watts, and Nickolas Bradford. They are retired officers who served under me." There was pride in Barrington's voice. "Lord Wallace served in Spain as part of Wellington's staff."

"We're sorry to hear about Mr. Sutton. Mr. Hawkins told us he died from a pistol misfire."

Wallace glanced at Barrington. "Don't look at me. I told you he was worse than any gossip. And he gets paid to do it. You can feel free to tell these men the truth. They know how to keep a confidence."

"Sutton tried to discharge his pistol. Unfortunately, it misfired." Collectively, the men groaned. They all knew what a misfire could do. "A misfire didn't kill him. Snake venom did."

Their whispered comments abruptly came to a halt. He had their full attention.

"The doctor confirmed the venom was from an African boomslang snake. He had some firsthand knowledge."

"You must be speaking of Dr. Price. He grew up in Africa. His father was a member of a London club searching for the source of the Niger River. He has extensive knowledge of the area," Peter said. "Do you have any idea what a boomslang snake is doing in England?"

"An accidental bite didn't kill Sutton. He died of a deliberate puncture. The doctor found a small wound in his back. Sutton was murdered."

"Any idea who killed him or why?" Nickolas voiced the question that was on everyone's mind.

Wallace heaved a heavy breath. "Issues at the factory are getting worse. According to Roddy, the disturbance and attack on the machines are not from our workers, but rather outside agitators. They've been vocal and made threats. They even visited Thornton Abbey and accosted Lady Katherine."

The men straightened and took on a different attitude. "Workers' disputes are happening across England. This is more serious. This is sinister."

"I agree. At the moment, we need to get through tomorrow and Sutton's burial." Barrington had taken on a grave expression. "Peter, find out about these agitators." He glanced at Wallace. "Who in Royston Mills looked out of place?"

"Aside from Whitaker? I'm afraid you must ask Roddy. I wouldn't know who belonged in Royston Mills and who didn't."

"Roddy and I have had many an ale together," Peter said. "I'll be discreet and find out what I can from him."

"Ask him about Jackson, the innkeeper. He appeared to be a good man. He may be able to give you more insight."

Peter nodded. "But not until after the pageant. It's the best part of the celebration."

"And here I thought the best part was the evening bonfire and soft bodies." Simon's comment had everyone snickering.

"I'll ask my brother, Edward, if he can locate any information. His position in Parliament may prove helpful. I think that is all for now. We can meet at Sommer Chase later and see if there is anything else we should be doing. I suggest we join the ladies and take our places for the pageant. Mrs. Bainbridge said she'd secure seats for us."

Barrington started walking toward the seats. Their discussion was over.

CHAPTER TEN

T HE BAILEY WAS alive with excitement as everyone took their places for the pageant, the last event of the afternoon. Clouds came in from the east. The sun, while low in the sky, ducked behind them and emerged every so often, dappling the bailey grounds.

The combatants carried shields to identify which side they represented. The 'Knights Templar' held shields of well-known families. Roddy, who played Stephen Thornton, carried a shield with the Thornton family crest. They fought against men carrying shields with the fleur-de-lis, the lily that stood for the 'French' army. Villagers filled the castle steps quickly, eager for a perfect view of the 'battle ground.'

Wallace glanced at the scene and found Lady Katherine in the front row sitting behind a wooden barrier. Her face brightened when she caught his attention. She gestured to the space next to her.

He nodded and made his way through the crowd, squeezing past those already seated, and reached the empty space beside her.

"You're just in time. They're about to start."

Wallace, still in his shirtsleeves sat and laid his tunic on his lap.

"There's a parade when our men take to the field." Lady

Katherine became more animated as she told him what to expect. "Everyone screams and yells. When the 'French' enter, there is booing and hissing. Someone starts the fight. The cheers are the loudest when our invincible knight enters. The fighting is almost over by then because the 'French' know they cannot win. It's quite enjoyable."

"You didn't play any games other than the Pall Mall." He straightened his tunic across his lap and waited for her to answer.

"Could anything be more exciting than *our* Pall Mall? You must admit, our field turned into an obstacle course and was definitely a challenge. But I came away with the prize." She touched the new ribbon she still wore in her hair. "It appeared you, on the other hand, did not have your fill of challenges. We feared a forfeit when one of our Sutton Textile runners injured his foot. The drama of a replacement runner made watching and cheering for our team more exciting."

"I'm not sure if I volunteered or if Roddy volunteered me. But it all worked out in the end." He couldn't help but smile at her enthusiasm.

"You surprised me. I didn't expect you to be in the relay. I had no idea you were a runner." She took a teal scarf that was tucked in at her waist.

"It was a skill I learned early in childhood." He leaned close and whispered in her ear. "I had to outrun the cook, or she'd take away the tart I stole from the cooling rack."

Her smile deepened to laughter. "The image of you running from anything, even a cook, is something I cannot comprehend."

"I made the mistake of standing my ground and quickly learned the wooden spoon she wielded was a weapon in disguise. I complained to my father. He became serious and told me, learn when to stand your ground and when it is best to fight another day."

Her smile became thoughtful. "What else did your father tell you?"

Wallace glanced from one side to the other then leaned in

close. "Next time, take a tart for him as well."

She threw her head back. Her laugh was infectious. He couldn't help himself. All he could do was laugh with her.

The minstrels took their place by the gate.

She touched his arm lightly. "We best be quiet. They're ready to start."

A trumpeter stepped forward and with a fanfare announced the start of the pageant. Excitement sparked through the air igniting the crowd as the combatants marched into the center of the bailey.

Roddy, solemnly holding the Thornton shield, approached the castle steps and stood in front of Lady Katherine. He held his sword high for all to see, *Invincible* painted on its blade. The crowd cheered again. This time louder than the last. He lowered the sword and presented it to Lady Katherine.

A hush went through the crowd.

Lady Katherine took her teal scarf and tied it to its hilt.

"God's speed."

The knight bowed to Lady Katherine. The crowd cheered as he rejoined his troop.

The next few minutes was a choreographed dance. One side taunting and teasing the other until someone struck the first blow. One strike led to another, then another. Wallace understood why everyone waited for the pageant. Most of the antics were humorous. A tap on the behind, a jest. All was in the name of fun.

It happened quickly. A glint in the eye of one of the "Frenchman." His stance. The way he held his weapon. Hate rolled off him in waves like an incoming tide. Wallace scanned the other "French" soldiers: several of them didn't play by the rules. No, four men made this pageant more deadly than planned.

One by one the strikes became less playful and more menacing. Injured "knights" fell to the ground and had a difficult time getting up.

The sun had gone behind a cloud throwing a shroud over the

battle area.

Unsettled, Wallace jumped out of his seat. His tunic lay forgotten on the step. He leaped over the barrier. Barrington and his friends were not far behind.

Roddy came out to cheers. The attack was immediate. The "Frenchman" struck the Thornton shield over and over, battering Roddy into the ground.

Wallace went into the fracas racing toward his foreman. Roddy was down without his sword or shield. He was no match for the seasoned warrior in front of him.

Barrington and others cleared the courtyard, putting an end to some of the skirmishes and held the other Frenchmen while Wallace went to help Roddy.

The Frenchman, his back to Wallace, had Roddy pinned to the ground and his sword raised over his head.

This was not going to end well. Wallace searched the ground for something to use. A flash of teal peeked out from beneath a discarded shield. He threw the shield to the side and grabbed Roddy's sword.

"À moi! Thornton à la rescousse!" Wallace shouted and thrust the sword high over his head.

To me! Thornton to the rescue! The Knights Templar battle cry echoed off the stone walls of the castle. The crowd stood and shouted it as loud as they could.

Everything stopped. The fighting. The noise. Everyone held their breath and waited.

Wallace stood in his shirt sleeves. His dark hair ruffled in the breeze. Every muscle taut and hard. He had enough of these troublemakers. They wanted to fight. Wallace had no intention of stopping them. He had every intention of finishing them.

The echo of the battle cry had barely faded when the man standing over Roddy turned and faced him. Ollie. Not one of the factory workers, but a man paid to agitate and disrupt. This was not part of the pageant. Someone intended it to be a brawl.

A single ray of sun fought its way through the clouds and

caught the polished blade Wallace still held high. A flash of light from the blade lit the bailey. A hushed murmur spread from one person to the next, to the next, and to the next, and then silence.

Wallace lowered his arm. He didn't give the man time to think or plan. There would be no mercy in his attack. Four more attackers broke through the crowd and came at him. But Wallace would have none of that. His sword moved from one stroke to the next. The warrior slashed on the down stroke and again on the backswing, sweeping his weapon to the side, repeating the deadly arc until he cleared his way to the man who stood over Roddy.

He focused on Ollie. From the looks of the man, he was used to people running from him, intimidated by his size and meanness. His tactic wouldn't work here.

No sense watching the man's sword. Ollie's eyes would tell him what he needed to know, who he would attack. Wallace or Roddy. When he would strike. And how he would strike. It was all in his eyes.

The roar of the battle cry faded from the bailey, but still rang in Wallace's head along with the image of Sutton's face before he died.

Ollie scoured the crowd looking for support. He found none. Barrington's men had removed the men who came with him. The man switched his focus to him and gave him his best intimidating stare.

Wallace planted his feet, straightened his spine, and came to his full height. He brought his shoulders back making himself bigger and wider. His body ached with built up energy.

Ollie took his foot off Roddy and helped him up.

Several Sutton men hurried into the courtyard and helped the foreman to safety.

Only a few short yards separated Wallace and Ollie.

Wallace knew what it was like before a battle. This was no different. He faced fear and danger with courage and a clear head.

Ollie started to breathe heavily, working himself up. He

stepped toward Wallace, his eyes not on him but someone amid the crowd.

Wallace would not retreat. He remained resolute and waited for Ollie to decide the next move.

Ollie halted mid-stride, gave an almost unnoticeable nod to someone in the crowd, then tossed down his sword.

The bailey erupted as Ollie walked away.

It took several minutes for Wallace to recover from his battle-ready position.

Barrington was the first to reach him.

"Do you have any idea who gave him the order to withdraw?" Wallace asked.

"No. The crowd was too thick. I will say everyone thinks this was part of the pageant. You are being hailed as the essence of the young knight. You have a Highlander-way about you. Committed and deadly."

"I'll take that as a compliment. Whoever is behind this had every intention of turning this into a brawl, if not a bloodbath. Roddy was no match."

"You've made yourself the primary target. After this they will come after you, not the factory, the factory workers, or Lady Katherine. But I think you knew that when you took him on."

"Ollie was the man who tried to start trouble at the abbey yesterday." He faced Barrington. "You are correct. Ollie and his leader will need to get through me first."

Barrington didn't disagree with him. "My men took the others to the castle to interview them. They'll report to us later."

The crowd gathered around him and Barrington while Whitaker and others helped clear the castle steps. Lady Katherine, Mrs. Bainbridge, and her ladies hurried toward them.

"Lord Wallace. What a wonderful pageant. So authentic. You and that man had everyone fearful something terrible was going to happen." Lady Euphemia fluttered with excitement.

"And when you gave out your battle cry, it was as if you called us all to action. I felt a part of the battle." Lady Harriet clasped her hands by her chest. "This was the best pageant I've ever attended. Alicia will be very upset when she finds out what she missed. Effie, Anna, and I are off to help Mrs. Russell. Thank you again. It was breathtaking."

The three women left, chattering as they headed toward the castle kitchens.

"Lord Barrington." Roddy came up to them. "The magistrate would like to speak to you."

Lady Katherine took the sword out of his hand, removed her scarf, and handed the sword to Roddy.

"That man wasn't playacting. He didn't intend to stop." Roddy whispered to Wallace.

He gave Roddy his full attention. The foreman was still shaken by the incident.

"If I was your commander, I would be proud of you. Another man would have panicked. You judged the situation quickly and acted accordingly. You and the others prepared for a demonstration, not a battle."

Roddy's eyes widened as he stared at him and took back some of his self-esteem.

"Did you see who in the crowd gave him the order to stop?" Barrington asked.

"No." Roddy shook his head. "But I can ask the others."

"That would be helpful. If you find out anything, tell me or Lord Wallace. The villagers believe this was all part of the pageant. Let's not tell them otherwise for now."

"Wallace, why don't you escort Lady Katherine to Sommer Chase? There is still more to come this evening. I'll meet you after I speak to Magistrate Rogers." Barrington and Roddy made their way to the magistrate who stood with the other Sutton men.

He understood Barrington's comment. The celebration continued into the night, and preparations needed to be made to keep everyone safe. Now, they had to act like nothing happened. He offered Lady Katherine his arm to escort her out.

"That was not part of the pageant." She spoke quietly behind a modest smile as he led her off the castle grounds.

"No." He nodded to people who cheered him as he passed.

"I followed the man's stare. I wanted to see who gave him instructions, but there were too many people. It could have been anyone."

"Barrington didn't find him either."

"I'm glad you were here to help Roddy and the others. This could have been ended badly, very badly."

Her concern was correct. At the moment, he wanted to remove her from the area. Wallace and Lady Katherine made their way to Barrington's Sommer Chase.

"WELCOME TO SOMMER Chase, Your Grace, Lady Katherine." Barrington's butler took them into the library which was behind the dining room.

Shelves filled with books stood on two walls and surrounded the fireplace on the third. A sideboard with goblets and decanters to one side was on the fourth wall. A fine Persian carpet covered the floor. There were two seating areas, one by the hearth and another at the far end of the room.

Barrington had turned his country home into a private men's club of sorts, a place where he and his close friends, most of whom served with him, could meet, exercise, and deliberate without interruption.

"You made it through the crowd. You are the man of the hour. Your name is on everyone's lips. According to the judge, the magistrate, and others, everyone assumes your actions were part of the performance." Barrington handed him a brandy. "You earned this."

Wallace understood Barrington's reasoning to minimize the situation. However, not telling the villagers about the attack left them vulnerable and unprepared. Worse than that, with a false sense of security, it made them all easy targets.

"Wilmore, tell Wallace what you found out when you questioned the men with Ollie."

"Four were with him in the pageant. Ollie hired them. They received their instructions this morning. Judge Scofield had them locked up until the magistrate can take them to Bamburgh Castle."

"None of us could see who gave Ollie his orders. I can tell you that once he left the courtyard, he disappeared. You'd think someone that large would be easy to find." Peter didn't hide the irritation in his tone.

"I followed him outside the gate but lost him in the crush of people leaving." Simon finished his brandy.

"Ollie met Lord Whitaker outside the gate." Everyone turned to Mrs. Bainbridge.

"Are you sure?" Barrington appeared to be caught off guard, a position the man didn't like.

"Oh, yes. Lord Whitaker had stopped to speak to me. He rudely looked over my shoulder and caught someone's eye. It was the look he gave them that cautioned me. So, I dropped my reticule and when I bent to pick it up glanced behind me. That's when I saw the man."

"Whitaker had a retinue of people with him." Lady Katherine went to the sideboard for a drink of lemonade. "They all left Sommer-by-the-Sea on the York coach. Whitaker was bold enough to say good-bye to me."

"Nothing's on that road until you reach Royston Mills," Barrington said under his breath.

"Coincidence?" Wilmore tilted his head.

"I'm not sure, but I will wait to pass judgement. His leaving may be a ploy. The man likes to play games. Simms." Barrington turned and faced his guests. "Gather a few men. Magistrate Rogers told me he requested assistance. He asked us to watch the roads coming into the village while he waits for reinforcements.

Neither of us want the evening's celebration disturbed."

"If you will excuse me." Lady Katherine stood. "I must prepare for this evening. Lord Wallace, the evening is also a re-enactment of sorts. We feast as my forefathers did five hundred years ago."

"I seem to have my orders as well." Wallace stood. "Lead the way, Lady Katherine." He turned to the others. "Let's hope these plans are for naught."

Chapter Eleven

Wallace peered into the looking glass, amazed at who stared back at him. How had Mr. Russell and Lenard worked their miracle? In a short amount of time, the two had transformed him into a fourteenth-century lord. He wore chausses that fit tight to his legs, a white shirt, with an embroidered tunic belted low on his hips.

"Do I pass muster?" Wallace continued to stare at himself, turning in various directions, checking every angle. "You don't think I look foolish, do you?"

"More handsome than most, but no, not foolish at all. You will be the belle of the feast."

Wallace, looking at his man in the looking glass, didn't miss his stifled playful smirk. Lenard knew how to bring him down to earth.

Wallace turned to leave.

Lenard extended his leg and gave him a gracious bow. "Have a good evening, milord."

Wallace left his room and headed for the drawing room, smiling, and shaking his head. He intended to review his sketches, but the notes for their new plans interested him more.

A quick review of the documents showed Sutton had added drawings of the inside of the mechanical. His partner clearly saw the internal workings, possible problems, but more importantly, he also saw areas in need of corrections.

He'd rather spend more time studying the plans but that would have to wait. On his way out of the room, he passed the covered lock and peaked underneath. Lockpicks and a detailed drawing of the lock's insides lay next to the mechanism. The challenge was interesting. He studied the sketch, then the tools. If the drawing was accurate, these tools would never work. This project required more intricate picks.

He replaced the cloth. The lock didn't matter now. With Sutton gone, its secrets were safe.

He went downstairs and directly into the parlor. Mr. Russell, who had kept vigil all afternoon, quietly left. Standing, looking down at Sutton, it was difficult to believe his friend was gone.

"I wish you would get up and..." He clasped his hands in front of him, alternately running his thumbs up each other in a restless motion. As soon as he realized his fidgeting, he brought his hands to his side as if he'd been scolded by his governess.

"Silly, isn't it. You laying there. Why didn't you tell me? Ivy-Rose is a grown woman more than capable of taking care of herself. You had a reason to make me take that oath. And don't tell me you didn't put that gossip in the paper, sealing it up like a nice package. But I can't deduce why." He stared at his friend's peaceful expression. Was Bennett having the last laugh? No, there was something urgent behind all this. "You are crafty, but mark my words, I'll put the pieces together."

He turned at a sound by the door half expecting to see Mr. Russell. Instead, Lady Katherine stood at the threshold in a black bombazine dress. As she crossed the room, her skirt elegantly swirled, the creases taking on a dark purple hue. The dress fit her snuggly and flowed to the ground. An intricately embroidered silk belt rested loosely at her hips. Her long black hair in a loose braid hung down her back. Around her neck was her single piece of jewelry, the silver locket. Even in mourning the woman was a beauty.

Was Lady Katherine really his? A nagging in the back of his

mind refused to be still. This woman would not marry because of an oath given to her dying uncle or a command given from her father. No. Lady Katherine Ivy-Rose Thornton, descendent of the great Knight Templar, Lord Stephen, would always make her own decisions. About everything.

You have given me two challenges that I wholeheartedly accept. I will find your murderer and I will marry Ivy-Rose. But listen to me, Sutton, wherever you are: I will not break her spirit. I will not force her. Your Ivy-Rose must come to me of her own free will. This I swear to you.

"I can come back later." She started to walk away.

"No, please. I'm sure Sutton's had enough of me today. He's the same as always, ignoring my banter."

A small hiccup of a chuckle snuck through her otherwise solemn exterior.

"You knew him that well." Lady Katherine moved next to him. They both gazed at Bennett. "He would be the first to tell you that you played a better young knight than he ever did. Bennett never enjoyed the re-enactment part of the celebration. *'Let the past rest in peace'.*"

For several minutes, both reflected coming to terms with their loss in their own ways.

Lady Katherine let out a deep breath. "But I swear by all that is holy, I will find out who did this to him."

"As will I." His voice was low and deadly to his own ears.

"You needn't play the chivalrous knight. I can—"

"Take care of yourself." Wallace turned and faced her. "Yes, I am aware you're more than capable. But it would grieve me deeply if I did not join you in capturing his murderer. I, too, have a score to settle. Let's make a pact to do this together." He glanced at Sutton. "I made him a pledge."

She relented and abandoned her brusque tone for a softer one. "I would be foolish not to agree. Ollie is much bigger than me." She tenderly touched her uncle's hand. "And he would scold me. So there. You have it. Our pact is made. But not before the end of our celebration. Tonight's events are the one part of the celebration Bennett enjoyed. Eating, drinking, singing, dancing, and the bonfire. This seems the best way to honor him before tomorrow. We should be on our way."

Wallace, his right hand on his heart, his right leg extended, tilted his head, and bowed. "This way, milady."

"Well done, milord." Her soft chuckle pleased him. They left the abbey and headed to the celebration.

"THE PREVIOUS CASTLE residents abandoned the place long before my family arrived here. It isn't part of my family's legacy." They walked into the bailey. "It does provide a service. Without a resident militia, the magistrate and Judge Scofield use the dungeons for detention. We also use the area on special occasions. Like this one."

More banquet tables had been added to the bailey along with a raised platform in front of the castle steps that led to the keep. She glanced at the table set on the dais draped with a garland of flowers as they headed to their seats.

"I know every aspect of the day's events. The evening is my favorite. Father, the great knight, and Mother, the beautiful princess, hosted dinner for the village. Afterward everyone danced and sang." The ghost of a smile touched her lips. "My father taught me to dance the cotillion here while Mother pulled Bennett to be her partner. He complained at every step. Other than dancing, he remained at my side, grumbling the whole evening. That is until the drinking and singing started. He was good at that."

They moved among the villagers. Wallace accepted compliments for fending off the "French." Lady Katherine received praise for another excellent celebration. Up ahead, Lord Barrington, Mrs. Bainbridge, and several village dignitaries waited for them at the dais. She had Lord Wallace sit to her right, as the highest-ranking nobleman. That was the excuse she gave herself, but for all her bravado he made her feel safe.

The trumpeter sounded a fanfare. The noise in the bailey faded until only the sound of the pennants flapping in the breeze could be heard. She stood, holding her goblet.

"Welcome. We are here this evening to pay homage to Lord Stephen Thornton who fought valiantly for his god and country. It is through his sacrifice and valor that Sommer-by-the-Sea has remained strong and safe." She raised her goblet. "To Lord Stephen. May he rest in peace and protect us."

"Hear, hear."

Lady Katherine drank her wine and again held up her goblet.

Well done, Ivy-Rose. Our grand Knight Templar may protect the village, but it is Ian who will protect you.

She stared wordlessly at Lord Wallace, her heart pounding.

Lord Wallace's pleasant smile slipped from his face. His eyebrows were drawn together in concern. She sat down before he did anything.

"What is it?" When she didn't reply, he scanned the area.

"Is your given name Ian?" She didn't face him, but rather stared out at the people in the bailey.

Wallace twisted around to face her. "Yes. Why do you ask?"

"You would think me mad if I told you." Lenard came to the table with a soup tureen. She stared at him as he served them a chilled soup. "Almost as mad as your valet serving dinner."

Lenard gave a small nod and moved on to serve the others at the table.

"Why would I think you mad?" Wallace gazed at her with his spoon poised in his hand.

"Bennett told me."

"Why would I think you mad if Sutton told you my given name?"

She shrugged and spoke offhandedly. "Because he *just* told me. In my head." If Katherine expected him to shrink back in horror or run from the table, she was disappointed.

"You may have found my name in Sutton's papers." Wallace tasted the soup and returned nods from Mr. Hawkins and several others who passed by him.

"I'm sure you have it right." She masked her inner turmoil and loss with a deceptive calmness.

"You're not mad." She startled when he put down his spoon and covered her hand with his. "I miss him, too."

Surprised by his admission, she stared at him and shrugged, biting the inside of her cheek to control the tears that threatened.

"I find myself speaking to him even though he isn't here. If we are mad, we are mad together." He took away his hand, picked up his spoon, and gestured toward hers.

Katherine raised the utensil and began to eat. Her melancholy softened as the villagers, some dressed as jugglers and some as jesters, entertained and made mischief. She laughed with them and sang with the minstrel who roved among the tables taking requests.

The dinner over, Katherine and Wallace walked along the battlements overlooking the village. "I hope you enjoyed the feast. Bennett would have suffered through the meal to get to the bonfire and drinking afterward. He and the minstrel were always the center of the evening's entertainment. As the night got on, and people had more to drink, the songs became bawdier."

She glanced at Wallace and found she had his full attention. "As much as he complained and found fault, he was also a visionary who gave praise and encouragement."

Wallace nodded his agreement.

"You don't look surprised."

"Sutton's hard outside shell was his protection. It kept people away. But there are those of us, and I am proud to count myself among them, who he allowed to see the real Bennett Sutton. His caring for the people who work for him, and those he felt responsible for, is the true essence of the man. The rest is much like the costume I'm wearing – a disguise to hide behind."

They stood on the rampart and watched as the sky turned

from pastel to indigo, the color blending with that of the ocean. If it wasn't for the reflection of the full moon on the water, the horizon would have gone unseen. They didn't speak, just shared the moments of a beautiful evening.

Noise from the bailey grabbed their attention. From their vantage point, it was obvious everyone was ready for the evening's events. They made their way down to the bailey as torches were put to the pile of wood to start the bonfire.

She grabbed Wallace's hand and pulled him along. "It's the same every year, but this is my favorite part of the celebration."

The mayor sat on a high stool at one end of the bonfire and overlooked the crowd. Children sat on the ground around him, the others on logs and blankets.

"The story begins more than five hundred years ago, with a son born to Lord Aldus and Lady Inga Thornton. He was not an exceptional boy. He was much like you." The mayor cast his glance at young boy sitting by him. "Or you." He glanced at another. "Or even you." He nodded and pointed to a third.

The mayor continued the story of how young Stephen grew up to be truthful and just.

As the bonfire reached its height and the hour got late, the servers poured wine for everyone. The mayor raised his goblet, saluted Lord Stephen, and told the end of the story. This story was not about a magical object. This story was about a brave man who gave his life for his beliefs. Katherine cried every year although she knew the ending of the tale.

As the last words of the story left the mayor's lips, the lilting sounds of the minstrel's lute filtered down from the castle keep and the minstrel made his way to the bonfire. With the musician's inspiration, and a little wine for encouragement, the sadness of the tale turned into triumph and a celebration with people singing and dancing.

"Milady, do you have a song you would like to hear?" The minstrel, Mr. Green, the seminary's music instructor, stood in front of her.

"'The Three Ravens', if you please."

"My pleasure." With a flare, he doffed his cap and gracefully extended his leg. He strummed his lute playing the opening chord.

"The one of them said to his mate,

Where shall we our breakfast take?

There were three ravens sat on a tree,

They were as black as they might be.

With a down, derrie, derrie, derrie, down, down."

The minstrel paused. It was an old game he played.

"More." Came the roar from the crowd.

The minstrel grinned and gazed at everyone, making them wait for the next verse. Finally, he relented.

"Down in yonder green field,

There lies a Knight slain under his shield."

He paused again and glanced at Katherine. "My lady, the chorus please."

"There were three ravens sat on a tree,

They were as black as they might be.

With a down, derrie, derrie, derrie, down, down."

Her alto voice was strong and clear.

The minstrel went through the crowd giving others an opportunity to sing the chorus. Some sang alone and others banded together in groups. By the end of the tale everyone was singing together.

The tempo of the music picked up. One of the men brought out a drum and lent the music a strong beat. Another took out a fiddle and joined the group. There was no way to sit still. If your body wasn't swaying, then your hands were clapping. If your hands weren't clapping, then your feet were stomping. And when you could no longer sit in your seat, you were on your feet and dancing.

"Milady?" Wallace stood in front of her.

She gazed at his extended hand. Was she up for the challenge? Susceptible to the music as everyone else, her body swayed to the music. A wide smile spread across her face as she accepted his hand.

They took their places with the others. Lady Katherine curtsied, and he bowed as the dance, a story of pursuit and surrender, began. For the rest of the dance, neither took their gaze off the other.

CHAPTER TWELVE

O N THE DOWNBEAT, Wallace gracefully stepped back. Katherine, unwilling to accept his retreat, stepped forward in pursuit and stood in front of him, demanding he not leave her behind.

His hands tightened around her waist as he moved forward, taking her with him returning her to where she started.

Wallace let her go and once again quickly retreated, leaving her staring at him with a gaze that enticed him to return.

Accepting her challenge, he stepped toward her.

But Katherine didn't move.

It was his turn to refuse being ignored.

His hands once again encircled her waist. She could feel the warmth of his fingers on her skin through her gown. With a sweeping move, he easily lifted her high.

She glanced at him from up in the air, her hands braced on his shoulders. Her stomach in a frenzy not from the meal, but from the man. Artfully he spun them around.

The blur of those circling them created a wall, a private space for no one else but them. His penetrating gaze didn't waiver. Thrilled by his attention, her heart was close to bursting.

Those around them squealed with delight, but Wallace and Katherine didn't notice.

Setting her down where he had been standing, he pulled her

close. Her heart pounded so loud, certainly he heard it over the music.

Stepping to her side, they played a game of cat and mouse until once again he stood in front of her.

The teasing game left her breathless, wanting more.

His hand rested on her hip, while his other held her hand high over her head. Leaning close to her, he threatened to brush his lips against hers.

She bit her lower lip and sensed his eager affection.

His breath bathed her cheek, releasing a flutter of butterflies in her stomach.

Katherine stepped away from him as if rejecting his advance but refused to let go of his hand.

He pulled her back, spinning her under his arm until, once again, they stood a breath apart.

She cleared her throat, pretending not to be affected. But that couldn't be further from the truth.

Wallace brought her to his side and tucked her in, protecting her.

Katherine stayed in his arms, never wanting to leave. Their dancing flowed from one step to another as if they belonged together.

The first in the line of dancers, they separated, and sashayed to the back of the line where they took their places and began again.

With the repeat of each set of steps his touches and gazes became more tender, if that was possible. She tried to control the dizzy sensation running through her. The more she tried, the more she lost ground until the last chord of the dance played. Everything came to a halt.

"Your Grace. You take my breath away."

Wallace didn't let go of her hand as they made their way through the crowd to the refreshments. They stood by the castle wall far from everyone. She stared at his chest. She dared not glimpse at him afraid what he would see in her eyes would give her secret away.

Coward.

It was the thrill of the dance. Nothing else. The only way to put this to right was to look at him and see him as he was, not with all this dreaming. *Look at him.* She put on a smile and lifted her face.

Her breath caught. How had she missed it before?

"ARE YOU WELL, Lady Katherine?" Flushed from the dance, but nothing more. He found the brightness on her cheeks becoming. He asked if she was well when he was the one who needed attention.

Wallace hadn't danced in years and surprised himself when he offered her his hand.

"You're deep in thought." Lady Katherine handed him a goblet of wine.

"I enjoyed our reel. I'd forgotten how much I enjoy dancing."

As a young man, his friends would tease him. *If gentlemen had dance cards, yours would be filled before you stepped into the dance hall.* That was before he retired from the service and took his brother's place in the family. Now, he had no desire to dance. He had no desire for anything. He had built a wall to keep others out, but Lady Katherine was shattering it one stone at a time.

Had he only known her two days? How could his heart be so utterly lost? An attraction was acceptable, lust was understandable, but this? This longing was undying.

He didn't move away. He couldn't. He found her smile was more than inviting, it was bewitching. And her eyes, her extraordinary violet eyes blazed with desire.

His gaze focused on her lips, plump and moist. One moment he was staring at them, the next… He bent down and gently brushed his lips across hers. His muscles twitched and tightened with a rush of emotion he hadn't experienced in years.

His arms went around her bringing her close. *Kate, dear beautiful Kate.* He traced her soft lips with his tongue and tasted the honey sweet mead. He raised his mouth from hers and looked into her penetrating eyes.

Her brows furrowed with an unspoken question. He kissed her forehead and tucked her head against his chest. Her heart beat almost as fast as his.

He knew he was lost and didn't care.

TRUST HIM. CONFIDE in him. Love him.

Her head against his chest, she relished listening to his quickened heartbeat and pushed away her doubts. Wallace kissed the top of her head as he stroked her back soothing her to distraction. Her eyelids slid closed as she basked in the gentle strokes.

The dancing over, the minstrel played softly and took requests. Mr. Green glanced at Katherine and nodded. He didn't need to ask what she wanted. He played the introduction to the duet they sang every year, *Scarborough Fair.*

She looked up at Wallace. He nodded and took her hand bringing her back to the others. The minstrel and Katherine sang the first verse together. She then pointed to the next singer. Some had their favorite verses; others didn't care. It was time for the next to last verse. Tanya, the proprietress of the teashop chose Wallace. Everyone gave him an anxious look. He sang the verse in a smooth, rich voice. Katherine and Wallace sang the final chorus, together.

"Love imposes impossible tasks,
Parsley, sage, rosemary, and thyme.
But none more than any heart would ask,
I must know you're a true love of mine."

There was a brief silence after the last chord faded, but only for a moment. Everyone cheered. Some asked for more. Katherine shook her head and Wallace graciously agreed.

"Thank you, Your Grace." Mr. Green turned to her. "Lady Katherine. Your voices are well matched. I fear you may have me replaced." Those close enough to hear laughed. The minstrel went to the next group.

Barrington and Mrs. Bainbridge approached them.

"I thoroughly enjoyed your duet." Mrs. Bainbridge sat next to Katherine. "Reese was humming along. It was quite comical."

"Are you saying you wouldn't want me to serenade you?" Barrington put on a wounded expression that made them all laugh. "No, you are right. I have no talent for music. I do have a talent for catching criminals.

"The men have reported in. One of the magistrate's men went along Knight's Lane all the way to the crossroads and confirmed, Whitaker and his friends took a coach. He saw them enter Baycliff Woods. I think we can rest easy this evening."

He got to his feet. "Come Honoria, it's time I brought you home."

"Thank you for another wonderful celebration." Mrs. Bainbridge kissed her cheek. "You are generous as always."

"It is my pleasure." Katherine looked around. "Everyone enjoys the day."

Barrington put his arm around the headmistress as they went on, Barrington humming the folk song.

"You sing very well." Lady Katherine stared at the bonfire.

"My mother required my brother and I to have musical training. My brother chose the violin. I chose voice."

He laughed to himself.

"Is that humorous?"

"My reason for taking vocal training was. I wouldn't have an instrument in the military, but I would have my voice." They said nothing for a few minutes.

"Ivy-Rose." The minstrel stood in front of her.

"Mr. Green?" She kept her smile serene although the use of

her hated middle name had her insides jumping as if she walked barefoot on the hot sand.

"A poem from an admirer, milady."

With her nod, the minstrel continued.

"Thank you. This anonymous person requested that I recite the poem specifically to you."

"Very well."

"*I made my demand under the pine. You kept saying that you must decline. You can say no and decry, you can stamp your foot and deny. But I have proof and you must pay for your crime.*"

She felt the color drain from her face.

Wallace wasted no time. He put his arm around the minstrel and began to take him away.

"No, I'm coming with you." Lady Katherine stood and hurried after them.

Wallace didn't say anything. He tried to remain calm.

"But Your Grace." Mr. Green didn't struggle as Wallace moved him along. His voice pleaded for an explanation.

"Quiet. We'll talk in private." He turned to Lady Katherine. "Is there someplace we can go where we'll be alone?"

"This way." She led them to the castle.

When he tried the door, he found it locked and glanced at her.

"No bother." She pulled a hairpin from her hair and worked the lock until she heard the click.

If Wallace thought her skill odd, he kept it to himself.

Lady Katherine took a lit torch next to the door and led them into a small room.

"What is this about?" The minstrel stammered obviously bewildered at the turn of events. "I simply read what I was given."

"Who gave you the words to recite?" Wallace demanded grinding the words out from between his teeth.

The minstrel took out a paper tucked in his belt and handed it to him. "It came with a shilling. You can see the instructions." He pointed to the text. "To read to Lady Katherine at the bonfire."

"Who gave it to you?" Wallace's glare drilled into the minstrel.

"I don't know. I found the note and shilling tucked in my lute."

"I don't understand." Lady Katherine glanced at Wallace. He glared at her frowning. She took a breath fearing he would act at any moment.

"I left my lute against the wall while I dined. I found the note and shilling when I unwrapped the instrument to perform. I didn't see anyone near the area. I asked those around me and neither had they."

"Your Grace, Mr. Greene is a music instructor and plays the minstrel every year for the pageant. I am sure there is nothing malicious about him. Both myself and Mrs. Bainbridge will speak for him."

The warrior standing in front of her changed before her eyes. His angles softened. His face relaxed. She let out a sigh of relief.

"Mr. Greene. I'm sorry for any inconvenience."

"I should have realized it was some sort of prank. Please forgive me if I have caused you any discomfort."

"No. Not at all. You're correct. It was a prank." She let out a long-exhausted sigh. "At another time I may have tolerated it better, but not this evening. You best hurry back before there is no one left for you to sing to."

Mr. Greene gathered his dignity and looked from Wallace to Lady Katherine. "I will come to you at once if I find out who penned the note."

"That would be helpful and appreciated." Lord Wallace walked him to the door and didn't move until the man was well away. She came to his side.

This evening, everything appeared cheerful and innocent. But that was deceptive. He sensed the undercurrent, and it was getting stronger.

"Do you want to tell me why the poem upset you?" He still

gazed out the door.

"No. There is nothing to tell." Her immediate emphatic response caught him short.

"Perhaps I should demand an answer rather than politely ask." He glared at her, then closed the door. "Never play cards. Your emotions are clearly marked on your face. Tell me what upset you."

Lady Katherine crossed her arms and turned away. For her, the discussion was over.

Wallace couldn't let the conversation end. He had to convince her to tell him. Trust him. This was getting complicated. He took a deep breath to calm himself although every muscle wanted to grab her by her shoulders and make her look at him. Instead, he stepped in front of her.

"Can't you see I'm trying to protect you?" He leaned in close to keep her attention. "I can't do that unless I know where the threat is from."

"I know you want to protect me. There are some things that I cannot tell you. They are important only to me, for me to deal with and no one else."

"They're important to someone who enjoys taunting you. And from the looks of things, this person is very successful. The words in that message were carefully crafted and the meaning plain."

"Please." Her single whispered word and pained expression tugged at him.

"Katherine, not only to you." His voice was low. She could hardly hear him. "This is important to me as well."

She stood there very shaken by his declaration and suddenly anxious to leave, but there was no escape. Awkwardly, she cleared her throat.

"It would be best for me to return to the abbey."

"If you wait a moment, I'll let Barrington's men know I'm leaving.

"No." Her response came out more charged than she

planned. "No," she said in a quieter tone. "I know the way."

Wallace studied her for several heartbeats, his gaze never leaving hers.

"I can't do that. Not after all that's happened today. If you prefer, I'll have one of the others escort you."

She let out a deep sigh.

"I've been independent for a long time. I'm not accustomed to being sheltered. That is all. If there is anyone I trust, it is you." She put her hand on his chest. "Even more than my uncle. You would never force me to do anything. Bennett connived and planned all the time leaving me to deal with the results. I'd be happy to have you escort me back to the abbey."

They walked through the bailey and out the castle gate. Wallace nodded to Barrington's men who remained at their stations.

"On the way, will you tell me where you learned to pick a lock?"

"Perhaps."

Wallace lifted one eyebrow and glanced at her. He was glad the smile evident in her one-word answer played out across her face.

CHAPTER THIRTEEN

A SOFT MELLOW male voice faded along with the last strains of Scarborough Fair as Katherine opened her eyes. She stared at the garden mural on her bedroom ceiling. Overall, yesterday's celebration had been a success and last night's bonfire a delight. Perhaps breakfast outside this morning. She got out of bed and pulled open the curtains.

Her mouth dropped open. There was no sunshine. The skies had opened. Large puddles filling the wheel ruts spoke of an all-night rain and from the look of things the rain would probably last all day as well.

Her eyes caught sight of the hearse and her heart slammed in her chest. The respite the annual celebration provided only delayed the inevitable. Bennett Sutton would be laid to rest today. Her gaze moved from the carriage to the sky. How fitting. A miserable day.

A wistful smile touched her lips. Bennett understood her, convinced her mother to let her go to the seminary. He was the one person who knew what happened in London, rescued her, and never mentioned the incident. The smile faltered thinking about the poem Mr. Green recited. Now, on her own, she needed to rely on her abilities. Best not to worry about that now.

Standing at the window, she looked at the castle tower on the hill. There had been surprises all evening. Lenard serving dinner made her smile. Dancing with Wallace without stepping on his toes was an accomplishment. His arms around her. His kisses.

Her fingers touched her lips and for a moment, last night's dream seemed attainable. Lord Wallace. Brave. Trustworthy. Honest. Was he the next knight? Her knight? Her mouth twitched with amusement.

A perfect evening crushed by a perfectly horrid person. When would she learn dreams were for children? And choices come with consequences. Sometimes ones you live with forever.

Stop it! Stop mourning for something you never had.

Yesterday's pomp and ceremony was over. The summer will end soon enough, and the spring and summer rituals will need managing. There are the farmers, the shepherds, and the factory. The responsibilities were heavy ones.

One more responsibility needed to be added to the top of her list. Find who murdered Bennett and make sure he's brought to justice.

A cold chill ran up her spine. Katherine lowered herself onto the edge of the bed. Are the incidents related? The idea caught her off guard.

No. He wouldn't dare. Unless he was more desperate than he was all those months ago. This message was an omen, and not a good one, of things to come.

She glanced upstairs, but the fleeting sense of rescue faded. Bennett couldn't come to her rescue now.

"That's why he sent the poem," she murmured through clenched teeth.

She paced in front of the window. They needed a clever plan to catch him, but first, she needed to get through today.

"Calm down. Think. Deep breath. That's right. Another. You're not alone. Trust Wallace." Bennett's voice faded away in her mind.

Dressed for the day, she stood in front of the long mirror, staring at herself in the black bombazine dress, a black veil fixed to her hair, and holding a pair of black gloves. With everything in place, she left her room.

Hesitantly, she went down to the foyer relieved to see the parlor door closed and Mr. Russell blocking anyone from entering.

"Good morning." She went to walk by him but came to a halt when she looked at the man's face. "Mr. Russell. Are you well? I'd venture a guess you haven't slept all night."

"Thank you for your concern, Lady Katherine. I had a choice of sitting with Mr. Sutton or guarding the house outside. I preferred to sit with Mr. Sutton."

"I should be thanking you for seeing to this."

"Forgive me. Lord Wallace took care of the details. I volunteered."

She shouldn't be surprised, not after the way he took control yesterday. She was foolish letting her feelings show. It would be better if she didn't like him, even hated the man. It would be so much easier to turn away. The idea made her want to cry. But it had to be done.

"That doesn't change my gratitude. Also, I won't need the carriage. I'll walk behind my uncle." If Mr. Russell had concerns about the weather, he kept that concern to himself.

Katherine entered the breakfast room and sat at her place, her tea, scone, and bilberry jam in front of her. She poured the tea but left everything else untouched. The thought of eating didn't agree with her.

WALLACE STOOD AT his window and stared out at the drive. His discussion with Barrington as they stood guard last night still fresh in his mind.

"You *what?*" Barrington exploded.

"Hush, you'll wake everyone." Wallace glanced at the house, relieved no one stirred.

"What do you mean you didn't tell Lady Katherine about

your oath? I suppose you didn't tell her about the deed to the house either."

"No. When should I have told her? When the agitators visited? At the cemetery yesterday or at the celebration? Perhaps after we danced." He certainly wasn't going to tell her after their brief intimacy nor mention that to Barrington.

"It will not go well for you if she finds out on her own, or worse, from someone else."

"I am well aware, especially after last night."

"Last night?"

"She thinks I am honest and trustworthy. Would never lie to her."

Barrington didn't say anything. He didn't need to.

"But that is only one of the issues. After you and Mrs. Bainbridge left, the minstrel recited a poem to her at someone's request. The person used her middle name she dislikes, and few know."

"That should narrow the list of suspects."

"I think Lady Katherine has more information. She refused to tell me the name of the person who the poem refers to or the poem's significance. She insisted the issue was personal in nature and for her to bear." Wallace thought for a moment. *'I made my demand under the pine. You kept saying that you must decline. You can say no and decry, you can stamp your foot and deny. But I have proof, you must pay for your crime.'*

"What crime? A lover's spat? Surely, Honoria would know if Lady Katherine had an admirer."

Now, hours later he still had no idea what the woman was hiding. Two days ago, the possibility of a suitor or a husband would have been a welcome turn of events. But now? No. Now that he met her, spent time with her, kissed her, he had no intentions of walking away.

He gladly volunteered to stand guard during the night. He would not sleep anyway. His mind kept turning over the poem's puzzle. Now, in the light of day he still didn't have an answer. But he did have a plan.

Wallace left his room, noticed the door to the drawing room ajar and stepped inside.

"Roddy. I didn't expect to see you here."

"Your Grace. Lady Katherine asked for the daily reports."

"The ones you used to bring to Mr. Sutton?"

Roddy looked like he did when the cook caught him taking a tart. "The reports go to Lady Katherine. She shares them with Mr. Sutton."

Wallace schooled his face to hide his surprise.

"Lady Katherine would rather work at the factory, but Mr. Sutton refused. Instead, I bring what she needs here." Roddy's voice wavered a bit.

"And?"

Roddy paused, planning his answer with care. "There are times, rare ones." He added quickly. "That Lady Katherine comes to the factory." Roddy shuffled from one foot to the other. "She's a daring and determined woman and comes when the factory's closed, and then dressed as a boy. I'm amazed at her knowledge of the mechanicals. Sometimes she spends hours watching them work and makes suggestions on how to make them better. Mr. Sutton was none the wiser." Roddy appeared anxious. "She wouldn't be pleased with me if she knew I told you."

"You did the right thing. Your secret is safe. Neither of us want anything to happen to Lady Katherine and with the workers upset—"

"Your Grace. Sutton Textile workers are not upset. Our working conditions are better than most and we're paid fare wages. The arguments are not coming from us. They are coming from Ollie and his men."

"Do you know if any of them were at the bonfire last night?"

Roddy shook his head. "I didn't see any."

Someone gave the minstrel the note. Was there a traitor in their midst?

CHAPTER FOURTEEN

KATHERINE DRANK HER morning tea. She understood Mr. Russell watched over Bennett during the night and even the necessity of the vigil outside. The attempt to create the brawl at the pageant as well as the agitators' visit put everyone on edge. A flash of irritation had her put down her cup a bit harder than necessary. Gears turned in her mind unlocking a different solution. The men outside did not stand vigil, but rather guarded Thornton Abbey.

Would Bennett ever rest in peace? Thankfully, her father had the family build the mausoleum. With the granite doors closed and iron gate locked she could rest easy Bennett and her ancestors would be safe.

"Good morning, Lady Katherine. I hope you slept well." Wallace came into the breakfast room, poured himself a cup of coffee, and took a seat across from her.

"Yes. I wanted to thank you for seeing to Bennett. I wouldn't want him to spend his last night in the abbey alone. I would like to think you arranged it because of the funerary ritual. I fear the near-brawl and Ollie and his friends' visit made a guard necessary."

"I would have done it for the ritual. Ollie's visit and yesterday's events gave us more reasons."

"Who guarded the house last night? I'd like to thank him."

He hesitated, his cup not quite at his lips.

"Barrington and I stayed outside. I'm sure I speak for him when I say we did it from our heart. We both admired Bennett Sutton."

"I'm touched by your devotion." Her first impulse was to rush into his arms and hold him close. Instead, she stared at the black gloves in her lap.

Her sense of loss for Bennett, and denial of her attraction for him, had her beyond tears. He stared at her and instead of looking at him she glanced out the window. Mr. Russell, two others from her staff, and Roddy closed the back of the carriage.

Wallace followed her gaze. He drank his coffee and put down his empty cup. "If you're ready to leave."

Ready? Not to say good-bye to Bennett. The knot in her throat was hot and choking. But a delay would not bring him back. Her duty was to put him to rest. She gave a quick nod.

"Is Mrs. Bainbridge joining us?"

She got to her feet. "She's gone on ahead."

Together they went into the foyer. He took an umbrella by the front door and escorted her outside.

The rain had turned into an annoying mist. Lady Katherine didn't remember taking her place behind the hearse. She let Wallace steer her around the large puddles. Her mind was blank. Not a thought of Bennett, of the day, the near brawl, of Ollie, the poem, Wallace's tenderness…Her breath caught as the pain of sending him away became too great. *Concentrate. One foot in front of the other.*

She often made the quick trip to the church on foot. Today, the journey seemed endless.

"Not much further." Wallace spoke softly.

She nodded and glanced up as the cemetery gates came into view. The carriage entered the churchyard and moved down the path. Mrs. Bainbridge came to her side holding an umbrella.

Wallace went on ahead. She continued to the mausoleum with Mrs. Bainbridge and her friends.

Her small party turned the bend in the path, and she hesitated. Once again, the Sutton Textile workers, their families, a few villagers, and friends flanked the path to the mausoleum. She hadn't expected so many people, especially this early in the morning.

"Do you need a moment?" Mrs. Bainbridge's soft voice broke through the fog.

Katherine let out a deep breath. "No. I must get this done. It won't be any easier if we delay."

Her eyes focused on the ground. Each step more difficult than the last.

I am so angry with you. Going to Royston Mills was a gamble. You knew it was and still you went. Even after the threats. I should have been with you. I would have made sure nothing happened.

Katherine glanced at the solemn faces of the people around her. A hard, dry cough brought her attention to a group on the left where Bromley stood with some of the villagers. Ollie and his friends stood behind them. Bromley and those men weren't here to mourn her uncle or to support her. Intimidation was their goal.

Wallace waited up ahead, near the iron gate. Judge Scofield had his ear. Her eyes caught his and his face changed. The judge must have noticed. He abruptly stopped speaking and stepped to the side.

She exchanged a fleeting glance with several people. But her stomach sank at the sight of the open stone doors. In a few minutes, they would close, and Bennett would be inside forever.

Keep going. One foot in front of the other. She didn't know how she managed it, but they reached the mausoleum. The vicar reached out to her, inviting her to enter the tomb.

Katherine put her hand on Wallace's arm. He stepped forward, tucked her arm over his and walked with her into the mausoleum.

The vicar's voice, as soothing as it is, did not work its magic today. Barely able to make out the words, she stood in front of Bennett's crypt with her head bowed and Wallace's arm at her back.

The service over, the vicar left her and Wallace standing in front of Bennett's resting place in quiet prayer.

After several moments, Katherine approached the stone and placed her hand on it. "Rest in peace. I will miss you always." She glanced at the stone on the right. "And don't give your brother-in-law a hard time."

She moved to the right and placed her forehead on her father's stone. "Don't be angry that Bennett is with you. You love him, and someone needs to watch over him." She kissed the stone and stepped away.

Katherine and Wallace walked out as streaks of sunlight came through the trees. She took a deep breath and felt the relief of this task being completed. People stood quietly in clusters as Wallace walked her through the gauntlet and out of the churchyard.

"Thank you. I planned to go inside alone." Katherine took the comfort he provided.

"I'm glad I was able to make it easier for you." His voice was low and warm.

Go ahead. Tell him what's behind the poem. He's not scared off easily.

Her lips remained tightly closed.

You're almost back at the abbey. What is your plan. Avoid him?

She took a breath and gathered her thoughts. Tell him? Not today. She gave him a sideways glance. No, not today.

Wallace opened the garden gate and walked up to the door that was draped with black crepe. Inside, the parlor furniture was back in place. The gloom of the day was inside as much as it was outside.

"Would you like to sit in the parlor?"

"Please forgive me. I don't think I'd be good company."

"Of course."

She started up the staircase.

Wallace left the abbey and headed into the village.

"Lord Wallace. Come in." Judge Scofield led him into his office and gestured to a chair.

"How is Lady Katherine?"

"As good as can be expected considering."

"Burying kin is never easy. Lady Katherine is a strong woman and will see things through."

"So I'm learning."

"The papers are in probate. With Lord Barrington's brother in London, I hastened the filing. I may have word as early as next week. I'll inform you and Lady Katherine when to arrange for the reading of the will. All the interested parties are in Sommer-by-the-Sea. Your partnership agreement is sound. Everything is in good order. We can address the business at the same time."

"That's good news." Wallace paused.

"Is there something else?"

His plan sounded fine when he put it together. Now he had some concerns, but Sutton gave him the responsibility of caring for her. He swallowed his doubts, determined to protect her.

"Are there any issues in which Sutton or Lady Katherine may be involved that could be used against them?"

Scofield's expression shifted from congenial to startled. Wallace didn't need the judge to respond. The answer was plainly written on his face.

"Why do you ask?" The judge's demeanor was more like a solicitor than a friend.

"Someone played a prank on Lady Katherine at last night's bonfire that upset her."

"A prank, you say? Who would do such a thing with her burying Sutton? Did you ask her?"

"Of course, I did. She told me it was—"

"None of your business." The judge sat back and the friendly smile returned to his face.

"Yes. Last night, someone paid the minstrel to recite a poem to her. She was visibly shaken. It was an anonymous request. No one can identify who left the minstrel the request."

"I'm not surprised. People filled the bailey." The judge sat closer to the desk. "I've known Lady Katherine since she was a young girl. She values truth and honesty. I have the impression you haven't told her about the abbey and the oath."

The judge's statement was unexpected but correct. Wallace stood and paced in front of the desk, one hand on his hip.

"The London papers will be arriving soon. There isn't much time left."

He didn't say anything. Nor did he look the judge in the eye.

"You have the look of a doomed man. Is the thought of fulfilling your oath so terrible?"

"No, not at all. Lady Katherine is… perfect."

The judge raised his eyebrow and smiled. "Yes, she is. I do understand your hesitancy. But I wonder if there would ever be a suitable time."

"I had a similar conversation with Barrington. He agrees with you."

KATHERINE CLIMBED THE stairs. Rather than rest, she entered the drawing room. The factory reports waited for her. They would be a welcome diversion.

As she worked through the reports, the numbers startled her. The fleece deliveries were lower than expected. She read the report from the shepherds then did an analysis. What she found did not look good.

Among the papers she found a note from Roddy about damaged and missing mechanical parts. The numbers were higher than usual and wondered if they had new workers who didn't know how to operate the machines. She looked through the list and put it aside.

The broken parts could provide a clue where the problems lie. She pushed herself away from the desk and began to pull the gears and fragments of the machines out a crate to see if the issues were with the mechanical, or the worker.

Inexperienced workers were a preferable answer than sabotage. Roddy insisted the workers were happy and content. Did he exaggerate? She made a note to speak to him and the staff. She would have to come to her own conclusion.

She removed another piece of the mechanical from the crate and continued her investigation.

The morning rain was long over, the afternoon was also spent. The sun cast purple shadows across the room.

"Lady Katherine."

"Yes, Mr. Russell." She didn't lift her head.

"Dinner is served."

She looked up, almost annoyed at the interruption.

"Mrs. Bainbridge has gone to Lady Brandt's for dinner this evening."

Katherine said nothing.

"Should I tell His Grace you will not be joining him this evening?"

Startled to see the candle in his hand, she glanced out the window trying to reconcile how long she'd been at her desk. There was nothing more she could do this evening. She put down her pencil.

"No, I'll be right there." One last glance at her work and she put the papers together and went downstairs.

It was unreal sitting at the dining room table. Lord Wallace sat to her right. Bennett's seat on her left was vacant.

Mrs. Russell laid the table with all the dishes for all the courses. There was a tureen of cold artichoke soup, mackerel with fennel and mint, small meat pies, roasted root vegetables, and a fresh fruit compote for dessert. The footman brought a pitcher of a drink with spiced sweet ginger and a dish of licorice, Katherine's favorite sweet.

"If you're finished eating." She glanced at Lord Wallace, then her plate.

She didn't remember what she ate, if they had a conversation, and if they did, what they said. Her eyes went to the doorway, waiting for Bennett to come down the stairs and tell her something funny, something impossible, something absurd.

"I need a few minutes of your time." Her heart ached more today than when Lord Wallace told her he had passed away. She pushed her grief aside and focused on her guest.

"It's more comfortable in the library."

Not waiting for a reply, she stood leaving her meal uneaten, the room deserted, and thoughts of her uncle abandoned.

Wallace followed her and closed the library door behind them.

"You have had a very difficult two days."

The last thing she wanted to do was discuss those days. A terrible guilt weighed heavy on her shoulders and at the moment, not facing it was all she could think of.

"I should never have let him go to Royston Mills without me."

"Don't be absurd. What would you have done?"

She turned and faced him. Her guilt and anger came in waves. At times, a little sharp twinge, at other times overwhelming pain. It seemed to be an endless ebb and flow.

"He would have listened to me. I could have... controlled him. Stopped his drinking at least." She was wringing the serviette still in her hands.

"Katherine." The use of her given name and his stern voice made her snap around and give him her attention. "His death is not your fault. Besides, there were others with him."

She chewed on her lip and stood in front of him and felt like a lost soul. Looking up at him she saw the compassion and concern in his eyes. Her breath caught as she tried to swallow around the growing hot knot in her throat.

"But none knew him as well as me." Her voice was a whisper. She couldn't stop the tide of oncoming grief that swelled. She took a breath and the tears trickled down her cheeks.

Wallace took her into his arms and held her close.

"It's all right to feel, to miss him, to be sad," he whispered into her hair. "Go ahead and cry. You're the bravest person I know. Even the brave, especially the brave, are allowed to cry."

She sobbed quietly in his embrace while he stroked her back and spoke about Bennett in a soft tone. The vibration of his chest soothed and comforted her.

Finally, the tears subsided, and Katherine took deep breaths trying to regain her control.

He gave her his handkerchief but didn't let her go.

"I don't know how to thank you."

"None are needed. You helped me as well."

She glanced at him surprised to see his damp eyes. "Aren't we a pair?"

"You blame yourself for not being with him. I blame myself for being with him and not doing enough. Yes. Aren't we a pair? But in truth, does it matter? What is done is done. We cannot bring him back. All we can do is move forward. Perhaps that is where we can help each other."

Could she collaborate with him? Just until they found who murdered Bennett. No more kisses. She stepped away from him. No more embraces.

"I'm sure this isn't why you wanted to speak to me."

"I spoke with Judge Scofield. He's been able to expedite the necessary filings."

"Why didn't he speak to me? Why you?"

Her pouncing attack startled him. "I was Sutton's partner. And for no other reason than not wanting to create any more stress for you."

"Is that all?"

"Anything else can wait."

It wasn't what he said or how he said it. Lord Wallace did an excellent job of keeping his thoughts to himself. But he did have more to say. To her, it was as obvious as his mysterious hazel eyes that beckoned her. All she could do was wait. He would tell her when he was ready.

CHAPTER FIFTEEN

THE REST OF the week fell into a routine for a house in mourning. Roddy came to the abbey almost every day with news from the factory. At least that was the reason he gave her. But she didn't have the heart to work on the mechanicals, tackle the challenge lock, or go near the drawing room.

Callers arrived in the late morning. Some left their card to acknowledge their sorrow while close friends stayed for a brief visit. Katherine remained at home reading and responding to the condolence messages that filled the morning mail. The outpouring surprised her. Most of the mourners recognized Bennett as a bold, forward, uncompromising person who could also be friendly, pleasant, and agreeable as long as it was on *his* terms. He did have another side that few ever witnessed.

Bennett longed to move away from the confines of the past and into the possibilities of the future. At times, his drive toward that glowing light caused him to take more risks than necessary. She could see where his eccentric behaviors and over-willingness to speak his mind would put off people. The messages proved her wrong, they soothed her. They were a testament to the man and for that she was thankful.

Today a message arrived from her dear seminary friend Lady Alicia Caulfield who lived in London.

"Caulfield and I have seen with the deepest sorrow and sympathy

what has befallen you. We learned of your uncle's passing only this morning. We cannot find words to tell you how our hearts are aching for you. Your Uncle Bennett was very special. With our deepest love, Alicia."

The last message in the bundle came from one of the seminary's guest speakers, Mr. Edward Bramah.

"I write in the hope that you are finding your work is of some help in getting though your grief. I do indeed know what it is to lose a loved one. It's been a year since the passing of my dear father, Joseph. I feel for you with all my heart. I will tell you this emptiness will pass.

"To find purpose, I threw myself into my work. So, I will renew the challenge I gave you. Focus your energy on finding the answer to opening the challenge lock."

Katherine lowered the letter to her lap. His heartfelt note made a point. Doing nothing made the emptiness worse. Her sole activity these last days was sitting at her writing desk responding to each note on black trimmed stationary. Her brief messages acknowledged the writer's concern, except the one to Mr. Bramah.

"Your kind note appeared in my morning mail. I shall remember you henceforth as a man who has been through a similar experience and remember the kind friend who stood by and spoke words of encouragement. Words can in one sense do nothing in such cases, but they, or the sentiments the words express, can bring a person out of that dark place and remind them that they are not alone.

"I accepted your challenge before and renew it this moment. Thank you for your most dear note. I look forward to presenting you with an opened lock."

Rather than sit in the parlor and stare out the window or sit on the terrace and stare at nothing, Katherine marched up the stairs. Without hesitating, she entered the drawing room, removed the cloth from the challenge lock, and started working.

By the afternoon, she had improvised a tool and found and secured another pin. Gratified, she still had no idea how many more pins needed to be found before the lock would open.

⋙✦⋘

LORD WALLACE GAZED out the office door at the factory with pride. The three-floor building, on the Baycliff River, did more than spin yarn. Using waterpower, Sutton Textile carded, spun, and wove cotton and wool into fabrics.

Wallace spent the first days after Sutton's funeral going through the factory papers. They were well organized, for the most part. There were notes from their correspondence with an American industrialist. The man's ideas about creating housing for workers near the factory appealed to Wallace and was the primary reason he pursued the partnership.

Sutton's interest in him arose from his property that was not far from the factory. The final agreement between them included deeding the property to the company. They were ready to begin construction when the issues at the factory started. Learning the troublemakers were not his workers, but rather paid agitators, put the difficulties in a different light. *What was the agitator's goal?* He needed to get to the bottom of this.

Wallace worked his way down the pile of folios and came to the last one. *Personal.* Reading Sutton's personal correspondence was not necessary. He bent down to open the drawer to put the folio away when the file slipped from his hand. Several papers fell to the floor.

He bent down to retrieve them and stared at a document from Lord Kinsleye, Ryder Whitaker's uncle. The letter was dated before he and Sutton became partners.

Four people vied to be Sutton's partner. He was leaning toward one in particular, but the name of that party was one of the best kept secrets in London. Wallace let out a chuckle. Everyone thought they were Sutton's choice. Lord Kinsleye surprised him when Sutton mentioned His Lordship gave him a stellar recommendation.

Wallace read through the papers, curious why this information would be out of the filing drawer. He found little of interest, the unsigned draft of a contract drawn up by Lord Hughes of the prestigious London legal firm of Hughes, Swift, and Lacy. The other papers documenting Lord Kinsleye's death appeared unimportant.

Lord Kinsleye's sudden heart attack and later death shocked everyone in London. Kinsleye died two weeks before he and Sutton struck their final agreement. Lord Kinsleye was a good man. He couldn't say the same about his nephew.

After witnessing Lady Katherine's reaction to Whitaker, he realized they both had similar opinions of him. Although her reaction did appear harsh.

Wallace's heart pounded. A nagging in the back of his mind refused to keep still. Whitaker was brash enough to draft that poem to her and coward enough to have someone else deliver it. He focused on the documents in his hand. Why did Sutton have this information out? This was old news. Or was it? His hands squeezed to fists.

Pencils and drawings fell to the floor as he swept everything off the table and spread the documents out like a campaign map. He searched for something, anything to connect the documents to the minstrel's poem. After what seemed to be hours, he stared at his results and drummed his fingers on the desk.

What did he have? Receipts. An invitation to a soiree at Kinsleye House. Personal cards from several business associates. Notes from Lord Hughes regarding the contract. Receipts from the modiste for Lady Katherine's gowns. A personal note about rescheduling a cancelled meeting.

"Nothing!" He threw the pencil onto the desk.

Wallace didn't like Whitaker in London or Royston Mills and liked him even less in Sommer-by-the-Sea. He slammed his hand on the desk and looked at the door. He could demand an answer from Lady Katherine. He rubbed the back of his neck. He knew her answer before he asked the question.

Wallace gathered the documents and put them in a folio.

Roddy had everything in hand at the factory. Barrington and his men could keep a watchful eye over Lady Katherine. A trip to London and a meeting with Lord Hughes was in order. He left the office, closed the door behind him, and started out for the abbey.

WALLACE ENTERED THE drawing room. "Mr. Russell told me I'd find you here."

Lady Katherine glanced up from the table strewn with tools and the solidly closed lock.

"I didn't realize it was late. I do get lost in the challenge."

The last week had been draining for him, each day watching her withdraw more and more. Conversations were punctuated with long pauses and blank stares. The usually busy woman read and answered the posts but nothing else. Roddy brought her reports, but they went unread. Seeing her now working with the lock and with her cheeks flushed with color was encouraging.

Several times he thought to tell her about the deed and his oath to Bennett, but he wouldn't add to her distress.

Staring at the tools on the table, he gave her a questioning glance. Katherine nodded her permission and he picked one of them up.

"That is a triangle pick. It's the most versatile. The next is a rake pick. This tool rakes all the pins in the lock at once to push them into place allowing you to turn the rod. The last is the hook pick. That one lifts each pin individually into the correct position one at a time. Are you interested in locks?"

He returned the tool to the table.

"You never did tell me how you got involved in picking locks."

"When I was young, Bennett kept his secret things in a locked box which I couldn't open. However, he kept getting into mine.

No matter what I did, he'd find my case, open it, and leave me a note claiming victory. He didn't bother to hide his precious box. He taunted me, leaving it in full view for everyone to see.

"I decided to give him a taste of his own medicine. I learned to pick the lock. It took me a while, but when I did, I left him a short, succinct note. *Victory is mine.*" She laughed at the memory. "Bennett wasn't angry. On the contrary, he was quite proud of me. I enjoyed the challenge, but it was the workings of the lock that fascinated me. That's when I started drawing them.

"At the seminary Mrs. Bainbridge encouraged a diversity of instructive methods including guest lecturers.

"Mr. Bramah, the famous inventor's son, visited us and spoke about mechanicals. I asked about their insides, how they worked. As he spoke, I drew them. He was surprised and excited when I showed him my work. So much so that a few days later this arrived." Katherine gestured to the lock. "One of his father's challenge locks."

"I wondered why a wealthy heiress knew how to pick locks. You always surprise me."

Lady Katherine was a surprise in many ways. He should have known the lock wasn't Sutton's. The man had no patience for that type of work.

"Everyone has a secret or two. I am sure you have yours. Do you have anything you would like to share with me?"

Wallace glanced at the papers on her desk. *Tell her. Your biggest secret. What better time than now?*

He picked up a pair of drawings from the pile and handed one to her. "This one is mine."

Coward. He was only making this worse by avoiding the discussion.

Katherine stared at his drawing.

Honorable and trustworthy. Not after he told her his secret. She'd never speak to him again. No. He couldn't bear the thought.

She let out a sigh. "I thought Bennett's abilities had improved much too quickly. I wasn't sure who created them." She put the drawings down and glanced up at him. "Where did a lord learn to make such detailed drawings? I thought all lords learned was how to be a lord."

He gave an embarrassed laugh. "I am the second son in my family. From as early as I can remember my father told me I would be a military man.

"While Geoffrey learned how to be a duke, I sketched. It became my hobby. When I was in Wellington's command and he remained in London, I sketched the battlefield and enemy encampments for him. From there I went to drawing their weapons. It was only a small leap to mechanicals."

"Your brother?"

He watched as her mind worked, putting the pieces together.

"I'm sorry. How rude of me. Please forgive me."

Something in her tone overwhelmed him. He saw the shared pain in her face as well.

"My father and brother were among those lost when one of my father's ships went down in a gale off the coast of Kent five years ago." His voice was matter of fact, but his stomach still swirled at the thought.

He gazed into her violet eyes. "We've both lost people close to us. We are a pair."

He tried to laugh but it came out as a hoarse, strained sound. If they continued along the path of this conversation, it would only lead them to a dark place. He took a cleansing breath.

"I'm sure Mr. Russell will be here any time to call us to dinner."

She didn't say anything. Instead, she put her tools away, covered the lock with the cloth, and rose. "Shall we?"

She came around the desk and stood in front of him. He turned to move on, but she stopped him with a light touch.

Startled, he gazed at her.

Tell her. Now. If she gets upset, you can go back to the factory. Tell her.

"I'm leaving for London in the morning."

Coward.

"Oh." She stared, unblinking, her eyes wide open, as if frozen in place.

"You'll be safe. Barrington will have someone close by." What else could he say when he hoped it wasn't her safety she was thinking about.

"Will you be gone long?" Her tone was even, her glance secretive.

"A week, perhaps a few days more at most."

Her eyes brightened. "I may have solved the challenge by then."

She looped her arm in his. "I wonder what Mrs. Russell has made for dinner. I don't know the last time I was this hungry."

Chapter Sixteen

Lord Wallace climbed the stairs to Lord Hughes' office in The Temple, not far from the Embankment. He hadn't seen George Hughes since his father's and brother's funeral.

He gave his name to the clerk who slipped quietly into the adjoining room. The next moment, the door flew open, and Lord Hughes hurried out.

"Wallace, it is good to see you." Hughes' thick, white, wavy hair hadn't changed. He was clean-shaven, although he preferred the well-trimmed beard he'd had the last time they met. His Lordship's steel gray eyes twinkled. Hughes put his arm around him and squeezed. "Please, come in. Did I tell you it is good to see you?"

The clerk, as well as the four other people in the office looked dumbfounded at His Lordship's display.

"Milord, it has been too long since we last spoke."

Hughes paused at his clerk's desk. "I'm not available unless Parliament is under attack."

The boy nodded, his face still blank. Hughes went inside.

"You appear well. You must be a head taller since we last met. Or am I now a head shorter?" They both laughed as the solicitor closed the door and gestured for him to take a seat. "How is your business venture? I follow the happenings of some of the factories in Northumberland."

"We've been fortunate. We take care of our workers. Pay them a decent wage. At the moment, our people are still dealing with Sutton's sudden death, but we are all getting through it."

"I offer you my sincere condolences. Is that why you've sought me out? Judge Scofield handles Sutton and his business."

"Yes, I am aware. You represented Lord Kinsleye when Sutton considered him for a partnership." He took out the unsigned contract. "I found this in Sutton's papers."

"Lord Kinsleye stopped the negotiation and stepped away. Why are you interested in an incomplete negotiation now with both men gone?"

"Ryder Whitaker is making a nuisance of himself and threatening Lady Katherine Thornton."

Hughes' jovial manner faltered for a heartbeat, enough for Wallace to realize something was not right. He moved to the edge of the chair and leaned toward his father's friend.

"I am doing my due diligence. Lady Katherine, Sutton's niece, is now my responsibility."

"I understand congratulations are in order."

Wallace smiled. He never thought that gossip tidbit would benefit him. "Then you understand why I need to identify where there is an exposure so I can take the appropriate precautions."

Hughes chewed on that information for a moment, his elbows on the arms of his chair, his hands tented in front of him. After several moment he lowered his hands. "Lord Kinsleye is gone and thankfully I do not represent his nephew. The records will show that Whitaker found his uncle dead of a heart attack during a house party at the Kinsleye House in London. I wish there were more facts to tell you.

"People developed their own assumptions. I will speak for myself. You know who and what Whitaker is. He makes no effort to hide his obsessive overindulgent behavior. Lord Kinsleye reduced his inheritance to a modest allowance and a title without any land. He also cut Whitaker and any wife or subsequent children, legitimate or otherwise, out of claiming any inheritance.

"Whitaker came to me to contest the will. As the only living relative, he claimed the money belonged to him. He did not win. Lord Kinsleye did the right thing. I'm also of the opinion there is more to his uncle's death than meets the eye, but I cannot prove it."

"I can't say I'm surprised that you have questions. In many ways, Whitaker has a captivating charm to some, but to others he is vile." Wallace sat back, vindicated that his intuition had led down the right path.

"I cannot tell you anything about Lady Katherine. Other than I had one dance with her at Lord Kinsleye's soiree. Her authentic charm and grace captured the *ton*. I had hoped for a dance at Almack's, but sadly she and Sutton left London after the soiree, cutting her season short. I hope I have given you some insight."

"Yes." Wallace rose and extended his hand. "Thank you for your time."

Wallace left Lord Hughes on his way to Blackhall House. It was late morning. He planned to leave for Sommer-by-the-Sea on the packet that left on the afternoon tide.

He still didn't know what Whitaker held over Lady Katherine. He hurried along as a sense of urgency pulled at him.

After a quick change into travel clothes, he and Lenard departed for the trip north.

"I picked up the package you wanted. It's in your luggage."

Wallace nodded. "Did you have any difficulty?"

"Not at all. Your design surprised the jeweler. He had never seen anything like it."

"I should hope not." Wallace could not hide the smile at the private picture in his mind.

"I asked the staff here if they knew anything about the incident at Kinsleye's soiree. Some remembered the events clearly. Edwin Key, the footman, knows Lord Kinsleye's cook. I arranged for you to speak with her. She was at Kinsleye House the night of the party."

"An eyewitness of sorts. Let's hope she can help us."

"Edwin said she retired and lives near the Fox and Bowl Inn. We're almost there."

Several minutes later, they pulled up at the tavern. From the outside it appeared well kept, from the dark wood exterior to the painted window box with bright yellow flowers. The only woman inside sat at a table in the back.

They walked up to her. "Mrs. Fitzgerald, this is Lord Wallace."

She stood and made a small curtsey. One look at her and Wallace's heart went out to her. She sat with them wetting her lips and smoothing her skirt.

"Lenard, please bring us some tea and biscuits." He glanced at Mrs. Fitzgerald. "I'm happy to have the tavern keeper put something into the tea if you'd rather."

Mrs. Fitzgerald stared at him for a heartbeat or two before a wide smile spread across her face.

"No, thank you, Your Grace. But I do appreciate the offer."

Wallace stared at her for a moment.

"Mrs. Fitzgerald, have we met?"

"I worked in your mother's kitchen in York. You used to steal—"

"Tarts." He blurted out. "Sweet apple and cinnamon tarts. You used to chase me out the door with your wooden spoon."

The woman laughed. "I learned very quickly to make four extra ones. And here I thought you wouldn't remember me."

"It's the Mrs. Fitzgerald that confused me. You were Miss Nettie Carter."

"I'm married now."

Lenard brought the tea and biscuits.

"This is Nettie Carter-Fitzgerald. She served as the pastry chef at my mother's country home in York."

"Pleased to meet you, Mrs. Fitzgerald."

"You sit right down, Mr. Lenard. I'll gladly serve you both tea."

"Lenard mentioned that you are retired." He put his hand

over the cup when she offered sugar.

"It wasn't long after Lord Kinsleye passed. The family decided to close the house and I had met Mr. Fitzgerald." She poured Lenard his tea.

"What can you tell me about Lord Kinsleye and his nephew?"

"The staff knew what went on in that house. His lordship's nephew was a horror. We all stayed as far away from him as possible. The two would argue whenever they were together. His lordship spoke to his solicitor and had the boy taken out of his will."

"Mrs. Fitzgerald." She turned to Lenard.

"Do you know anything about Lady Katherine and His Lordship's nephew?"

"Lord Whitaker was taken by Lady Katherine. He pursued her from the start of the season. Always back to his uncle for more money. 'Something for Lady Katherine' he'd say.

"The staff hoped she would change him. I myself had little hope of that ever happening. People don't change that drastically and that's what it would take.

"No one understood why she was so taken by him. Lady Katherine had the pick of them all. The talk of the *ton,* she was. Everyone envied Lord Whitaker with her on his arm.

"Lord Kinsleye's butler, my husband Shamus, told me the night of the soiree, Lord Whitaker and his friends played pool in the billiard room. He bragged how he planned to spend her money. He didn't stop there.

"When Mr. Sutton and Lady Katherine arrived, they overheard Lord Whitaker talking to his friends about Lady Katherine as if..." She looked down at the table. "Not like a young man would speak about a woman he wanted to marry."

"If this is difficult, you needn't go on." Wallace kept his voice gentle, but inwardly he seethed with cold contempt.

"No." She picked up her head. "I've had this bottled up in me for a very long time. Mr. Fitzgerald told me to forget about all this, but I cannot." She took a breath.

"Mr. Sutton and Lord Whitaker argued. Lady Katherine, the poor dear, scurried off to the lady's salon to calm down. Mr. Fitzgerald had one of the downstairs girls go into the salon to make sure she was all right. The girl helped her with her hair and to dry her eyes. The poor thing was so upset she must have made a wrong turn when she left the salon. She wound up in the wrong hallway.

"Mr. Fitzgerald heard Lady Katherine call for help. Lord Kinsleye was in distress and thirsty. She gave him tea while Mr. Fitzgerald summoned the doctor. Lord Whitaker arrived and immediately accused her of poisoning his uncle."

"Mr. Sutton was at Lord Whitaker's heels. He hurried Lady Katherine away. Everyone focused on Lord Kinsleye. The doctor said Lord Kinsleye's heart was failing and to make him comfortable. He passed away before morning.

"I'll never forget the look on Lord Whitaker. He had a coldness about him. Right after Lady Katherine and Mr. Sutton left, he told who ever would listen Lady Katherine gave his uncle poisoned tea."

Mrs. Fitzgerald finished the last of her tea. "That's all the story that I know. That man has no interest in working for his money. Lord Kinsleye worked hard to make his business a success. His nephew thought he would marry an heiress and do nothing."

"Thank you for your help and for telling me the truth of the matter."

"Your Grace, there is no thank you needed. It's me who should be thanking you. I kept this bottled up so long. I needed to get it out and to someone I trust."

"Can we see you home?"

"I am home. This is my tavern. The tavern keeper is my Mr. Fitzgerald." She nodded to the side of the room.

Wallace got up and walked Mrs. Fitzgerald to her husband.

"Mr. Fitzgerald. Miss Nettie Carter is very special to me. She used to make me apple cinnamon tarts."

"Aye, Your Grace. She does the same for me and our four little ones. My Nettie is very special indeed. I'm glad she's gotten rid of that shadow. You should know that Lord Whitaker proudly announced to his uncle the day before the soiree that he never had any intentions of marrying Lady Katherine. She was 'simply a diversion.'

"After his nephew left, he had me get Mr. Hughes. His Lordship arranged for Lord Whitaker to get an annual stipend and nothing more. He signed the papers that very afternoon. Before the first guest arrived for the soiree, he told the boy to enjoy the party and order him to be gone before first light. Now isn't it strange that Lord Kinsleye would be dead by then?"

"Very strange, indeed. Thank you, Mr. Fitzgerald." He turned to his wife. "You both have been very helpful."

Wallace and Lenard said their good-byes and took their leave.

"Whitaker isn't after Sutton Textiles. The man never has two shillings to rub together. I think he's after Lady Katherine's money. I agree with Mr. Fitzgerald. I find it highly suspicious that Lord Kinsleye tossed out and disinherited his nephew hours before he died. Lady Katherine is guilty of being in the wrong place at the wrong time.

"We almost have all the pieces. I understand the connection between Lady Katherine and Whitaker, but what proof does he have that she is responsible for Kinsleye's death?" Lady Katherine had the answer. All he had to do was convince her to share it with him, then he'd be able to put this to rest.

CHAPTER SEVENTEEN

"**Y**ES, MR. RUSSELL?" Katherine sat in the drawing room examining the lock. She found ten pins but still had no idea how many more remained.

"Lady Euphemia, Lady Marianna, and Lady Harriet are here to see you. They're waiting for you in the parlor."

"Please tell them I'll be right with them. Ask Mrs. Russell to bring in tea and a plate of biscuits."

The week went by quickly. Mr. and Mrs. Russell kept the house running smoothly. Mrs. Bainbridge kept her in order, eating meals, walking daily, and receiving visitors. Each day, the headmistress conveniently went to the seminary for a few hours, giving her time to work on the challenge lock.

Then again, if the days were so full, why were they so empty?

A week, he said he'd return in a week. Since yesterday morning every odd sound outside had her at the window. Surely, Wallace would return today.

Katherine went to the window and closed the curtains. This urgency to be with Wallace was nothing more than a substitute for Bennett. Nothing else.

Several times she tried to banish him from her thoughts. But it wasn't Bennett's empty chair at the dining table she stared at. It wasn't Bennett's presence she anticipated walking into a room. In her heart of hearts, it wasn't Bennett at all.

Katherine straightened out the tools on the table, covered the lock, and joined her friends.

"Good afternoon." Katherine searched the room. "Mrs. Bainbridge isn't here?" Glancing at each friend, her smile faded.

No one touched any of the biscuits. She expected the plate to be half-empty with Effie here.

"What's wrong? Mrs. Bainbridge?" Her heart thumped as she waited for an answer.

"No, she is fine. We didn't come here to see her. We wanted to speak to you, alone. How could you?" Effie huffed with her arms crossed in front of her.

Katherine studied each of her friends. Confused, she approached the less emotional Anna.

"What is this about?"

Anna looked at her clasped hands in her lap then up at Katherine.

"We thought we were close, no secrets between us. We understand you're under a great deal of strain with your uncle's death. But this?"

Katherine took a breath, then began to get angry. "I clearly have no idea what the three of you are talking about. I do not keep secrets from you, just as you do not keep them from me."

Effie got to her feet so quickly Katherine stepped back. Her friend handed her the *London Gazette*, a circle drawn around an article.

She took the newspaper and read the noted item.

"The very eligible and handsome Lord Wallace, 4th Duke of Blackhall, is finally off the market. He's made his vow. Does Lady Ivy-Rose T. even know she snagged the wealthiest and handsomest man in London? And does Lady RH realize she's missed her opportunity? This should be something to watch unfold. All the best to the happy (?) couple. No matter who becomes the next Duchess of Blackhall."

Katherine slowly sank down into the chair. Her friends looked at each other than at her.

"You're the only Lady Ivy-Rose T. we know. And Lord Wallace is mentioned."

"Hush," Hattie snapped and elbowed Effie. "Eat a biscuit."

Katherine re-read the article a second, then a third time. *Who is Lady RH?* Did someone else have his heart? Her breath came in spurts.

"Are you all right? You haven't said a word." Anna knelt next to her.

Katherine clenched her hands, her fingernails digging into her palms. She turned and stared at her close friend.

Anna studied Katherine's face.

"You had no idea, did you?" Anna's voice faded to a hushed silence. Her expression changed from hurt to horror.

Numb, Katherine swallowed around the hot knot building in her throat and shook her head.

"The rake," Anna muttered.

"I can think of more descriptive things to call him." Katherine put the *Gazette* on the table next to her and stood. Is Wallace no better than Whitaker, dallying with her?

"Who is Lady RH?" Effie asked finishing one of the sweetmeat biscuits. "Anna, pass the tea, please."

"We thought you were cutting us and didn't know why. I should have known something was wrong." Hattie's tone was odd, yet gentle.

"I would never cut any of you." Breathing hard, Katherine glanced from one friend to the next. How could they think she would treat them so badly? "Each of you is important to me. I can't explain that article."

With every breath she gathered her wits and her anger built. "But I have an idea who can. He's just not here at the moment. I assure you as soon as he arrives, I plan to find out."

"There is more to this article than we're reading." Hattie picked up the newspaper and read the piece again. "This isn't a recent article. Look at the date."

Anna glanced at Hattie. "You're right." She turned her attention to Katherine. "When did you meet Lord Wallace?"

"A fortnight ago when he brought Bennett home. Why is that

important?"

"Because this newspaper is dated seventeen days ago." Hattie showed her the paper.

"How is that possible?" Katherine grabbed it from her and examined the date.

"He wouldn't know your middle name."

She tossed the paper onto the table.

"Bennett." Katherine stood with her fists at her side. He was the only one who would dare. "If he wasn't dead, I'd kill him."

"This sounds like…" Hattie's voice trailed off. All eyes were on her.

"Like what?" Effie asked.

"An arrangement."

Katherine was too startled by Hattie's suggestion to make a comment. Did Bennett offer her to encourage Lord Wallace into the partnership? Her heart hammered, her breathing ragged at the thought Bennett would consider making such a vile arrangement. He went too far this time.

"This does sound like one of Bennett's pranks." Anna wrapped her arm around Katherine's shoulder. "Will you be all right?"

"I will. You are truly good friends." She gathered each in her arms. "I would never—"

Anna squeezed her tight and spoke softly. "Hush. Not another word."

"You all will be the first to know if I am to be a duchess. I'm sure when Lord Wallace reads this, he too will be upset."

"That is a relief." Anna stepped back. "We should go. I'm glad we got to the bottom of this. I'm sure Lord Wallace has an explanation. Don't be harsh on him. Your Uncle Bennett is to blame."

Katherine listened as the ladies chatted on their way out of the house.

Bennett may have put the article into the paper, but Lord Wallace knew about the article if not when Bennett posted it, certainly before today. More than Bennett's prank bothered her.

How could his kiss be so passionate if his heart belonged to someone else? She stiffened, momentarily mortified. *Is Lady RH the reason he went to London?*

Her head hurt trying to put the pieces together. If their intimacy was simply the heat of the moment… She spun around physically seeking a different direction. No, his attention was sincere. *You thought Whitaker was sincere.* How did she let this happen, again?

Katherine took a steadying breath and left the parlor. She stopped in the dining room, then went to work on the challenge lock. Anything to keep her mind off the article.

She stared at the lock, but it was Wallace's face staring back at her. *How could you? Keep focused.* She took up her pick, stared at the blurry lock, and struggled to keep tears from falling.

Steady. You've done this a hundred times.

With a trembling hand, she aimed the pick at the lock. The more she tried to control the tremors, the more violently her hand shook. Disgusted, she tossed the instrument onto the table.

Her usual orderly mind ran rampant, flittering like a butterfly from one thought to the next. One minute she wanted to scratch out his eyes, the next she wanted to be in his arms.

Images of him in the bailey, the epitome of the valiant knight, dancing with him, their playful banter, and his kiss. She closed her eyes. *His kiss.* It all ran through her head.

Confused, angry, but mostly hurt, Katherine tried to regain some control. How foolish she'd been. She knew better but didn't want to listen to her head.

She let out a deep breath. No more dreams. Only reality. Lord Wallace was not perfect. He was a man with flaws.

She rushed out of the room and down the hall. Finally, inside her room, she stood with her back against the door. *A man with flaws.* One who didn't love her. But God help her, she loved him.

Katherine sank to the floor in tears.

IN THE DARKENING early evening, Wallace and Lenard made their way from the dock, across the village, and to the abbey. No one greeted them when they arrived.

Lenard took their things upstairs. Wallace went to the parlor and library but found both rooms empty. It was nearly time for dinner. He'd best wash off the ocean voyage before he saw Lady Katherine.

Wallace stood at the washstand and cleaned up.

"Dinner will be served shortly. A message from Judge Scofield arrived for you."

Wallace had his shirt off and soap up to his elbows. "Read it to me."

"As a beneficiary of Mr. Bennett Sutton's estate, you are required to be present at the reading of Mr. Bennett Sutton's will." Lenard looked up. "The judge scheduled the reading for late tomorrow morning here, at Thornton Abbey." Lenard refolded the message and put it on the dresser.

"The house is unusually quiet. It wasn't this still before the funeral. Mrs. Russell hardly said a word to me." Lenard laid out a clean shirt and Wallace's coat on the bed.

"It's your imagination. After all the tumult in London, Sommer-by-the-Sea seems quiet." Wallace took the towel from Lenard. "I'll finish cleaning up. You go ahead and eat dinner."

"I'll find out what news there is about the factory." The valet left for the kitchen.

Gone a week. He missed being with Katherine and even Mrs. Bainbridge. A sense of calm came over him. He didn't realize how anxious he was to get back to the abbey. He enjoyed Blackhall House, but he much preferred to be here. Perhaps it was the quiet open air that he preferred. He smiled to himself. That wasn't the truth. He wanted to be with Katherine.

Armed with his new information about Kinsleye's death and Whitaker's behavior, he felt better prepared to discuss the situation with her, when the time arrived.

He put on the fresh shirt, slipped into his coat, making sure the packet from the jeweler was in his pocket, and hurried to dinner.

With long strides he entered the room and came to an abrupt halt. It was empty. The table set for one.

"Lady Katherine will not be down for dinner this evening," Mr. Russell said when he entered the room.

He stepped toward his place and saw the London Gazette. Without looking at the newspaper he knew what had happened.

Wallace turned, hurried to the staircase. He took the steps two and three at a time. He should have told her. Why hadn't he? He hurried down the hall and stood at her door.

He closed his eyes. No matter what he said, she would not forgive him. Hoping he was wrong, he knocked on her door.

"Lady Katherine. Let me explain."

She didn't answer.

"Katherine, you don't understand. I thought you were a child, not a grown woman."

Silence.

"I tried so many times to tell you, but it seemed cruel with you in mourning." The excuse sounded weak even to him. "Kate, you're killing me. Please, we must talk."

He heard the click of the lock. His heart jumped when the latch moved and the door opened.

"Not half as much as you killed me." The pain on her face shot through him. Her voice was dead, her eyes swollen with no feeling, no anything.

"I never imagined you would toy with me." She started to close the door and hesitated. "I thought you were an honorable man. Obviously, I put my trust in the wrong person."

He had no reply. He stood in front of her wishing she would yell and scream, show some emotion.

"Please remove yourself from Thornton Abbey as soon as possible. I want to be free of you." She closed the door softly.

SHE STOOD WITH her forehead against the door. With all her heart she wanted to be in his arms. Dismissing him was the hardest thing she had ever done.

"Kate, I had no intention of hurting you. I can't blame Sutton. You should have heard this from me and no one else."

Tears ran down her cheeks. She didn't move. There had to be more to this notice than it appeared. But why didn't he tell her? The struggle went on until her hand went to the latch. She pulled the door open.

He was gone. Her heart jumped from her throat to her feet and back up again. *Go to his room.* But her feet wouldn't work. She closed her door.

Her food went untouched. She took to her bed, but hours later she still tossed and turned.

Ivy-Rose, you are being foolish. Wallace isn't what you think. Trust me, Ivy-Rose. Trust Wallace.

Should she? Trust him?

For hours, she fought for some sleep. But her eyes wouldn't close. Her mind wouldn't stop. Staying in bed was useless. Katherine went to the window and stared at the brightening sky. Soon it would be a vivid red and orange.

The hour was early, but she had to put an end to this. Let him have his say and she hers. A war of silence would get neither of them anywhere.

Katherine grabbed her shawl and hurried to his room. Gathering all her strength, she knocked on his door.

"Lord Wallace."

He didn't answer.

"Lord Wallace." Her voice was a bit frantic. She knocked again. The door moved. She pushed it open and stepped inside. The room was empty. She glanced at the closet.

Empty.

He was gone.

CHAPTER EIGHTEEN

"Yes, Mr. Russell?" Her butler stood at the door to the drawing room.

"Judge Schofield and Lord Barrington are in the parlor along with Lord Wallace."

"Tell them I'll be right with them." She worked on the challenge most of the morning but didn't make any progress. Her failure added to her mood. Katherine was past being upset and all the way to angry. Angry at herself for being emotional and foolish yesterday, the day before that, and the day before that.

Eager for the formality of reading Bennett's will to be over she covered the lock and left the room. With any luck everything would go back to normal, and Lord Wallace would be gone.

Katherine walked into the parlor and froze more confused than ever. Every thought this morning was directed at hating him, yet here he stood. One glance at him and her resolve faltered. God help her, she was glad he was here.

Whatever glimmer of hope she had was quickly extinguished. He barely acknowledged her arrival. As a gentleman, he stood with the others when she entered but kept talking to the judge.

Katherine took a seat. Everyone followed.

"If you're ready, I'll begin." Judge Scofield didn't wait for a response.

"We're here to read the last will and testament of Bennett

Franklin Sutton. As the executor, Lord Reese Barrington is here. The beneficiaries are Lord Ian Geoffrey Wallace, 4th Duke of Blackhall, and Lady Katherine Ivy-Rose Thornton.

"For her patience and ability to laugh with me, and never at me, I give and bequeath to my niece, Lady Katherine Ivy-Rose Thornton, who has been my companion and north star, the entirety of my personal finances accumulated at the time of my demise. These funds are to be added to her already extensive trust.

"My sweet girl, the Thornton line is now in your keeping. I'm sure your offspring will be fine, clever, and will carry on the proud name of Thornton. In everything I've done, I have kept your wellbeing in mind. At times, it may be a mystery to you, but have faith. Know that you are loved. And please, when you lay me to rest, put me beside your father so I can bother him for all eternity, as he deserves."

The judge paused, allowing her to take in the personal message.

Angry as she was at Bennett, his words made her laugh as much as they brought her to tears.

"In addition, I bequeath all my shares of Sutton Textiles, a total of forty-nine percent, to my niece, Lady Katherine Ivy-Rose Thornton."

"Lord Wallace holds the remaining fifty-one percent of the business." The judge waited for her question.

"Why isn't this an equal partnership? Bennett was the founder of the business." She directed the question at Wallace.

Lord Wallace gave her a disinterested glance then turned to the judge and nodded.

"The partnership shares are split according to your uncle's demand. He felt since Lord Wallace took the risk and backed the enterprise with his money and provided the land next to the factory and along the river, it entitled him to a larger share. Lord Wallace accepted a one-percent advantage."

Katherine glanced at Wallace. "I didn't realize the purchase of the land had been completed. I didn't find anything in the ledger."

"You won't find a purchase." He didn't look at her, but kept his nose buried in the papers.

Look at me, she silently demanded. He didn't budge. *Look at me,* she screamed in her head.

He glanced at her and quickly returned to his papers. "The land was my personal property. I signed the deed over to the company. You'll find the land listed under assets."

Katherine thumbed through the pages and found the list of assets with the additional land.

"As a longtime friend of your family," the judge held Katherine's full attention, "I must tell you that you have a solid partner in Lord Wallace."

She glanced at the financial documents again.

"Is there any restriction on selling the company shares?"

Wallace and the judge gave her their attention. "You want to sell your shares?" Wallace asked.

"No, buy yours. Between the funds Bennett left me and my trust there should be more than enough to complete the transaction." She put the papers on the table next to her. "If we are done here, I'll ask Mr. Russell bring in some refreshments." She sat at the edge of her seat about to get up.

"No. We are not done. About Thornton Abbey." The judge studied the papers in his hand.

"What about Thornton Abbey?" Hesitating and blinking in bafflement, her glance slid to Lord Wallace. He busied himself with the documents.

"Before your uncle's death he signed his portion of the house to Lord Wallace. He now owns forty-nine percent of Thornton Abbey."

"Forty-nine percent?" Wallace glanced at Lady Katherine, who sported a satisfied smirk. Wallace shook his head. "I thought Sutton's wording was strange. I didn't realize the abbey was a partnership. I assume Lady Katherine owns the remaining fifty-one percent."

"Yes. You appear to own the part of the abbey that my uncle refused to maintain and is in dire need of repair. But let me understand this." Lady Katherine spat out the words contemptuously. "You thought you owned all of Thornton Abbey and said nothing to me. Were you waiting, planning when to turn me out?"

Wallace shot to his feet. "You go too far. Sutton gave me a document deeding me the abbey. I gave the paper to the judge and asked him to find a way to discredit it. I did not want, nor do I need, your home."

"We're done here." Katherine got to her feet, then.

"No, we are not." Wallace handed her a document. "This is for you to review."

Katherine inspected the paper quickly, then looked up outraged.

"You are crying off. Stating the notice in the *Gazette* was a complete sham, a bad joke on you. You make me a laughingstock of the *ton*." She lowered the document, appalled at his nerve.

"My reputation is impacted more than yours." Wallace took the document from her. "And people will take sides as they are wont to do. You may be the victim, but you will have the advantage. More importantly, you will be free of me as you requested."

Yes, that was her request, but she never thought… she didn't want… She didn't know what she wanted.

"I'm showing this to you as a curtesy. I really don't need your approval. I can simply ask your friend Hawkins to publish it and this part of Sutton's fiasco is over. I should have realized your uncle was up to something when he made his demand."

"Lord Wallace." Judge Scofield didn't hide the irritation in his tone. "Lady Katherine deserves to hear the truth, all of it."

Wallace sat down and gave the judge's directive some thought.

"Sutton was in a state when he demanded I vow to marry you. He thought he was dying. I and the others with me thought he was being overly dramatic. I made the oath to placate him, put him at ease. I've known Sutton since Cambridge. We never spoke of family. When he told me he had a niece in a seminary, I thought you were a student, not one of the teachers who was nearly as old as him.

"When we met, I thought it was impossible that you were not spoken for. I couldn't understand why Sutton would demand me to make such an oath. Was he trying to protect you? Possibly from the person behind the poem Mr. Green recited?"

He didn't miss her eyes widen and her quick intake of breath.

"I am not a piece of property to be traded as you would your favorite mare. How dare you and Bennett enter such a transaction? And now this? My body and my house. What else do you want? What else is left?"

Her anger became a scalding fury and didn't diminish. Lifting her eyes, Wallace's seductive gaze unnerved her. *How does he do it?* Heat her body with a glance. To cool him down, she returned his leer with a hostile stare.

"There is no need for you to cry off, Your Grace. I'll toss you out. Leave you to Lady RH. I give you to her, with my blessings."

Katherine thought that a nice touch. "How does it feel to be treated without a care, like unwanted property?"

"That is enough, Lady Katherine." Judge Scofield's tone went straight through her. "Your parents would never forgive me. You may be independent and capable, but you live in a society where that would ruin you."

"But not Lord Wallace."

"You're quite correct." Wallace got up and stood in front of her, glaring down. "My reputation would not be harmed. But let me make this very clear: I have never demeaned or caused anyone, man, woman, or child, harm. And I'm not about to start now. As for Lady Rosamond Henley, we had one dance at a house party years ago. As a matter of fact, she saw the recent notice in the newspaper and left a lovely note for me at my London address. The woman thought it was quite funny to see her name associated with mine." Wallace went back to his seat.

"I'm sure she did." Katherine got up, opened a desk drawer, and tossed him the key. He caught it without any difficulty.

"Your key. You can maintain your own side of the house with your own staff." She sat down.

"Enough," Barrington bellowed. The command in his voice froze them both. "I'm through listening to you scratch at each other. I understand you both are angry." Barrington got to his feet. "There is more at stake here than a prank and Wallace's placating Sutton, who knew he was dying.

"Lady Katherine has received threats and so has the factory. Whoever is behind them may also be responsible for Sutton's murder. Under the circumstances, the best way for you both to save face is to announce your engagement. You can say you didn't make your betrothal public because of the recent death in the family. That will quiet the *ton*. Wallace staying at the abbey gives Lady Katherine protection and helps avert any attack."

Lord Wallace and Katherine glared at each other, stunned.

"Lord Barrington, it's one thing for a short-term guest, but it would be indecent for Lord Wallace to stay here."

"Would you rather get an emergency license or make a quick trip to Gretna Green?" Barrington didn't hide the irritation in his tone.

"No. No. That won't be necessary." Katherine's voice dropped to a whisper. She glanced at Lord Wallace but couldn't tell what he was thinking other than he didn't like being reprimanded.

Barrington called for the butler. Mr. Russell arrived before Barrington let go of the bell pull.

"Please ask Mrs. Bainbridge to join us."

Barrington faced Katherine. "I will ask Mrs. Bainbridge to remain with you."

"What happens when this is all made to right? The scandal would ruin her." Barrington stared at Lord Wallace.

"Don't worry Wallace. When you and Lady Katherine expose

the murderer, everyone will hail you both as heroes."

There was a soft knock and Mrs. Bainbridge entered.

"You are the first to hear the good news, my dear. Lord Wallace and Lady Katherine are engaged."

She looked at the intended bride and groom.

"Oh dear. They don't appear to be happy."

"Give them time. I'd like them to go about as newly betrothed."

"That's enough Barrington. You go too far." Lord Wallace was adamant.

Katherine was about to agree when her mouth dropped open. She swung around and faced him.

"Why? What's wrong with me?"

"I wouldn't want a woman like you." He struggled to keep his tone even and controlled. His steady gaze traveled over her face, then moved over her body slowly. "Now I understand why Sutton had to trick me into marrying you."

Wallace stormed out of the room.

"Honoria, would you mind?"

"Say no more, Reese. I will enjoy continuing as a referee between the two." She looked at Katherine.

"It would be lovely having you remain as my guest," Katherine said still looking after Wallace's retreating back.

CHAPTER NINETEEN

LORD WALLACE STARED out the parlor window and stroked the velvet case in his pocket. Over the last two weeks their tempers had cooled, and they had settled into a congenial yet tenuous working arrangement. At the moment, he didn't want to address the deeper issues for fear of jeopardizing the fragile arrangement. Lady Katherine appeared to be of the same mind.

As partners, they decided to go over the factory documents together. Wallace learned a great deal about the factory, their staff, and the advancements Sutton and Lady Katherine set in motion. Lady Katherine came away with a better understanding of the company's finances and trade contracts.

Their social life changed as well. Ever since she gave Hawkins an exclusive interview announcing their engagement, congratulatory messages and invitations filled the morning post. Each afternoon the two went through the correspondence and decided which invitations to accept and which to decline.

The clock on the mantel struck half past four. He glanced at the door as she glided into the room.

"Waiting long?" Lady Katherine glanced in the mirror above the sideboard and adjusted an errant curl. A hairpin, with a mind of its own, fell to the carpet.

"Not at all." He bent and retrieved the pin and gave it to her. He gazed at her reflection in the mirror. Lady Katherine was a beautiful woman, but when dressed for an evening, she was magnificent.

"I hope this gown is to your liking. You requested the color not the style." She turned to face him.

Her teal silk and lace gown was of the latest fashion. The skirt with a modest train fell softly around her curves, and was enough to be striking yet still leave much to the imagination. The lace bodice with its square neckline was the perfect frame for her silver locket.

"I will be the envy of every man."

"Your Grace." Katherine dipped a deep curtsey.

He took her hand, helped her up, and handed her the velvet case.

"What is this?" She took the velvet box and stood looking at him with a blank expression.

"I bought this for you when I was in London." He gave the design to the jeweler with precise instructions. Her surprised expression excited him.

She opened the box, looked at the contents, then stared at him in astonishment.

"Do you like them?"

A pair of ebony hair sticks. The light caught the swirls of small aquamarine gems winding around the wooden shafts.

"They are beautiful." She didn't take her eyes off them.

"And very practical. Let me show you." He took one hair stick from her, unscrewed the rod, and pulled out a long thin piece of metal.

"Lockpicks?" Her laugh was infectious. "A small rake. How clever."

She put the hair stick back together and moved to the mirror. With care, she put both in her hair.

"They look beautiful on you. My design startled the jeweler." He stood behind her enjoying her excitement.

"I'm sure he was." A laugh bubbled up. She swung around and kissed him.

"I'm pleased you like them." He wanted to reciprocate. It was difficult being with her and not holding her. But their truce was hard won, and he didn't want to risk her refusal or spoil the moment. "We can test them on your lock in the morning."

"Yes. Right now, we best leave."

They left the parlor and headed toward the door and nearly walked into Mr. Russell.

"Excuse me, Lady Katherine. A message just arrived for you."

"Put it in my room, please."

The butler nodded and started up the stairs.

She looked up as he reached the landing.

"Do you want to see who it's from." Wallace's glance moved from the butler to her.

Kate let out a sigh. "No. It can wait until morning. We're already fashionably late."

Moments later they were in their carriage and on their way.

WALLACE HANDED HIS fiancée down from the carriage in front of the home of Tobias and Edwyna Nicolls.

"Do you know the Nicolls well?" Kate smoothed her gown standing next to him.

"More by reputation. We met once in London." They started walking to the door. "Nicolls owns a trading company and recently approached Sutton for an exclusive trade arrangement."

"He didn't realize you were Bennett's partner? Oh." Lady Katherine stopped several paces from the steps. "He thinks you asked me to marry you to secure your business. I was curious why the dinner is in our honor."

"I'm not sure. His information is from *The Sommer Sentinel*. In Mr. Hawkins' defense, his articles are about us, not our factory. Nicolls must be contemplating expanding his business. He doesn't trade in textiles.

"Why on earth are they having a dinner in our honor?" She adjusted her skirt.

"Nicolls knew Sutton, but he is not so sure about the current owners of Sutton Textile. I am sure he wants to get to know us."

"I'm just as certain Mrs. Nicolls has read the *Gazette,* as well as the *Sentinel,* and wants to separate the fact from fiction."

"Ah, our Mr. Hawkins. The man must work through the night to keep us in the news. I like the man less every time I see our names in one of his columns."

"I suppose it's not often Mr. Hawkins has an opportunity to publish an exclusive story." Wallace offered her his arm which she graciously accepted. "I understand the *Gazette* is in contact with him."

"Yes. He tells everyone, multiple times." Katherine leaned toward him. "In the same conversation."

They arrived at the door laughing.

The footman ushered them inside. They stood at the threshold to the parlor. The room went eerily quiet. Wallace kept a protective hand at her back.

Mrs. Nicolls excused herself and came directly to them.

"Lord Wallace. Lady Katherine. Welcome to our home. Let me introduce you to the others."

"This is my husband, Tobias. Lord Wallace and Lady Katherine."

"It is good to meet you, Mr. Nicolls. I speak for Lady Katherine when I say thank you for honoring us at dinner tonight."

"Yes, well, Wyn, I mean *Edwyna* and I are happy you joined us."

After introductions to the five other couples were complete, Mr. Nicolls pulled Wallace into a business conversation.

Katherine was getting used to losing Wallace to the men at dinner parties. She stood with the women and gazed at him from across the room. It wasn't difficult for either of them to play the newly engaged couple. But, in truth, her heart lurched when he glanced at her and winked. She reciprocated with a smile, the one she knew took his breath away.

⟫⟫✳⟪⟪

"HE IS HANDSOME." Katherine turned to Mrs. Nicolls. "You two make a beautiful pair. How long have you known His Grace?"

The woman had a pleasant expression but Katherine wondered if she was on a mission for her husband.

Wallace and Nicolls came over with glasses of wine.

"His Grace and I met when he and my uncle became partners."

"Partners? I didn't realize..." Mrs. Nicolls looked from Wallace to her husband.

Katherine hadn't lied. She learned about Wallace when Bennett took him on as his partner. Did it matter that she hadn't met him face to face until a few weeks ago?

Mrs. Nicolls stepped close to her. "We've all been excited for you. It must be difficult in the midst of your recent loss. I admit, I didn't know whether to send a note of condolence or congratulations."

She gave her hostess a weak smile and let the remark pass.

The dining room doors opened, and everyone took their seats. During the meal there were countless toasts to the happy couple, which Wallace graciously accepted.

"Edwyna and I moved here from Boston in February. This is the first time we experienced the Invincible Celebration. The memorial at the cemetery was touching and the fair was well done. I found the pageant most exhilarating. I thought we were in the middle of a battle."

"I'm glad you enjoyed it." It amazed her that people still talked about the near brawl.

"Those men should be with us against these factory workers. Don't the workers understand they *must* make way for the future? We're through with their lazy, incompetent ways."

Mr. Nicolls' topic of discussion surprised her. She would have thought business was discussed amongst the men and not in the company of women. Katherine glanced at Wallace. His poker face expression gave nothing away. It took all her strength to hold her tongue.

"The village should maintain a militia. Keep the complaining factory workers in line. Don't you agree, Lady Katherine?"

Katherine weighed being quiet against voicing her opinion. It took only a heartbeat to decide. She put down her fork and straightened in her chair.

Wallace leaned close to her. "Be gentle. You don't want to scare him too much."

"Feel free to join in any time."

"Oh no, my dear. This is all yours. I promise to step in if it comes to blows. I wouldn't want you to hurt our host, too much."

Encouraged, she gave Mr. Nicolls her full attention.

"Our factory workers are neither opposed to the mechanicals nor are they incompetent. We've had mechanicals at Sutton Textile for nearly a decade. Our workers are skilled with the mechanicals and every stage of the process. Productivity increases every year without any loss in quality. What factory workers are against are factory *owners* who refuse to hire guild members and pay a wage that is not enough to support their families." Katherine waited for her host's response.

"Your Grace, do you pay your workers enough to support their families? Does anyone ever get paid enough?" Nicolls' sarcastic remark enraged her.

"Mr. Nicolls, Lady Katherine is my partner at Sutton Textile." He turned to her. "As she will be my partner in life. She can answer your question."

Blushing, she squeezed his hand, and faced an astonished Mr. Nicolls.

"Yes, we do pay our workers an honest wage, one that will support their families. We provide schooling for their children.

And if needed, medical treatment."

From the corner of her eye, she noticed Wallace slide back in his chair with a broad smile across his face.

"The seemingly endless war against Napoleon's France has brought poverty to homes and to far too many people for the first time."

"The workers break the mechanicals that help them earn an honest wage." Mr. Nicolls was not about to give up.

"If any mechanicals are attacked, they are the ones owned by those who ignore standard labor practices. Those factory owners who really don't care about their workers or the quality of their goods. The workers want training, apprenticeships, and decent wages."

"Lady Katherine. I don't want to correct you. But you have it all wrong. The workers I met don't want mechanicals." Mr. Nicolls held his position.

She let out a deep breath.

"Obviously, Mr. Nicolls, you haven't met our workers."

"I tell you, if I had your invincible sword I would go into battle against the workers and come out the victor."

Everyone around the table laughed.

"I'm sorry, Mr. Nicolls. You will need to get in line. You're the second person this week who asked for the sword."

Wallace leaned toward her. "What do you mean?"

"We can speak about it later."

The rest of dinner was less lively. Mrs. Nicolls was able to change the subject and keep the conversation flowing.

Dinner over, Katherine retired to the parlor with the women while the men had their brandy and discussed business.

"Are you and His Grace planning a large wedding?"

"Not at this time. We have set aside all our wedding plans at the moment with the recent passing of my uncle."

"Of course." One of the other women said. "But surely you have some idea about your wedding. Every girl starts planning their wedding as soon as they can walk."

"Ladies, leave the bride alone. Perhaps she wants to keep her plans to herself. Lady Katherine, don't let these nosey hens bother you."

The group chuckled. The conversation moved to the local modiste and the fashions for the coming winter season.

An hour later, the door opened, and the men joined them.

They didn't stay much longer. They said their good-byes, thanked Mr. and Mrs. Nicolls for the dinner party and went to their waiting coach.

"I'm aware there are unscrupulous owners who will do anything to get around the labor laws and care nothing about their workers. Was Bennett one of those men? Surely, he did what was right for our workers and upheld the law."

Lord Wallace hesitated before he responded. "To reduce costs Sutton and I once talked about taking shortcuts, even considered hiring non-guild workers."

She said nothing for a few minutes. "Do you think a small factory as ours can compete in a market where others take shortcuts? If we cannot, should we close Sutton Textile?"

"No. Not at all." Lord Wallace glared at her. "You would let people like Mr. Nicolls win the day. Closing Sutton Textile will not make the problems go away. Creating a business that adheres to the law, provides for workers both in the factory and the home is what they need, not only to survive, but to thrive. And produce goods that they and we are proud of. That is how we fight the Mr. Nicolls of the world. Sutton was willing to fight."

"But you said yourself he was willing to take shortcuts." She narrowed her eyes at him more confused than ever. Had she misunderstood?

"In the end, Sutton and I decided we would never take shortcuts. I believed in his strategy and plan then and I still do. And he was following through. When I went through the factory papers, I found documents regarding the teachers Mrs. Bainbridge provides for the factory school. Your name is prominently listed."

"There are others, not only teachers, who are hired or donate their time to serve the Sutton Textile community." Katherine held his attention. "Lady Harriet Manning provides medical assistance to our workers and their families. Bennett made it very clear to me that over time, that as more needs were identified, we would find ways to meet them."

"Sutton Textile is more than a textile business venture for you." He leaned his head back and gazed into her eyes. "I spent years in the belly of a war. I was very good at tearing people and places apart. Now I want to build, give people opportunities to thrive, make things work, and be proud of what I've done."

"We both have high aspirations for Sutton Textile. We can't both be wrong."

The carriage pulled up to the abbey steps. He handed her down and escorted her inside.

"I was proud to be your escort this evening. We're lucky Sutton wasn't there. I can imagine him in a full rage and walking out."

Katherine wagged her head as they walked up the stairs to the second floor.

"Good night, Your Grace."

"Please, call me Ian. Your Grace sounds too formal under the circumstances."

He looked like a little boy asking for a second tart rather than a handsome man offering an intimacy.

"Of course… Ian. And what would you like to call me?"

"Not Ivy-Rose." He gave her a small cheeky smile that made her laugh. "I'd like to call you Kate."

Her eyes got misty. "That would be perfect, Ian."

"I do have a question for you. At dinner you told Nicolls he was the second person to ask you for *Invincible*. Who was the first?"

"Everyone asks about the sword, especially after the celebration when *Invincible* is on their mind. Nothing more."

He gazed at her, but Katherine had the distinct feeling he didn't believe her. She leaned close and kissed his cheek. His hand caressed her face. Her eyelids fluttered closed at his soft caress.

He took her hand and brushed her knuckles with his lips.

Restraining from his kisses made them more desirable, more precious. He released her hand and stood in front of her, his arms at his side. She wanted more than a kiss on her hand.

"Good night, Kate."

She reveled in the sound of her name from his lips. She dared not stay with him a moment longer. Reluctantly, she turned and walked toward her room, afraid to look back for fear of running into his arms.

CHAPTER TWENTY

KATE STARED OUT her window as the sun peeked over the horizon. She finished dressing and sat at her dressing table eager to set her new hair sticks in place. Catching a stray tendril, she picked up a hairpin and glanced in the mirror. On her dresser was the note Mr. Russell brought up last night. They were meeting with Mr. Graves and Mr. Hunter, the sheep farmers, this morning. She hoped they hadn't cancelled their appointment.

She went to the table and picked it up. She stared at the handwriting, Ryder Whitaker.

Kate ripped open the message.

"Katherine, I ask for your forgiveness. My uncle was right. At times, I can be a very petulant child. Regarding the proof I have. I want to give it to you to destroy. You would never believe me if I told you I destroyed it. Meet me by the mausoleum at nine o'clock. Ryder."

She and Ian moved past the disaster Bennett caused by pledging to be truthful with each other. Where did truth begin? Certainly not with the past. Some things were too personal.

Kate glanced at the note. Would the man ever leave her be? She didn't want to accept Whitaker's invitation, but she didn't dare risk him speaking with Mr. Hawkins or approaching Ian. She stuffed the note in her pocket.

One last look in the mirror and she was ready to face Whitaker. She finished her tea and left the abbey.

She stomped down the lane. Whitaker's poem echoed in her head. *Pay for your crime.* She went on. *Pay for your crime.* A bit further. *Pay for your crime.* The cadence of her steps accentuated the words. She couldn't get away from the nagging, clawing word. *Crime. Crime. Crime.* Her hands over her ears, Kate ran the final distance trying to rid herself of the word.

She hesitated at the gate long enough to catch her breath and gather her wits. Ready to face him, she made her way to the mausoleum.

"Lady Katherine, how good of you to join me. I will admit the cemetery is not my first choice for—" Whitaker leaned close, leering at her. "A rendezvous."

She pressed her lips together. She dared not speak. It only provoked him to go on. Silence was her best weapon.

Whitaker paced in front of the mausoleum. His hands rubbed the back of his neck or flailed in the air.

"We both are aware the part you played in my uncle's sudden death. I'm still not sure what poison you used."

The last time Whitaker suggested her involvement in Lord Kinsleye's death, Bennett had him flat on his back.

"Go ahead and tell her." Whitaker glanced at her over his shoulder as he muttered. "Tell her. Uncle Percival can't stop you now. You saw to that."

His incessant pacing stopped.

"I brought you here about the proof I have." His pacing resumed. "Yes, yes, the proof. You must pay for your crime," he babbled to himself.

"What are you talking about?" She kept her tone even and controlled. "I thought we came to terms with your threats nine months ago."

A maniacal smile flickered across his face before he resumed pacing back and forth.

She fought the rush of panic threatening to unnerve her.

Whitaker moved behind her, his mouth against her ear.

"Your kisses were sweet. Innocent. And those fleeting, or not so fleeting, touches. Remember them?"

Kate closed her eyes and said nothing. The indiscretion was hers to bear. Her mistake.

"We were quite the topic of conversation your first season, your only season. Everyone thought I would offer for you, but you left rather quickly."

His playful manner snapped. He grabbed her upper arm.

Kate remained still and waited for an opportunity to get away from him. There would be no one in the church this early to help her and no one at the abbey would miss her until later in the morning.

"You killed my Uncle Percival because he wouldn't give you what you wanted."

"The last time we discussed this—" She struggled but was able to keep her voice soft and calm.

"Sutton came to your defense. Where is he now?" His eyes brightened with a mad expression. "And don't expect *his dukeness* to defend you once I show him my proof. Murderer. If you want your precious Lord Wallace you'll do as I say, or I'll take the proof to him. You do know, he could have the same illness as Uncle Percival. What a fittingly horrid end."

He pushed her away, against the mausoleum wall, unable to get his hands off her fast enough.

She worked hard not to let him see how frightened she was. Instead, she stood tall and shot him a cold glare.

"Yes, I did make myself quite clear. I could consider surrendering the proof to you to do with as you like...for a price."

She moved away from him. Waiting. Listening.

"*Invincible.*" He spun around, pinning her with a crazed expression. "Give me the sword."

Unprepared for his demand, she stared at him in amazement.

"*Invincible* is worth a king's ransom." His eyes had a wild look. "And me? *I* would be invincible."

"You are aware the sword is a myth and doesn't exist. The story is a fantasy to give the villagers pride and confidence.

Nothing more."

His face fell but only for moment. "You can't fool me. Everyone knows your family has hoarded the sword and kept it for themselves. Now is the time to free the sword. And I am the one to do it."

"Oh, free and in your hands so you can steal the gems for yourself."

"The sword does exist." Whitaker pounced on the opportunity.

"No. Again, the sword doesn't exist and never did. But you go with your story and tell the world." Kate threw her hands into the air. "You'll not get anything from me."

She started to leave, then hesitated. In her stern voice, the one used for unruly students, she instructed him. "Here is my promise. Come near me and mine again and you will need someone to carry you out." Kate stepped in front of him and poked his chest at each word. "I do not need a legendary sword. Do. I. Make. Myself. Clear?"

The color faded from his face.

"Yes, I see, I have made myself quite clear."

Kate stomped out of the cemetery without looking back. By the time the abbey came into sight, she was calm enough to think clearly.

Whitaker was mad. His ploy with this proof of her guilt worked for a while. But the mention of his uncle, *'he saw to that,'* stuck in her mind. Did Whitaker poison his uncle? If so, he'd have no qualms killing anyone else, her, even Ian.

Kate hurried into the library. She threw open the door intent on warning Ian, but he wasn't there. He would be here for their meeting. All she could do was wait.

"GOOD MORNING." IAN entered the library, his steps long and

decisive.

Kate sat at the desk reading factory documents while she waited for him.

The mantel clock struck the hour.

She glanced at the clock. Mr. Graves and Mr. Hunter would be arriving any moment. She didn't have enough time to tell him about her meeting with Whitaker. It had to wait until later.

"Here are the documents for the meeting." She passed a folio to him. "While I was looking for them, I came across the plans for the medical office."

"Sutton and I spoke about the concept before we went to Royston Mills. While we were there, we spoke to Dr. Price. The doctor thought the concept was interesting. I met with several doctors in Cambridge for their opinion and the likelihood of attracting a doctor to work in a clinic rather than a private office."

"Dr. Manning has been seeing our workers in his clinic. He is a close friend and may be able to provide resources."

"Do you think we should provide a clinic for our workers?"

At first, she was too startled by his question to respond, but found her voice. "My opinion?"

"Don't doubt yourself." Ian sat by the desk. "You are a capable and intelligent woman. You base your opinions on facts, not gossip, as everyone found out last night. You even manage objections quite admirably. You're my partner. So, yes. I do want your opinion."

She said nothing for a few heartbeats. His belief in her abilities was unconditional and complete. And his acceptance was more important to her than she realized.

"We should see if your Dr. Manning wants the position," Ian said as he leafed through the papers.

Kate was aware the perfect candidate wasn't Dr. Manning. The better practitioner was Hattie, his daughter. But that's another story.

"I am going to be the envy of every man. Not only do I have a well-run business but a beautiful and intelligent partner. You may be the company's best asset. I enjoy watching you think. I can almost see the thought develop in your mind and the moment the idea catches fire."

"An intelligent woman is a drastic idea, at least for most men." Kate may be teasing, but Ian wasn't, and the thought excited her. "Bennett had his shortcomings. Working at the factory or anyone knowing a woman worked on the mechanicals upset him. I'm glad you're more forward thinking.

"Although I can sit here and banter with you all day, which is much more enjoyable then thinking about mechanicals, I'd like to discuss today's meeting." She handed him Bennett's diary open to the calendar. "You're meeting with two shepherds who sell us fleece."

"Yes, I read the production report. We do not have a contract with them. Bennett did business on a handshake." She pulled out the document. "Wool deliveries are lower than we expected and beginning to impact production. There are several questions you may want to ask them."

Kate stood to leave.

"Where are you going?" He glanced up at her. "Our guests should be here any time now. We'll both meet with them. You can ask your questions. You are available, aren't you?"

"Yes, I am."

They both turned at the gentle knock on the door.

"Come," they both said in unison.

Mr. Russell entered, trying not to smile. Lady Katherine, Mr. Graves and Mr. Hunter have arrived."

"Show them in, Mr. Russell." She came around the desk as the two men entered.

"Lord Wallace. May I introduce Mr. Bernard Graves and Mr. William Hunter."

"Your Grace." The men, their hats in their hands, nodded, then turned to Kate. Both were eager to speak to her.

"From Jenny, Lady Katherine." Mr. Graves handed her a wool scarf. "My girl said when you visited this winter you didn't have one. Her Mum taught her how to knit. The stitches aren't even."

Kate took the scarf and unfolded it. The stitches were indeed uneven, but the gesture was warm.

"The scarf is perfect. I'll make sure to thank her."

Kate turned to Mr. Hunter.

"How are the twins? They must be as tall as trees."

The shepherd glanced at her with a broad smile. "I'm not sure which are a bigger handful, the boys or the sheep."

Ian found it surprising Kate knew the business so well and the shepherds so personally.

"We're both sorry about Mr. Sutton's passing."

"Thank you." She turned to Ian. He gave her a brief nod encouraging her to go on.

"Please, be seated." Ian sat in the seat next to the desk, silently indicating she sit at the desk. This was to be her meeting. Everyone was quickly settled.

"We wanted to tell you, face to face." Mr. Graves kept his hands busy with the hat in his hands. "We must cut back on the amount of fleece we send to you."

"Why?" Kate clasped her hands, resting them on the desk.

"You've always been fair to us. But we don't have a choice." Hunter glanced at Graves. Both men were uncomfortable.

"There is always a choice. Tell me, why won't you sell us wool?" She gave Ian a sideways glance.

"People visited us." Graves sat at the edge of his seat. "Said they were factory workers. They asked for our support. Both of us come down to Sommer-by-the-Sea often enough to know who works at the factory. We didn't recognize any of them."

"When we didn't stop sending you wool, things started to happen." Hunter went on. "First, they stole wool. Then they sheared most of our sheep."

"But that wasn't enough. They burned our barns." Graves held Wallace's stare. "They threatened our homes and families next."

"Threatened…" Kate pivoted toward Ian. "We can't let this go on."

The two sheep farmers stood, anxious to be on their way.

"No. We cannot." Ian got to his feet. "Thank you both for coming here. You've taken a risk."

"As we said. You've always been fair with us." The men gave them a stoic nod.

"A handshake is still a contract. If anyone asks why you were here, tell them you came to sever your agreement with Sutton Textiles. You can tell them Lady Katherine and I tried to change your mind, but you would not bend. Also, by the end of the week you will have several new people on your farm, at my expense. Use them as farm hands but know that they are there to protect you and your family."

Graves glanced at Hunter, then back at Wallace. "We don't know what to say."

"You did the right thing coming to us." Ian walked the men to the door. "Mr. Graves, before you leave. Who buys your wool now?"

"Royston Textile." The men left the abbey.

"Who owns Royston Textile?" Kate asked Ian.

"Bromley manages the factory. I have no idea who owns it." He was thoughtful for a few moments, then turned to her. "I know we were planning to go into the village, but I must speak to Barrington. We need to arrange some protection for Graves and Hunter. I'll also ask about Royston Textile. I'll tell you all tonight at dinner"

He left before she said anything.

CHAPTER TWENTY-ONE

"**Y**OUR GRACE. A moment of your time." Mr. Hawkins hurried after Ian, following him across the commons.

The last person Ian wanted to speak to was the reporter. Every time Hawkins saw him, the man wanted information.

"Hawkins, not now."

The reporter caught his breath and gave him an urgent glance. He handed him a paper from his small notebook.

"I need to refute this. Please, read—"

"Yes, yes. I must go." Ian stuffed the paper in his pocket and hurried on to Sommer Chase.

For the next twenty minutes, Ian turned over the events of the last month in his head. When he looked at them in relation to each other, the outcome was different than looking at them individually. The more he thought about the various incidents, the more the emerging image held true. He hurried on.

Mr. Sanderson, Barrington's butler, ushered him into the practice room.

"You appear annoyed." Barrington finished his daily training and sat on the bench cooling down with a towel draped around his neck.

"Hawkins stopped me on my way here. I like the man less and less. But the gossip column is not what has me concerned. I met with the sheep farmers who supply our fleece. Another factory issue has come to light."

"The agitators aren't harassing your men." Barrington gave him his full attention.

"No. The farmers told us they can no longer sell us fleece. The more I put all the pieces together, Sutton Textile is under attack on two fronts, from inside and out. The attack and harassment of our workers, the picketing outside the factory, our sources for wool eliminated, and Sutton's murder. Even the near brawl at the pageant. This isn't the end, either. I don't know where or when to expect the next confrontation or who will be the target."

"Come with me into the library. What's the issue today?"

"The farmers came under attack for selling us fleece. They lost their barn and now their families are threatened. They need help. I'm concerned my helping them may cause them more problems."

They entered the library. Barrington sat at his desk and took out writing materials. "I can manage to get them assistance without implicating anyone from here. I have a contact in Edinburgh who can help."

"The fleece is now being bought by Royston Textile. All my dealings with them have been through Alfred Bromley, the factory manager. Sutton and I were to meet with the owner, but the duel got in the way."

"I wonder if your partnership has anything to do with this. When asked, Sutton only referred to his partner as 'His Grace.' We all believed Sutton was playing one of his games, but if you're correct, not disclosing the name of his partner was a necessity."

"You think the attacks are focused on me? If you're correct, then they will try to reach me any way they can." Ian's mind raced. He knew what it was like to be a target. His responsibilities for Wellington had him in the crosshairs many times. He could take care of himself, but... a shiver of dread rushed through him. "Kate."

Barrington shot to his feet.

Wallace, a look of defiance on his face, stared at Barrington. "If someone wants to get to me, they may get it in their head to target my fiancée."

"James and Peter are at the abbey. Go back and make arrangements. I'll go to Bamburgh Castle and bring more men here."

⇛⊁⇚

THE SILVER BELL above the door of Madam Pembroke's modiste shop tinkled. Kate found Anna sitting in the back of the shop.

"Effie's here for a fitting for a new summer gown. She should be out any moment. Should I tell Madam Pembroke you're here to buy a wedding dress?"

"Absolutely not." Her friends had teased her ever since she shared the real story of her engagement with them.

She sat down and Anna put several magazines with bridal gowns in her lap.

"This design is nice." She held the image up to show Anna. "I could ask Mrs. Pembroke to dye the thing black."

Anna giggled. "You wouldn't dare. The poor woman would succumb to the vapors."

Kate read the *London Gazette* she found in the pile and shot to her feet. The magazines cascaded to the floor.

"How dare they print this rubbish." She threw down the paper.

"Who? What?" Anna picked up the offending paper.

"Who would have thought that the future Duchess of Blackhall would be a woman won in a card game. Oh, dear. Who would have thought that Lady Ivy-Rose T, a belle in Sommer-by-the-Sea was that type of woman? But then, she, like many others, is just a pawn in the larger game played by men of power."

"Must you read the article out loud for everyone to hear?" Kate said between clenched teeth.

"Oh dear. Surely this isn't true. This is not at all like Lord

Wallace."

"Isn't this dress wonderful?" Effie swept in front of them wearing a lovely summer gown made of a lawn cotton with small bunches of forget-me-nots scattered across the material. The signature empire waist gown had a bodice trimmed with delicate lace as well as on the band below. The sleeves were puffy caps. All in all, the gown fit Effie well and looked wonderful on her.

Kate heard only muffled sounds and snippets of her friends' conversation. She took the paper from Anna, read the article again and got angrier. She tucked the newspaper under her arm.

Ready to leave, she stopped when she glanced at her friend.

"Effie, the dress is beautiful on you. When I saw the material at the factory, I knew you would like it."

"Do you really think so?" Effie spun around again and faced her. The smile on her face dropped as she glanced at the rolled-up paper, then at Kate. "Are you leaving? I thought we would stop at the tearoom."

"Not today. I must get back to the abbey." She hurried out the door.

So much for truth. What else hadn't Lord Wallace told her?

"Good evening, Lady Katherine, Mrs. Bainbridge." Wallace took his seat at the dining room table.

Kate had waited all afternoon for him to return. Now she kept her eyes on him and the paper.

Ian glanced at the *Gazette* on his plate and moved it away. She rose, picked up the paper, and put it back on his plate.

"The newspaper wasn't there for you to read. This time it is there for you to eat."

"Katherine." Mrs. Bainbridge was outraged.

"The village is abuzz with gossip regarding Lord Wallace and me from him being a rake to me stealing Lady RH's man. Now this. Being won at a card game. At least Mr. Hawkins didn't print this in the *Sentinel*." She turned from staring at Wallace and directed her attention to Mrs. Bainbridge. "I would think you would support me on this."

Hawkins. Ian had a sickening feeling. He never did read the paper the man gave him. Now he picked up the *Gazette* and read the circled column.

"Both statements are a gross exaggeration. I told you about Lady RH. I danced with her once at a house party. I remember the dance very clearly. My toes regretfully cannot forget. As for courting Lady RH. Definitely not. The party honored the lady's eightieth birthday. She chose me as her partner for her birthday dance." Ian looked for her reaction. "All London knows Lady RH. I'm sure you can understand why associating her and me in a courtship is ridiculous. Her grandson is older than me."

Kate's mouth hung open.

"Of course, I didn't win you in a card game, I won the house in the card game. I gave Sutton my oath to marry you when he took ill. You could interpret that as being my consolation prize when he called off the duel."

Her mouth hung even lower. With his absurd explanation she didn't know whether to laugh or cry.

"I understand why you're angry. I'm not pleased you are being made the brunt of this gossip."

Ian pulled the paper out of his pocket and read it. Hawkins did indeed give him the article from the *Gazette*.

"Mr. Hawkins attempted to inform me. It was already posted in the *Gazette*." He wagged his head. "There is some truth to this report."

Mrs. Bainbridge stood. "For some reason, I'm not sure if it's to protect yourselves or each other, but you have held back information. No relationship can survive on half-truths. You do not need a referee. You need to be honest with each other about everything."

They glared at each other. Neither said anything.

"If not for a relationship, for your partnership. If you keep these secrets, you and your business will fail."

"I don't have anything to hide. I tried to be considerate. This is," Ian pointed to the *Gazette*, "true to a point, but without context can be misunderstood."

"Give me the context. From the very beginning." Kate sat next to him. "I'll listen."

"Sutton and I were in Royston Mills to speak with the textile factory owner. We arrived the day before the meeting. A group of men demonstrated outside the inn. They were the same men who visited you and interrupted the pageant."

She listened carefully.

"Sutton was upset and drinking too much. I needed to keep him occupied. We played cards. Sutton played recklessly, taking risks a beginner wouldn't ever take. When he lost, I tried to forgive the debt, but Sutton would have none of it. He wrote out a note and gave it to me. I couldn't get him to cancel the debt. I suggested another game, winner take all. I intended to make sure he won.

"Sutton refused and started an argument. I took his abuse even when he slapped my face in front of a room full of people. He called for satisfaction and left me no choice. But I didn't give up trying to stop the circus. I never loaded my pistol.

"Sutton finally came to his senses and called off the duel. Everyone was leaving the clearing when there was a flash, and his pistol went off.

"Your uncle thought he was dying. In his delirium, he made me promise to marry his niece Ivy-Rose. Without an obvious fatal wound, no one thought he would die, not even the doctor.

"By evening his situation surprised the doctor and everyone else. Sutton's last words to me were to swear again to marry his niece and protect the coffer with a silver lock. When the article appeared in the paper the following morning, I was shocked and angry. I quickly put the pieces together. Sutton had to be the person who put the article in the paper. But that didn't matter. I could not deny I gave him my word. I swore my oath in front of everyone at the dueling field.

"That is everything. We will never know Sutton's reasoning, but I understand now how worried he was for you."

"I don't know what to make of all this." His honest tone, the story, some parts he had told her, were consistent. Every instinct told her he was telling her the truth.

"Kate." Ian held her hands. "I didn't like being manipulated either. But I also feel an obligation to Sutton. Your uncle died thinking I would take care of you. I couldn't go back on my word. I thought to be your guardian, see you through school, and well settled. And now, I want so much more than that.

"I've told you the truth. It's your turn to tell me everything. From the beginning."

"Excuse me, Your Grace." Roddy, with Mr. Russell quickly coming up behind him, stood in the shadows at the door. "You're needed at the factory."

Wallace took one look at Roddy and got to his feet. It wasn't like the man to stand in the shadows. What was he hiding? As he got closer, he looked at him carefully. It was obvious his foreman had been in a fight.

"Kate, don't leave the abbey. I'll explain when I return."

She listened as the front door closed, not having told him about Whitaker.

CHAPTER TWENTY-TWO

"WHAT DOES LORD Wallace mean, you haven't told him the truth? What are you withholding from him? You can tell me anything. It won't go any farther than these four walls." Mrs. Bainbridge sat patiently and waited.

So many thoughts vied for attention in her head. So many actions needed to be faced. So many failures needed to be confessed.

"There are times I can be as stubborn as Bennett. The notion I could manage the situation is far from the truth." Kate gazed at her mentor. "I am as delusional as Whitaker."

A terrorizing notion washed over her. The burden was too great, and the consequences too deadly.

"Problems began with my season in London. Whitaker spent a substantial amount of time with me. The *ton* believed there would be a proposal."

She needed to go on and put the rest into words. Relive the pain.

"Bennett and I attended Lord Kinsleye's soiree. We overheard Whitaker speaking with some friends saying some terrible things. Some about me." Kate couldn't lift her head or look at Mrs. Bainbridge. "Mostly about me. In a frenzy, I went to the lady's salon. Bennett's confrontation with Whitaker ended with Ryder on the floor, his nose bloody. As for Bennett and me, we were on our way back to Sommer-by-the-Sea."

"Somehow I find that very pleasing." Mrs. Bainbridge patted her hand. "I don't care for Lord Whitaker."

"There is more to the story." Kate took a deep breath. "I lost my way returning from the lady's salon and found myself in Lord Kinsleye's library. He didn't feel well and had a terrible thirst. I helped him with tea and called for assistance.

"When the butler arrived, Lord Kinsleye's condition worsened. The butler called for a doctor. That's when his nephew arrived, Bennett with him.

"Bennett and I didn't stay for the soiree. We left that evening for Sommer-by-the-Sea. On the way, Bennett told me Lord Kinsleye cut his nephew out of his will and told him before the soiree he was to be gone before first light."

"Several weeks later, Alicia wrote informing me Whitaker was telling anyone who would listen that I poisoned his uncle. Bennett didn't tell me until much later that Whitaker came here to speak to him. For a price, Whitaker would clear me of any wrongdoing. That was nine months ago. I didn't hear from or see him until he approached me in the bailey and again today."

Kate didn't miss Mrs. Bainbridge's quick intake of breath.

"Yes, I spoke with him this morning. Again, he declared he has evidence proving I murdered his uncle.

"He was mad, muttering to himself and pacing about. He no longer is demanding money. If I give him *Invincible,* he will give me this evidence. If I don't give him the sword, Ian will suffer the same fate as his uncle."

Mrs. Bainbridge sprang to her feet.

"Why did you keep all this from Wallace? You must tell him. This isn't some squabble between you and a rejected suitor. This is much more deadly."

"I tried to tell him this afternoon, but Ian ran out. I planned to tell him now, but once again some issue called him away."

"You should have told someone, if not Ian, Barrington, or me."

"I thought myself capable of managing Whitaker and the situation." Kate glanced at Mrs. Bainbridge and saw a deeply troubled expression.

"You have been on your own for a long time, depending on yourself. You have followed your own path with excellent results. I am proud of your accomplishments. Not many young women could do as well. But at a certain point we must recognize the extent of our own abilities and be confident in ourselves to reach out to those who can assist us. This is not your weakness. It is your strength."

Kate lifted her head.

"Promise me you will speak to Lord Wallace. You must tell him everything."

"Yes. I will."

Was it too late? What if something happened while he was at the factory? She would never forgive herself.

LONG AFTER DINNER, Kate laid in bed waiting to hear Ian return. Determined to tell him everything. Her conversation with Mrs. Bainbridge repeated in her head. Her eyes heavy, they were almost closed. She took a deep breath ready to nod off. The fragrance of the lilac outside her window mixed with the odor of smoky pine wafted into her room. Her eyes sprung open.

Instantly alert, Kate hurried to the window. A red haze tinged the dark sky in the direction of the factory.

"Fire."

James and Peter hurried below her window.

"The factory." Kate pointed toward the horizon.

"James, you stay here. I'll tell Barrington and the others." Peter was on his horse and speeding down the lane.

Mr. and Mrs. Russell, still in their bed clothes, came to her door, Mrs. Bainbridge behind.

"Fire at the factory, Mr. Russell. They'll need our help. Mrs. Russell, we'll need to be prepared for injuries."

"I'll help." Mrs. Bainbridge hurried off with the couple.

Where was Ian? Kate ran to his room and threw open the door. His bed hadn't been slept in.

"Lenard?" There was no answer.

Kate hurried back to her room, opened her closet, and put on the breeches and shirt she wore on her secret visits to the factory.

She hurried to the stable, grabbed a halter, not bothering with a saddle, and mounted her horse, ready to leave. That's when she spotted Lenard amongst her staff.

"Where is Lord Wallace?" Would he hear her over the commotion of people gathering supplies and hitching wagons?

Lenard paused, loading a wagon. "At the factory."

Without waiting for him to say anything else, she pulled the horse around and hurried out of the yard.

Please let him be safe.

Kate veered off the road and took the short cut across the field, her horse full out as they raced up the rise.

She came to a halt at the top of the ridge. Her horse danced, eager to go on. Kate took a moment to look down at the black sooty smoke engulfing the river and factory below.

Bringing her horse under control, they burst down the rise toward the factory grounds.

Kate found Ian's horse tethered outside the factory gate by the stone fence and quickly tied her mare there. The horse secure, she ran into the yard and stood rooted to the spot. Tools and debris filled the yard as if someone had turned over all the tool cases, then scattered them covering every space.

The summer evening was warm, but the heat in the yard was stifling, the smoke choking. Flames licked out of the first-floor window. The whooshing sound as the fire grew, igniting its next article, punctuated the crackling sound of the fire. Wooden timbers creaked and groaned from the heat. And the odor. Burning fleece and cotton added to the acrid odor that burned her nose and throat.

The wind shifted and a gray smoky haze blanketed the yard. The air was so thick she could see only a few yards ahead.

Workers were everywhere, some dragging things out of the building and trying to move as far away as possible. Others running into the building, to help, to save.

As volunteers arrived, they helped the men who had started a bucket brigade drawing water from the sluice. She went to help but noticed the buckets scraped the bottom of the sluice. There was hardly any water at all. The headgate must be obstructed.

She knew the channel and the headgates well having made several detailed drawings of them. Removing the obstruction and opening the channel would provide more than enough water to control the fire, if water was available before the fire got out of control.

More volunteers arrived. She ran along the sluice, came to the headgate, and found them padlocked. Kate reached for her hairpin. There wasn't one. Spinning around, she looked in every direction for something to use. Among the debris on the embankment she found a sledgehammer. That would have to do. She brought her oversized 'lockpick' back to the headgate.

The padlock dangled from a chain holding the gates tightly in place, a good position for her attack. Kate climbed on top of the headgate and swung the sledgehammer like a Pall Mall mallet.

The jarring strike bounced off the gate, but only left the lock dented. The shackle still held. Another swing, and another, this time with more force. Still, the padlock held.

A glance at the factory confirmed the second floor was almost completely hidden by black smoke. There was no telling where the fire had spread.

This was getting her nowhere. Her heart pounded as she decided on a new strategy. Counting to three, she swung the sledgehammer back and over her head, and with all her might brought it down onto the body of the lock.

The smashed padlock landed in the empty sluice. She

dropped the sledgehammer to the side and sprang open the latch. Water cascaded down the sluice.

Kate ran along the embankment and reached the factory as the water wheel began to turn.

A second bucket line quickly formed. Volunteers were everywhere doing their best to fight the fire. She scanned the yard for Ian but didn't see him. Desperate, Kate turned in a circle, looking and searching, but he was nowhere to be seen.

"Where are you?" she muttered under her breath. He would be where no one else would go. Her gaze landed on the building. Kate closed her eyes and moaned. He was inside.

She ran to the open factory door and made her way in. The first floor was ablaze. Water splashing from the water wheel hissed, striking the hot stones, creating clouds of steam that filled the building.

Kate tried to go deeper into the building, but the smoke, heat, and steam were too much. Coughing and rubbing her eyes, she emerged and searched for another way in. She hurried toward the mechanical room.

The debris blocked the door. She was about to look for another way in when loud banging reached her ears. Someone was trapped.

"Over here. I need some help. There are people inside." She and several others hurried to the door. They pulled away the debris and found the door locked. One of the men, an axe in hand, broke through. Three workers, coughing and gulping air, stumbled out.

"That door is never locked when people are inside," the man with the axe said as he helped move the people to the far stone wall.

A screeching sound had everyone stop in their tracks and stare at the broken door. A loud crash sent cinders flying out the doorway.

She turned to one of the men they rescued. "Where is Lord Wallace? Did you see him?"

"Inside. Second floor," he said between spasms of coughing and gulping for air. "Getting people out."

She started for the door, but someone pulled her back.

"You can't go in there. The floor above just gave way."

What did that matter? Ian was inside.

"Katherine."

She swung around. Barrington came up behind her. He stared past her. She turned and followed what held his interest. Steam gathered and rolled upward angrily around the mechanical room door. The cloud of steam mixed with smoke grew as more water hit the hot stones. Kate tilted her head and took in how the fire backlit the steam and flickered with a soft orange, otherworldly glow. While the clouds of steam appeared soft and gentle at the edges, swirls of steam churned in the center.

Slowly the silhouette of a man came out of the mist with a stride she would know anywhere.

"Ian." Her voice was a whisper. She started to move but Barrington held her back.

He came closer. He had a piece of material around his mouth like a highwayman. His arm was around someone, helping him out of the building.

"Ian." She turned to Barrington. "He has Roddy." She wrestled out of Barrington's grip and ran to him.

Kate slipped her arm around Roddy's other shoulder. She needed to move them both to safety. Barrington took over organizing the factory workers and volunteers to put out the fire. Dr Manning and Hattie arrived carrying medical supplies and went right to work.

With the foreman between them, Ian and Kate moved him to safety against the stone fence with the other casualties.

Dr. Manning and Hattie rushed over to evaluate the extent of Ian and Roddy's injuries.

Hattie helped her father remove Roddy's bloody shirt. "These aren't from the fire." Hattie glanced from Roddy to Ian for an answer as she ministered to Roddy's injuries.

"He's been beaten," Ian said between coughing spasms. He turned to Kate. "Hold this walking stick."

"You're fortunate. Your burns aren't severe. I don't think they'll blister." Dr. Manning finished examining Ian and turned to Kate.

"A cool compress and rest."

Dr. Manning went on to the next casualty.

"No broken bones." Hattie held Roddy's attention. "You'll be sore and have a great deal of bruising. The cuts are not deep. I've wrapped what I could." She signaled to one of the men to come over. "Help Roddy to his wife."

Hattie turned to Kate. Her eyebrow raised as she looked her up and down. "The latest style?" Hattie shook her head. "Let me examine you."

"No need." Kate waved her off. "You go and help the others. They need your care more than I do."

Hattie gave her a skeptical look. "You'll have someone find me if you need me."

"Of course. Go on."

Hattie moved toward a group of people waiting for attention. She acknowledged Barrington as they crossed paths.

"Where did you find the walking stick and why is it important?" Kate sat next to Ian holding onto the cane.

"Roddy wouldn't leave until we found it. He said the man used this to beat him while others held him."

Barrington came over to them. "Thank goodness the sluice was operational. We were able to put the fire out quickly. The men are raking through the cinders and wetting them down. Other than a partial collapse of the floor on the east side of the factory, the building appears sound. What happened?"

"Roddy was on guard. I was working on one of the mechanicals when I smelled smoke. I alerted the others. By the time we found Roddy he was unconscious, and people were smashing the mechanicals. They ran when they saw us. We worked on putting out the fire rather than go after the scoundrels."

"Between your men and mine, everything is under control." He let out a deep sigh, but his tense expression said much more. "You and Lady Katherine go back to the abbey. Try to get some rest. And don't worry about the factory. I'll set guards." Barrington went off to organize the situation.

The terror of the night under control, Kate and Ian got to their feet and started out across the yard. "You shouldn't be here."

"Why shouldn't I be here? The factory is forty-nine percent mine."

"You argue about everything." He shook his head and followed her to their horses on the other side of the wall. He tied the walking stick Roddy retrieved in the factory onto the back of his saddle.

Before she could put together a response, he turned and had his strong, solid arms around her. She didn't try to pull away. He smelled of smoke and ash. She didn't care. He was safe and she was in his arms.

"Kiss me." Her voice was fragile and shaking.

His eyes turned a passionate blue. There was no smugness, only a tender gaze that made her stomach swirl. He bent back her head and kissed her softly at first. Their kisses became more intense, demanding. She could have lost him. The thought made her cling to him more. Every drugged kiss stoked a fire, took her breath away. They were unlike anything she had experienced.

Every inch of her body demanded him, throbbed for him. Her fingers gripped his hair and pulled him closer. Her heart raced so fast, surely it would explode. And the wanting, she had never wanted anyone like this before.

He stepped forward, still kissing her, pressing her against the stone wall. The full weight of his body against her, all of him against her.

The touch of him, the taste of him, even the smell of him drove her mad. His kisses were intoxicating, like a rare brandy, and all-consuming. In a frenzy, she returned his kisses, refusing to be denied, demanding he never stop.

Ian pulled away and she gazed into his eyes. Those beautiful hazel eyes were a brilliant, passionate blue.

Whatever held her together flew apart in every direction. She knotted her fists in his shirt and pulled him toward her. Something wild, wonderful, and wanting rushed through her. Closer. She needed him closer. She wanted more, demanded more.

"I am yours," he whispered.

The heat of his breath, the fire of his words shattered her into a thousand pieces.

Neither of them moved until the world was back on course. The sounds and tumult of the chaos around them gradually came into view. Still they remained in each other's arms.

"I don't remember ever being that scared." Her voice was a whisper.

"Fires are very dangerous." He stroked her back and nestled her head under his chin.

She pulled her head back and gazed at him.

"The fire didn't scare me. The thought of losing you did." She felt his heart race and his muscles tense. "When I saw you, I didn't know whether to kiss you or scream at you."

"I felt the same way. I told you to stay at the abbey." His voice was soft, resigned as they stepped apart. "Not to control you. For your safety."

He took her hand and led her to their horses.

"I am not the only one in jeopardy." He had to be aware of the threat. "You are as well."

"No more so than usual." They mounted up and headed toward the abbey.

"Please, Ian. Whitaker may appear harmless, but he's more dangerous than you imagine." How could she make him understand? She'd have to tell him about their meeting. "Whitaker gave me an ultimatum. He demanded I give him *Invincible*."

He gave her a sideways glance. "When did that happen?"

She turned to him. "This morning. I met him at the mausoleum."

"And he demanded *Invincible*."

"Yes. If I don't give it to him, you'll suffer the same fate as his uncle and probably blame me for that, too. He was mad, muttering to himself and pacing." She paused to gather her strength. "He claims he has evidence I killed his uncle."

"The crime. He's your poet." He mumbled under his breath. "What evidence does he have?"

"I can't imagine. He approached Bennett nine months ago with a similar claim and demanded money. He never produced the evidence. And before you ask, Bennett paid him with a bloody nose."

They went on in silence the rest of the way to the abbey.

"You go inside." He helped her down, kissed her forehead, and handed her the walking stick from the back of his saddle.

"We have much to discuss, but first, I want to speak to James. I agree with you, Whitaker is dangerous, and arrangements must be made. I don't see him managing Ollie and those men, nor do I think he attacked Roddy. He must be working with someone. Not knowing who is where the danger lies. So far, that walking stick is all the evidence we have. Go on ahead. I won't be long."

Kate went into the library and examined the walking stick, concentrating on the worn engraved brass knob. It was a familiar insignia, but she couldn't place the family.

Debrett's had a list of all the families and their insignias. She searched the library shelf, took down the book, and brought it to the desk.

Before she could put it down, it slipped from her hand, skidding across the desk sending several items onto the floor.

The damage already done, she picked up Bennett's pocket watch and fob. His flask was beneath an errant paper and button by the leg of the chair. The items all accounted for, she put them aside to deal with later.

She scanned the pages and was three-quarters of the way through the book. Nothing. Her mind was working on where to search next when she turned the page and stopped. She was reaching for the brass knob when she glanced at the button and realized the two designs were similar. She picked up the button and placed it next to the likeness in the book.

A swell of rage raced through her. Flashes of conversations, scattered images, Bennett lying dead in the parlor burst in her mind. Her breathing was slow and steady as she tried to take back control.

"Kate. What's wrong?" Ian held her by her shoulders, his face inches away. She blinked, trying to clear her mind. His concern finally penetrated through the fog.

She moved back for him to see for himself.

He bent over to get a better look at the book, at the button, then back at her.

"Kinsleye."

She handed him the walking stick. The insignias were the same.

CHAPTER TWENTY-THREE

IAN WOKE WITH images of Kate's violet eyes and their stolen kisses fading away. He couldn't deny the mutual attraction between them, nor did he want to. Absent-mindedly, he licked his lips for any essence of her that lingered.

"I will not ask why you are smiling." Lenard put a small tray with a hot cup of coffee on the dresser. "Lady Katherine's brave. Barrington had to hold her back from running into the factory."

He sat up. "She will need more than an invincible sword for this situation."

"One of the men saw three men leaving the factory in a hurry as they came to help put out the fire. Your friend Ollie was not among them." Lenard laid out his clothes and began polishing Ian's shoes.

"Kate confirmed the insignia on both the walking cane and button are the same."

"The button?" Lenard, the shoe brush mid-stroke, stared at Ian who was washing up.

"The button we found in Sutton's bed at the inn. It was not his." Ian glanced at his valet. "It belongs to his killer."

"And the insignia?" Lenard dropped his hand with the brush to his lap.

"Kinsleye. I'm not fond of Ryder Whitaker but never thought he'd have the stomach for murder, a cleverly planned murder at that."

It made him all the more wary about what evidence he had that would implicate Kate in his uncle's murder. The evidence against Whitaker appeared to be substantial without his attempt to blackmail Kate.

"What do you plan to do?" Lenard put the finishing touches on Ian's shoes.

"That's a good question. Barrington will be here soon. I'll discuss it with him."

Lenard helped him on with his coat. Ian finished the last of his coffee and left the room.

On his way to the parlor, he found the drawing room door ajar. Roddy should be home resting and recuperating from his injuries, not here. He walked into the room intending to send the foreman home.

"Katherine? I didn't expect to see you here."

"I couldn't sleep. I needed a diversion."

The cloth remained draped on the challenge lock. The daily reports were in a stack, unread. Kate sat at the desk with a pencil in hand working on the mechanical drawings.

"May I?" Ian pointed to what she was working on.

She sat back and gave him a half-hearted gesture.

He picked up the drawing, read her comments, and became absorbed in her work.

"You are correct about the ability to add more spindles to the frame. Have you calculated how much more thread we can make if we do? Roddy should be able to tell us the damage to the mechanicals before noon. Is it possible we can make up for the woven material we lost?"

He glanced at her, waiting for an answer and was rewarded with an enthusiastic smile.

"Yes, we can." She moved closer to the desk. "By adding these spindles, we can increase the output by twenty percent without much strain on the workers. I checked the inventory. We lost about thirty percent of the raw material, but there is a shipment of cotton due in tomorrow.

"The carding mechanicals on the first floor sustained most of the damage. I asked Roddy to reach out to the families and have manual carders ready in case we need them. He mentioned this morning one of the spinning mechanicals needed a substantial amount of repair. That mechanical took the brunt of the attack."

Ian straightened and glanced at her. "That's why you're looking to increase the output on the other mechanical."

"Yes. We should know more about the spinning mechanicals on the second floor. Thankfully, the power looms on the third floor were not damaged."

"Good work." Ian paused for a moment and glanced around the room. He should have realized before. "This isn't your uncle's workroom with a desk for your challenge lock. This is your room."

"Yes. My visibility at the factory was an ongoing argument between Bennett and me. I wanted to work at the factory, but he wouldn't hear of it. When it came to adjusting pieces of equipment, Roddy brought them here.

"There were times, rare ones, when Roddy couldn't dismantle the mechanical for my convenience. Those times I went to the factory."

"The others didn't notice you? Wait. Let me guess. The pants and shirt you wore at the fire."

A flush ran up her neck.

"I go to the factory after closing, and yes, I dress as a boy. I was close enough to Roddy's older son's height and stature.

"Roddy was always with me, waiting for hours, sometimes, while I made an adjustment. Bennett and other workers were none the wiser. Roddy was not sure that if the factory workers knew I worked on the mechanicals he would have a real revolt on his hands. We didn't want to test his concern."

"These are your drawings, not Sutton's. Why didn't you tell me?"

"Bennett had the insight but not the ability or possibly the patience to put his thoughts down on paper. We worked together. He gave me your comments and I edited the drawings to include them."

"These are quite good." He murmured more to himself than to her. There was so much more to this woman. Would he ever know everything about her?

"That's an excellent working arrangement, but you haven't answered my question. Why didn't you tell me the part you play in our business? Especially now."

"Ian. You are an astute businessman. What would happen if our contacts, the people who buy our finished goods, found out a woman had a major role in its production?" She paused. "Let me answer the question for you. They would rather turn away then work with a woman."

"You've provided many answers, but you conveniently left one out. I assume you didn't tell me how involved you are in Sutton Textiles because you didn't want me to tell you to stop.

"I can understand your perspective. Still, Sutton should have told me."

The color on her face drained.

"No, Kate. It's not what you think. Your visibility to others may have been a consideration for Sutton, but not for me. I'm beginning to see how clever your uncle was. He knew I would insist you take your rightful place in the company."

"I have never met a man like you. Willing to accept a woman as a business partner."

"I'm *not* willing to accept a woman as a business partner. I *am* willing to accept a clever, intelligent person who understands our business and can think for themselves. The fact you're a woman has nothing to do with it."

He pulled her out of her chair and took her into his arms.

"The fact you are a beautiful, passionate woman who can make my heart race with a smile." He ran his knuckles down her cheek. "Who is as eager for me as I am for her." He held her close, fitting her in his embrace as if she were a missing piece in a puzzle. He leaned in closer.

"The touch of her lips." Brushing them with his own, he kissed them finding them impossibly soft.

Kate put her arms around him.

He deepened the kiss and pulled her closer still. Would he ever get enough of her? He could feel her heart beating as quickly and steadily as his own.

Ian pulled away and gazed deeply into her violet eyes. "You are my perfect partner."

"I worried about you last night." Her voice was lower than a whisper.

"Forgive me. I couldn't leave Roddy. I have never left any in my command behind."

"I wouldn't expect you to. I knew you would come back to me. When I saw you come out of the mist, I was excited, proud, and relieved."

"You are truly a Thornton. You didn't need a sword. You had a sledgehammer. You made me proud. Lenard described how you smashed the lock on the headgate with a sledgehammer. It's the least ladylike action I could imagine you doing but it made so much sense. I knew you would take the necessary action to protect others."

She put her head on his chest and they stood together quiet and content for several moments.

"I would carry you away, but Barrington will be here soon." He tenderly kissed her forehead. "We should go meet him."

THEY FOUND MRS. Bainbridge entertaining Barrington in the parlor. The captain stood and approached them.

"You both look well considering last night. I received information I think will surprise you." Barrington had their attention.

"Alfred Bromley of London is the owner of Royston Textile.

We've also been able to identify the men who demonstrated here at your factory. They are paid by Bromley. I have sent a man to see if he can find anything in Royston Mills. I instructed they conduct an extensive search."

"That is a surprise. I thought Bromley was the foreman and took his orders from Whitaker." Ian glanced at Kate than back at Barrington. "How is Bromley involved in this?"

"That was my thought as well. But there is more. Alfred Bromley has a bit of a dubious background." He pulled a paper out from his jacket.

"Mr. Bromley often came here." Kate read the paper Barrington handed to Ian. "He and Bennett discussed business issues. They both thought themselves clever for establishing a factory here in the coal region rather than the midlands. Bromley envied our factory having direct access to the river. They discussed how to convert to steam power since we have easy access to coal and water. Bennett may have considered him for partnership at one time, but I'm not sure." She turned to Ian. "That was long before you became a partner."

"Our Mr. Bromley had a hard life as a youngster. Even as a young boy he could charm people out of their money. What they didn't give him willingly, he found a way to remove from them." Barrington gestured to the document.

"A pickpocket?" Kate asked.

"Among other things. That is, until the man stole from one particular person. That person took him in. He thought the boy was clever, so he educated him, gave him a modest income, and money to start Royston Textiles. Bromley became admired in business circles. Not too long ago, he and his benefactor parted ways." Barrington took the letter from Kate.

"Is there a criminal element involved in all this?" Kate asked.

"We don't know. It may depend on who his benefactor was. We are still trying to find out."

"Come with us into the library." Ian gathered them together. "Kate will show you what she found."

Barrington and Mrs. Bainbridge followed Kate to the desk.

"This is the cane Roddy brought out of the factory during the fire. Take note of the brass knob." She gave Barrington the cane who passed it to Mrs. Bainbridge.

"This is the brass button we gathered up from Sutton's bed before we left Royston Mills. Notice the insignia." Ian handed the button to Mrs. Bainbridge.

"May I, Reese?" She put out her hand for the cane. She studied the two items, then glanced at Barrington. "The insignias are the same."

Mrs. Bainbridge handed the items to Barrington for him to inspect.

Kate put the *Debrett's* on the desk, opening it to the bookmarked page. She stood back and gave them room.

Barrington and Mrs. Bainbridge leaned over, read the page, then looked at each other.

"Kinsleye. Percival Kinsleye never used or carried a cane. That leaves Ryder Whitaker." Mrs. Bainbridge turned to Barrington. "I don't understand why Whitaker wants Sutton Textile to fail. Isn't that what will happen if these demonstrations persist?"

"My guess is Whitaker wants to take over Sutton Textiles. He can't buy it. He may want to play the valiant knight, send off the intruders, and save the day. His reward could be the lovely lady's hand in marriage." Ian bowed to Kate.

"That will never happen." Kate's determination was obvious from the tone of her voice and the glare in her eye.

"Not if I can help it." Ian gazed at her in that special way that melted her insides. He turned toward Barrington. He held the cane's shaft, pulled the handle, and swiftly pulled out a sword.

"I watched Whitaker at the celebration games. He was one of the contenders on the pell who hacked away at the wooden dummy. Unless the man is a good actor, he is not a swordsman even with a blade like this." Ian put the sword back into the cane. "If he is capable with a sword, he is more devious than we imagined. Whitaker cannot be ignored." He glanced at Kate.

Mrs. Bainbridge went to Barrington's side.

"I have some news as well." Ian placed his arm around her back. "Whitaker is more dangerous than you think. He may be involved with his uncle's death."

"This is worse than expected. I'll speak to the judge and tell him what we found," Barrington said.

"I'm going to the factory. I want to help the men clean and make the necessary repairs. We want to get the mechanicals running as soon as we can." Ian took the brass button from Mrs. Bainbridge and put it with the cane on the desk. "I'll bring the walking stick to the factory and see who claims it."

"I'll go with you. I may be of some assistance." Kate was eager to help.

"It would be better if you two aren't together in one place at the moment." They both turned to Barrington.

"Yesterday, all you wanted us to do was parade around the village together."

"Yesterday someone didn't try to kill His Grace. Both of you in the same place is too tempting. Please, until we capture the murderer, let's not give him any easy targets."

Ian turned to Kate. "He's right. You stay here with Mrs. Bainbridge. I'll send word if I need you."

Barrington turned to leave.

"Wait for me, Reese. I'm interviewing two potential students and want to get my papers at the seminary before I meet them." Mrs. Bainbridge turned to her. "I shan't be long. I'll be back in time for four o'clock tea."

Ian kissed her lips. The three went out the door, leaving Kate staring at them through the parlor window.

Her fingers on her lips, she could still feel his warmth, taste his sweetness. Letting out a deep sigh, she decided to work on her lock. It would keep her occupied until they returned.

CHAPTER TWENTY-FOUR

"A N URGENT MESSAGE, milady." Mr. Russell brought her a note on the salver.

"Lord Wallace asks that you meet him at the mausoleum as soon as possible."

Kate stared at the note. Her heart pounded. She stuffed the message in her pocket and grabbed her cloak. In minutes, she rode out of the stable.

Why did she let him go to the factory without her? She made the same mistake with Bennett. *Oh, please.* Not the same outcome.

Driving the mare hard, she took the shortcut through the meadow and headed to the back of the churchyard. At the gate, she tethered her horse next to Ian's and hurried to the mausoleum.

Inside her world came crashing down.

"Ian." She rushed to him, lying on the floor. "Ian." With care, she rolled him onto his back. Blood trickled down the side of his head.

"Can you hear me?" Kate ripped the bottom ruffle off her chemise and cleaned his wound. "It's Kate. Wake up. You've had a bad fall."

A rasping sound caught her attention. She turned in time to see the mausoleum door closing.

Racing to the door, she grabbed the latch to prevent it from closing. She pulled hard, surprised to find resistance. Someone pulled it from the other side.

"Vicar, it's Lady Katherine. I'm in here with Lord Wallace." The door almost kept closing. She kept pulling it. Her fingers began to slip. "Vicar. It's Kate." She fell backwards. Her grip gave way. She watched helpless as the door slammed shut and the lock clicked.

She glanced at Ian. He hadn't moved. Kate returned to the door and with a tender touch, ran her hands over the stone relief searching for the keyhole.

Nothing. Her conclusion? There wasn't one on this side. Why would there be? She almost laughed. No one here was going anywhere.

Gather your wits. Think. If there is someone outside, he doesn't want you to come out. You both are right where he wants you.

"Kate. Is that you?"

She rushed to him. The door forgotten. "Thank God you're all right."

He removed the torn cloth she placed on his wound. "I can assume you didn't send me a note to meet you immediately."

Confused, she said. "Me? You told me to come here at once."

He propped himself up against the knight's sarcophagus and glanced at the door.

"Closed. Not by itself," she added as an afterthought. "I didn't see who was on the other side, but they knew we were in here."

She took out the note for him to read.

"My note says much the same thing. I thought it strange you didn't pen the message yourself, but I didn't want to take a chance.

She took the message from him.

Ian stood and held out his hand.

"The key, please."

"I don't have the key, and even if I did, there is no lock on this side of the door. We may be here for quite a while. Mr. Hendrickson doesn't come here until Sunday to say his prayer."

Ian got to his feet and examined the door, especially around the door pull.

"There's an outline of a sword hilt. All we need is *Invincible.* Is there any more to the myth that could help us?"

"Not that I remember. What did Bennett tell you?"

"A silver lock and a coffer. Search everywhere on the door. See if you can find anything that looks like a lock."

They examined each marking on the door but found nothing. The base of the sarcophagus was next. They each took two sides and examined them as closely as possible.

Nothing.

Kate stood and started to search the wall at the head of the sarcophagus and came to an abrupt stop.

"What?" Ian came to her side. "Have you found something?"

"He's glowing."

The oculus in the dome filtered a ray of light that landed on the knight's face. No, his neck. He moved close to the sculpture and stared at the carving.

"Not a coffer, a coffin. And not a silver lock, a silver locket."

She removed her locket and placed it on the notch at the base of the statue's neck. A perfect fit. The silver piece caught the sun and sent light everywhere.

Ian studied the sculpture.

"The carving isn't one solid piece. The sword is separate. It's layered on top. There must be a way to remove it. Look for anything that could be a lock." Ian ran his hands along the stone sword.

Kate examined the seam, where the stone sword rested on the knight.

"Here it is." Kate glanced at him, a wide smile. She took her hair stick, removed the wooden cover, and worked the pick for a few moments until they heard the soft whisper of a click.

"I have one pin. The second is on the other side of the sword." Kate removed the second hair stick and unsheathed the lockpick.

In the silence of the room, she slid the second lockpick in, probed, and turned it. Her heart beat loudly as she listened and felt her way to capture and move the pin. A second soft whisper and the stone was free.

Carefully, Ian removed the stone sword.

Sunlight poured down on the polished etched blade and lit the room. The crystals and gems that remained embedded in the sarcophagus glowed with a heavenly light.

Ian went down on one knee, his hand on the knight's sculpture. Kate was right beside him.

"À moi! Thornton à la rescousse!" Ian spoke softly with reverence.

"To me! Thornton to the rescue!" Kate stood and gazed at the stone knight. "Thank you for one last battle. Rest in peace, Lord Stephen."

With reverence, Ian lifted the sword from its resting place.

"The balance and grip are perfect." He flourished the sword. "And as solid as the day it was forged."

"The sword was made for you. You're more like the knight than you know."

With *Invincible* in one hand, he grabbed her around the waist with the other and stepped to the door.

Ian took a deep breath, placed the hilt against the outline, and pushed against the sword. Nothing moved.

"Be patient," she said. "The mechanism hasn't been engaged in a hundred years."

Again, Ian pushed, this time a little harder. The stone gave way and slid back revealing a carved chest with a long thin keyhole.

Kate ran back to retrieve the hair sticks but stopped.

"Is something wrong?"

"No, not at all." She stared at the young knight.

Kate removed her locket. She hurried back to Ian and slipped it into the thin space as far as possible. Only the chain hung out. A definite click echoed in the room. The door lock opened.

Kate placed the locket around her neck.

Ian led them out of the crypt and to their horses.

"Let me have your cloak."

Kate did as he asked.

"Where are we going?"

"To Barrington." He wrapped the sword in her cloak and handed it to her.

They mounted their horses and raced across the field to the village and Sommer Chase.

They approached Sommer Chase's mews and hurried into the townhouse. Mr. Sanderson ushered them into Barrington's training room where he was fencing.

Barrington glanced at Ian. "Hold,' he called out to the others. He rushed over to Ian and examined his head.

"Sanderson," Barrington called over his shoulder.

"Right away, milord." The butler was gone.

"Come with me. What happened?" Barrington led them to the library.

Sanderson returned with a basin of water, liniment, and bandages. He began to minister to Ian.

"Someone locked us in the mausoleum and left us for dead."

Barrington turned to his men. "Go to the magistrate. He should be back from Bamburgh with men. Bring him here."

"It's a nasty bump on the head, Your Grace." Sanderson swabbed and applied liniment on the wound. "There isn't much more I can do."

"You have my thanks," Ian said as the butler left.

Ian got up to leave.

"Where do you think you're going?"

"To the factory."

"Not alone. Give me a moment and I'll go with you." Barrington left without waiting for him to respond.

"How is your head?" Kate checked the butler's handiwork.

"My head aches. Come sit with me until the hammering

quiets down. I interrupted you last night."

"You want to talk about that now?" She sat next to him, placing the wrapped sword beside her.

"It will keep my mind off my headache."

"You told me your truth. I need to tell you mine." Kate took his hand and hoped he would understand. "My truth has to do with Ryder Whitaker.

"During my first season, Whitaker was a very ardent suitor. Everyone expected a wedding date to be announced. I thought he might say something at his uncle's soiree. That didn't come about at all.

"Bennett was with me going into dinner. Whitaker and his friends were in one of the small ante rooms."

Kate paused trying to find the right words. What would he think?

Ivy-Rose. Tell him. Trust him.

"Whitaker boasted to his friends how he planned to use me and how wealthy he would be once my money and the factory were his."

Curses fell from his lips.

"He didn't stop there." Kate stared down at her lap.

"What did he do?"

She glanced at him with tears in her eyes. "He told them things, personal things, private things, some that never happened."

"Was Sutton aware?" His voice was hard and ruthless.

"He was with me and overheard him as well. He was furious." Kate gazed at a blank wall, unable to face him. "I couldn't remove myself from the situation fast enough. I ran to the lady's salon.

"I got turned around when I came out of the salon and lost my way back to the ballroom. Instead, I found myself in Lord Kinsleye's library. He was distressed and asked for a cup of tea. He said things would be made right. I thought that strange since I hadn't told him anything. Whitaker came in as I was refreshing his uncle's cup.

"At first Whitaker blamed what he said on too much to drink, men will say things, and I should be a good sport. I couldn't stand the sight of him or the sound of his voice. But when he tried to take me in his arms, a place I once thought was a refuge, I pulled away and called him out.

"That's when his entire disposition changed. In the midst of arguing, Lord Kinsleye called out. I went to him. He had turned a shade of blue and gasped for breath; I was horrified. Blood was everywhere. Whitaker accused me of poisoning him. Mr. Fitzgerald came in at once and called for a doctor."

"What did Whitaker do?" Ian's eyes were narrow slits.

"I don't know. Mr. Fitzgerald took me outside the room to calm me. He said Whitaker wasn't to be trusted and that he was up to no good.

"Bennett came in with the doctor. The next thing I knew, Bennett was tugging at me, pulling me along. We left the soiree and London."

"I never liked Whitaker. I like him even less now. I have more to tell you." Ian kept rubbing her back. "I haven't told you everything about Sutton's death. I didn't mention this because I thought it too gruesome.

"Sutton was poisoned with snake venom. When Lenard and I went into his room that night, he was bleeding profusely. Very much like Lord Kinsleye.

"I find two very similar murders suspicious. I know Bennett died of snake poison and find it more than a coincidence that Whitaker accuses you of poisoning his uncle." Ian got up. Kate held him back.

"Whitaker said he would tell everyone I killed his uncle unless I brought him *Invincible*. If I didn't bring it to him, you would be next. I think he would go as far as to blame that on me as well. No matter what I said or did, no one would believe me. It would be my word against his, a lord."

"Odd Whitaker didn't mention what evidence he possesses

that he waves in front of you." He paused.

He was quiet for a few moments. She could see he was deep in thought.

"No, Kate. He has nothing. And lords who murder go to the gallows like any other murderer. He needed to get us both out of the way. I don't know what he'll do." He got to his feet. "Tell Barrington to meet me at the factory."

"Ian. No. You're not well."

Ian was gone before she could stop him. She ran to the door as Barrington came in.

"Did Ian just leave?"

"Yes, I have to go with him. He's gone to look for Whitaker."

"You can't go after him. You must stay here." He held her back. "Don't fight me on this. Ian needs to know you're safe."

"You don't understand. He didn't take the sword."

"What sword?"

Kate grabbed her cloak from the sofa and unwrapped the weapon.

"*Invincible.*"

CHAPTER TWENTY-FIVE

IAN RODE THROUGH the meadow to the factory. Did Whitaker plan to prevent him and Kate from getting in his way? Or was his scheme more sinister – did he plan to kill them? If they put the pieces together correctly, Whitaker was more dangerous than either of them believed.

He rushed around the final bend. The factory gate was up ahead. Ian brought his horse to a halt. From his vantage point, the only sound was the churning water from the water wheel. The yard should be noisy and busy with people clearing the damage and making repairs.

He tied his horse outside the gate and, with his back against the wall, slid toward the opening listening for anything that would hint at what waited ahead.

He peeked around the gate, scanned the building, and saw nothing. The yard was half cleared. Debris and tools remained scattered on the ground close to the building entrance. Brooms and shovels lay discarded, giving the appearance the men left amid their work.

He took a deep breath. His next move mapped out. Acting and looking relaxed, he walked through the gate and headed for the factory door. On his way, Ian picked up a wrench resting on a ledge. It was better than nothing. He entered the first floor.

The hairs on the back of his neck stood at attention. Someone else was here with him.

He continued on. The men had done a good job cleaning this part of the factory. An idle broom stood against the wall with a pile of debris waiting to be swept up. There were wood, rope, and crates scattered across the work area. Of their two carding mechanicals, one was badly damaged. Pieces of the frame were in various stages of repair. The dented carder drum remained on the mechanical waiting to be fixed. The second mechanical had minor damages. The raw cotton and fleece that hadn't been burnt to ashes were in bales ready for disposal. The heavy smoke damage made the goods worthless.

A glint in the shadows caught his attention. A closer look and he let out a breath. It was light playing on the metal knob of the cane Roddy rescued. He had laid it across the foreman's desk earlier.

He crossed the floor and looked up the staircase and started up to the next level. Whoever was not here to destroy the mechanicals. Sutton's office was their likely goal.

Ian reached the landing. All was quiet. The spools of thread stood in crates draped with rope ready to be tied.

Approaching the office, the sound of drawers being shut and papers being shuffled reached his ears. Ready for action, he hefted the wrench. Now he watched and waited. Surprise was on his side as he stepped into the room.

"Are you adding theft to attempted murder?"

Whitaker's head snapped up. His mouth gaped open as the papers in his hands cascaded to the floor.

A cane leaned up against the desk. Ian noticed a different collar between the shaft and handle than the one Roddy retrieved from the fire. If Whitaker hadn't beaten Roddy, who had?

Whitaker grabbed his cane and swung it wildly at Ian. In a desperate effort, Whitaker rushed at him.

Ian fended off the assault and hit his attacker upside his head, sending him to the floor. He was right. Ryder Whitaker didn't know how to fight.

He picked up Whitaker and his walking stick and brought him downstairs. He tossed the stick to the floor away from his prisoner and tied Whitaker to a chair, ready to question him.

In the quiet of the factory floor the sound of a rough cough stopped Ian.

"You're not supposed to be here."

Ian, his back toward the intruder, smiled. "Bromley." He turned and faced him. "Sorry to disappoint you."

The man stepped out of the shadows with his coat off and his shirtsleeves rolled up.

"Repairing my mechanicals? No. Destroying them more likely. Didn't the fire do enough damage?"

Bromley glared at Whitaker. "When will I learn Whitaker can't carry out a simple order. Did you kill him?"

"No. I put him to sleep for a while."

Ian glanced at the desk and the cane in the man's hand. "You found your stick."

"It has a sentimental value. A gift from my benefactor." He unsheathed the blade and tossed the empty shaft to the side. "With an adjustment. You'd have been better off if you had stayed put in the mausoleum."

Bromley advanced.

"For you perhaps. Not for me or Lady Katherine."

"Lady Katherine?" Bromley's face paled. His steps faltered. "He was to bring her here, not to the cemetery."

"Whitaker never does follow directions. And if you're wondering how she is, my fiancée is well."

Ian glanced at Whitaker's walking stick on the floor. Bromley would cut him before he reached it. Bromley may be more skilled than Whitaker, but he wasn't a warrior. With the walking stick out of the question, Ian took a calculated step back between the mechanicals.

A smug grin spread across Bromley's face.

Ian knew that look. The intruder thought he retreated. Ian kept his emotions contained. Not retreat, regroup. He studied

Bromley's eyes and at the right moment took another step back and grabbed the broom. Using it as a weapon, he feinted to one side, spun around to the other, and struck the man's sword.

The force of the strike made Bromley's arm tremble, loosening his grip. He struggled for a moment but was able to keep hold of his weapon. Fear glittered in his eyes.

That's right. I'm not an easy target like Whitaker.

Bromley's hesitation quickly passed.

Ian twirled the broom in a figure-eight creating an impenetrable shield. He kept advancing forward, pushing Bromley back. He needed to get out from between the mechanicals and move the fight outside.

"Did I upset your plans?" Ian pasted a smug smile on his face and watched as Bromley bared his teeth and his nostrils flared. His intent? Anger Bromley into taking reckless chances. His strategy appeared to be working.

"I'm through with your interfering."

Ian fought on. He didn't let the difference in their weapons bother him. He swung the pole, jabbed at Bromley, catching him in his chest several times. And Bromley connected with the broom more than once, chopping it little by little.

When Bromley swung the blade leaving his side open, Wallace stepped in and let loose an upper cut, then retreated before his opponent recovered.

The grimace on his face set, Bromley came after him with quick strokes with his sword. Ian parried each one until he slipped on a piece of debris and fell to the floor.

A stinging sensation in his side caught him by surprise. A red stain spread on his coat.

"I brought down the great warrior." The man gloated, not realizing what he provoked.

Ian got to his feet and pushed forward, forcing the man toward the door.

Bromley raised his sword across his body, setting up a backhand strike.

Ian took full advantage of the opening and moved into Bromley's space where his sword was useless. He grabbed the man by the throat and threw him out the door. Bromley landed, sprawled on the ground amid the debris, the breath knocked out of him. His sword skidded out of his reach.

Ian kept his eyes on Bromley.

It could have been her scent, a sound, he wasn't certain what it was, but he felt Kate's presence behind him. Without knowing why, he reached his hand out to his side.

She filled it with the familiar feel of deadly steel.

The five-and-a-half-foot great-sword, with its polished brass handle and etched blade, was an intimidating weapon, an extension of his arm.

"To the gate. Now," he commanded.

She hurried away standing at the gate directly behind him.

The warrior stalked off and stood by Bromley's discarded weapon.

"Your sword." Ian flicked his foot sending it sliding toward him.

Bromley glared at him. His eyes filled with hate. He picked up his weapon and got to his feet. The men stared at each other waiting for someone to make the first strike.

A movement at the factory door caught Ian's attention. Bromley turned to see what was there. Both men froze.

Whitaker staggered out the door. He lifted his face and stared at them. Letting out a moan, he pointed to Ian. "No. The sword. *Invincible*. We're doomed."

Whitaker glanced around mumbling to himself.

God's blood, the mad man is looking for a weapon. Ian had to get to him before he did more harm.

Bromley took advantage of the diversion and swung at Ian.

He answered with a swift downward strike that cleaved Bromley's sword, leaving him with barely any steel but the handle. Ian stepped in for the final strike.

Whitaker found what he searched for. He grabbed an empty

spindle out of a toolkit, jabbing his hand in the process. He prepared to throw it.

"No. Whitaker. They're poison." Bromley's bellow filled the factory yard.

Whitaker pulled back his arm, aiming to throw the weapon at Ian.

Ian had to do something. If Whitaker missed him, the spindle would strike Kate. There was no way for him to reach her in time.

Whitaker's arm began to move forward.

Ian lunged toward the mad man, lifting *Invincible* quickly in one fluid movement, his focus on stopping the spindle's flight.

He was too far away and only able to catch the underside of Whitaker's arm and force a change in the spindle's path.

Whitaker let the poison spindle loose.

No longer interested in Whitaker, Ian spun around and tracked the spindle's path. It struck Bromley in his forearm.

Bromley stared at his arm and sank to the ground.

Barrington, with his men behind him, rushed in and took control.

Whitaker held his hand and wailed on the ground.

"Restrain Whitaker," Barrington ordered as he walked over to Ian.

Kate ran to his side and wouldn't let him go.

"Have one of your men take the toolkit." Ian gestured to the case next to Whitaker. "Handle it carefully. Those are the deadly spindles. They've been dipped in poison." He pointed to Whitaker and Bromley. "These are the men who killed Lord Kinsleye and Bennett Sutton. They are also responsible for the fire here last night."

"We'll remove Whitaker to a cell at the castle. He keeps yelling you have *Invincible,* demanding to touch it. I've sent for the doctor to see to them both."

Kate glanced at Whitaker as Barrington's men got him to his feet. "He thought the sword was the answer to all his problems. I have no pity for him."

"Neither do I." Ian held her close and kissed the top of her head.

He could have lost her.

"I didn't kill anyone. Whitaker is your murderer. His own uncle, then Sutton."

They went over to where Bromley sat with one of the men. The soldier removed the spindle, bandaged his arm, and emptied his pockets.

Kate glanced at Bromley, then at Ian. She held up a lockpick from among the contents of Bromley's pockets and handed it to Ian.

"A simple tool. That's how you got into Sutton's room in Royston Mills. I'm sure if we looked at your coat, we'd find a missing button as well."

Barrington approached him. "Where did you get the poison? And don't tell us you don't know. My men searched your office at Royston Textile and found the vials hidden in one of the mechanicals. Dr. Price already confirmed the vials hold snake venom. You're more guilty than Whitaker."

Bromley lowered his head, staring at the ground. He said nothing for some time, but took deep breaths until finally, he lifted his head. He looked first at them, then at the small bundle with the spindle they removed from his arm.

"I had everything planned. I would be Sutton's partner and marry his niece. I would have it all eventually, full ownership of the factory and a lady on my arm. Access to the wealthiest men and invited to the best houses. It was a simple plan. Except Lord Kinsleye told Sutton you were the better man, better than me. After I took in his do-nothing nephew."

"It may not be that Lord Wallace was the better choice."

Kate glanced at Ian. "Forgive me, Your Grace."

She glanced back at Bromley. "But it may have been your decision to take on his nephew. Lord Kinsleye fully disowned him. When you took him in, His Lordship disowned you as well."

Barrington signaled his men to take Bromley away.

Ian, Kate, and Barrington made their way out of the yard.

"Sutton must have known all along. Your betrothal announcement in the *London Gazette* put a stop to Bromley's plan," Barrington said.

Ian glanced at Kate. "He made me make that oath to protect you."

"And I thought Bennett was…" She buried her face in Ian's chest. She looked up at him. "With his last breath he protected me and gave me the only person who would not go back on his word. The only person he trusted."

Ian held her close. He too, had his doubts about Sutton. He should have known better. "We both owe him a great deal."

Barrington stood with them, his eye on Ian's sword. "Bromley's plan was for Whitaker to lock Wallace in the mausoleum and bring Lady Katherine to the factory, not the mausoleum. With her here with Whitaker, Bromley would come and rescue her. Then, with a swift swipe of his blade, get rid of Whitaker and be the hero of the day.

"A clever plan to do away with all his opposition, a pesky partner, and get his prizes, Lady Katherine and Sutton Textile. If Whitaker didn't change the plan, Bromley might have succeeded."

Barrington squinted, peering at the sword Ian held. "Whitaker is quite mad. He insisted you had *Invincible*. Quite mad if you ask me." A sudden indulgent glint flashed in his eyes. "What sword is that?"

"My army sword, of course," Ian lied.

Barrington smirked and gave him a nod. He paused and studied him. Finally, he held out his hand. "May I?"

Without hesitation, Ian presented him with the hilt.

"Magnificent. I always thought it was a legend." Barrington handled the weapon with respect. "You're correct, standard army issue."

Kate took *Invincible* and wrapped it in her cloak.

The rumble of horses and wagons broke the silence and grew louder. They looked up the trail as a wagon, with Roddy next to the driver, came into view. They stepped to the side as the wagons rolled past them into the yard.

"The storage areas are ready." Roddy called out. "Once the bales are stored, we need to get back to the cleanup and repair."

While the others took care of unloading the wagons, Roddy went over to Ian.

"I worried when I saw the gate open. I locked it myself when we left. I wanted to get the cotton shipment put away. We also had a message from Gates and Hunter. We should get their full order by the end of the week."

"Good work. When will you know about the mechanicals?" Ian asked.

"By the end of the day we should know if the carding mechanicals will be working. My plan is for them to be operational by morning. I'll have a full report for you tomorrow." Roddy left them and went back into the yard.

"I need to return to the castle before Hawkins starts to sniff around. I'll craft a statement for the *Sentinel*. Will the two of you be all right?" Barrington mounted his horse.

"Yes. Thanks to you and your men." Ian stood with Kate as Barrington rode away.

They mounted their horses and rode along in silence across the field. Kate held *Invincible* across her lap, still wrapped in her cloak.

She brought her horse to a halt. "I want to return *Invincible* to its resting place. Where it belongs."

"You are the keeper of the sword. Your wish is my command." Ian led them across the meadow, through the churchyard, to the mausoleum.

He pushed the tomb's door open. Light bounced off the limestone walls. Ian removed the stone sword on the sarcophagus while Kate lovingly wiped down the blade.

Her breath caught when she turned to wipe the other side

clean.

Inflexible in faith. Invincible in battle.

Kate laid the sword to rest. Ian replaced the stone cover on top and waited until they heard the soft click locking the sword away.

"I want to keep *Invincible* as a tale, not a prize for people to seek to make their own. I want it to belong to everyone."

"That's a fine plan."

Kate placed her hand on the sculpture. "Know you are re-membered and celebrated for your valor and your faith. And *Invincible* still protects Sommer-by-the-Sea."

They both stood at Bennett's crypt.

"My friend. I didn't see the reason for your actions. And yes, I doubted you and even thought you mad. I am humbled by your devotion to Kate and will work every day to be deserving of your trust." He gazed at her. "And hers. You have given me the greatest prize of all."

Kate stared into Ian's bright hazel eyes. "He gave the greatest prize to us both."

They walked out of the mausoleum and locked the door behind them.

⟫⟫⟫✦⟪⟪⟪

THEY SAT ON the boulder overlooking the sea.

"From the time I knew you were in Mrs. Bainbridge's semi-nary, I wondered what your special skill was."

"Have you decided?" She leaned against him, her head on his shoulder.

"You are a lockpick." His arm wrapped around her shoulder. "You unlocked my heart."

She snuggled closer. "You have a special skill as well."

He glanced at her, his hazel eyes full of mischief.

"You are *Invincible*. Somewhat like the sword, you are inflexi-ble in love, invincible in your devotion."

He lifted her chin and gazed into her passionate violet eyes. "Marry me, invincible Ivy-Rose."

Her breath caught, her heart skipping from her chest to her throat, and back again. "I am yours."

He took her in his arms and kissed her soundly.

THE END

About the Author

There was never a time when *USA Today* Bestseller, RUTH A. CASIE hasn't had a story in her head. When she was little, she and her older sister would dress up and act out the ones Ruth creative. Today, Ruth writes exciting and beautifully told legendary historical romances that are both rich and engaging. Her stories feature strong women and the men who deserve them, endearing flaws and all. Her stories are full of, 'edge of your seat' suspense, mind-boggling drama, and a forever-after romance.

She lives in New Jersey with her hero, three empty bedrooms and a growing number of incomplete counted cross-stitch projects. Before she found her voice, she was a speech therapist (pun intended), client liaison for a corrugated manufacturer, and vice president at an international bank where she was a product/marketing manager, but her favorite job is the one she's doing now—writing romance. Ruth hopes her stories become your favorite adventure.

Fun facts about Ruth:

1. She filled her passport up in one year.
2. She has three series. The Druid Knight is a time travel romance. The Stelton Legacy is a historical fantasy about the seven sons of a seventh son. Havenport Romances are contemporary romantic suspense stories. She also writes for the Pirates of Britannia connected world.

3. She did a rap with her son to "How Many Trucks Can a Tow Truck Tow If a Tow Truck Could Tow Trucks."

4. When she cooks she dances around the kitchen.

5. Her sudoku books is in the bathroom and that's all she'll say about that!

Social Media Links:

Website:
ruthacasie.com

Instagram:
instagram.com / ruthacasie

Facebook private reader's page, Casie Café:
facebook.com / groups / 963711677128537

Facebook Author Page:
facebook.com / RuthACasie

Twitter:
twitter.com / RuthACasie

BookBub:
bookbub.com / authors / ruth-a-casie

Amazon:
amazon.com / author / ruthacasie

Goodreads:
goodreads.com / author / show / 4792909.Ruth_A_Casie

YouTube:
bit.ly / 3hI5eQr

www.ingramcontent.com/pod-product-compliance
Lightning Source LLC
Chambersburg PA
CBHW061251210726
48293CB00003B/935